Klara with a K

A Novel
By
Sandy Berman

ISBN: 1497339928
ISBN-13: 9781497339927

For my husband,
Ozzie

AUTHOR'S NOTE

• *Klara with a K* is a work of fiction. With the exception of actual historical figures, the characters in this book are entirely the product of the author's imagination. Any similarity to persons living or deceased is purely coincidental. For the purpose of the book's chronological structure the date for the establishment of The Office of Special Investigations of the Justice Department was changed from 1979 to sometime in the 1960s.

Venerable are letters, infinitely brave, forlorn, and lost.

Virginia Woolfe

My dearest daughter,

The hardships are difficult to describe. The guards are finally allowing me to write and I pray my words will reach you. I am reluctant to add to your worry, but provisions are scarce and your brother is constantly hungry. If it is at all possible, please send a parcel with food and articles for our toilet.

Klara, although I am determined to survive, God may have other plans for your brother and me. You are my hope, little one. You may be called upon to act in a way or to do things that in another place, another time, you would never consider. Morality is fluid in a world gone completely mad. My dearest child, you have but one responsibility, and that is to live...no matter the cost.

I love you with all my heart.

Mama

Drancy Internment Camp, France, 1942

PART I

AWAKENING

ONE

The occupant of bed number 108 started to stir. For a few more moments, she remained teetering on the precipice of time, in the final seconds between sleep and consciousness when there is still an uncertainty whether the sounds and voices assaulting your senses are real or a delusion. Soon the sun began warming her face and the young woman realized that, against all odds, she was still alive.

Too stunned and too frightened to open her eyes or change position, she struggled for clarity. Her last memories were vague and elusive. Fever, chills, and then darkness. *Don't say anything until you can think straight*, she thought. *Is it possible? Am I actually safe?* Tears began to well up under the girl's still-closed eyelids. Klara Werner knew she had kept her promise. She had survived.

Bed number 108 rested against a back wall next to a window. Hundreds of identical cots had been hastily lined up to accommodate the staggering number of sick and dying found at the Buchenwald concentration camp when it was liberated by American soldiers on April 11, 1945. Klara, along with many of the other survivors, had been stricken with typhus, a disease that had already killed thousands.

As Klara's mind began to clear, she could make out English words among the cacophony of sounds emanating from every direction. Pleas for help in Polish, German, and languages she did not recognize mixed in with the violent retching of the critically ill and the clang and clatter of bedpans.

Years earlier, Klara had studied English in the Volksschule in Berlin, but that was before the Nuremberg Laws of 1938 had expelled her and all the other Jewish students, and required them to attend Jewish-only schools. Of course, that was several lifetimes ago, if one could measure time by the horror of one's experiences.

The hospital was filled to capacity. Half of the staff was busy caring for the patients. The other half was consumed with removing the remains of the victims for whom liberation had come too late. With all of the activity, Klara had time to take in her surroundings. The nurses' idle chitchat sickened her. They spoke of their lives outside the walls of the makeshift hospital. A run in a pair of stockings, a good-looking soldier, a possible date. Would such nonsense ever occupy her mind again? Was it possible that she, too, would once again worry about her outward appearance? Would she ever again think about the monotony of everyday life?

Worse yet, the nurses spoke about going home. For them, the war was over. Most would be leaving the camp in a few short weeks, a month or two at most. Once home, they would pick up the lives they had left behind. Back to the university or to a job. Back to loved ones, to family. That was what grieved Klara the most. She would never be going home again. There was no such place, no life to return to. No loved ones to embrace her ever again. She needed time to think, to adjust to this new situation, and to accept the inevitable. Apparently, she was going to live. As hard as she tried, however, she had little strength to concentrate. Her body and mind were far from recovered from the nightmare of the last several years. Soon the noises of the hospital ward began to fade and Klara allowed sleep and the memories of her childhood to overtake her.

TWO

In 1924, the year Adolph Hitler was released from Landsberg Prison, Fritz Werner graduated from medical school and opened a family practice in the upscale Grünwald area of Berlin. A year earlier he had married Gisela Goldman, and the young couple were expecting their first child. Beginning in 1933, with the appointment of Hitler as chancellor of Germany, the hopes and dreams of the Werner family began to unravel. Fritz was trapped in a world that made little sense, where good and evil exchanged roles and where the police became perpetrators of unimaginable crimes against law-abiding citizens, who were then being labeled as criminals.

"I am a respected member of the community, Gisela. You worry too much. Hitler is a buffoon. The German people will not put up with his maniacal tirades for long." Fritz Werner repeated this same speech nightly to his wife, who was determined to convince Fritz to leave Germany. Many of their friends had already immigrated to other countries in Western Europe or to the United States, and those who had not yet left were making plans to do so. Gisela was anxious to follow. With each new Nazi edict, life grew more and more difficult. Gisela feared for the safety of her two beautiful children, who were no longer welcome in the homes of friends they had known since early childhood. Fritz's arguments could not sway her, and Gisela, again and again, begged him to get their documents in order and seek visas to emigrate from Germany.

"Fritz, how many more indignities must we suffer? The Germans have already stopped you from practicing medicine on any non-Jewish patients. Your sister's marriage to her Christian husband is no longer legal under the despicable 'Law for the Protection of German Blood and German Honor,' and your own children are prohibited from attending school with their friends. Are you blind?" screamed Gisela. "Most of our friends have already left. Soon it will be too late. The Kohns, the Schneiders, the Baers—all of them have already been issued their papers. They will be leaving in two weeks. If you won't do it for me, then do it for the children!" Gisela wailed, as tears streamed down her face.

"Ernst is only ten years old and I have not seen him smile in weeks. He no longer plays outside; he is too afraid of the neighborhood children. Did you know that his best friend, Karl, didn't invite him to his birthday party? Stupidly, I called to ask why, and his mother didn't even apologize. She said only that Karl was no longer allowed to play with Ernst, and then the line went dead. This from a woman I have known and socialized with for years! And what of our beautiful Klara? Fourteen years old, and made to leave the public swimming pool where she's played with her friends for the last six years. Does she not deserve better?"

"Enough!" yelled Fritz. "Your nightly rants are driving me mad."

Gisela could no longer contain her frustration. Uncontrollable now, she pounded on her husband's chest and pleaded for him to be reasonable. "You've forgotten who you are, Fritz. You are no longer Fritz Werner, a German citizen. You are Fritz Israel Werner, just as I am Gisela Sarah Werner. We have no rights; they have all been stripped away. All of us, each and every one of us, have been forced to adopt these new 'Israelite' middle names. You're a Jew, do you hear me? A Jew! Just like the old men from the Orthodox shul who have always embarrassed you. We are no longer Germans. Perhaps we never were."

Gisela cowered as Fritz's face reddened with uncontrolled rage. "You will never speak of this again," he said. "You compare me to the stoop-shouldered rabbis from the shul, those who do nothing but pray all day and who remind our Christian neighbors why they hate us? Those Jews give all of us a bad name. We are Germans, and we will stay." With that, Fritz picked up his medical bag and stormed from the house.

Gisela stood for several minutes staring at the closed door she knew would never reopen with a repentant husband. Fritz would return in a few hours as if nothing happened, expecting that this verboten subject would not be discussed again. It was almost as if Fritz believed that if the persecution were not mentioned, it would simply go away. With each new pronouncement, another layer of security was being stripped away from her once self-assured husband. Like all Jews, he was ostracized by his former coworkers and friends. Perhaps because she knew him so well, Gisela understood that Fritz was as frightened as she, but his fear was compounded by the dread of having to start over in a new country with absolutely nothing. If they emigrated, they would be allowed to take only the barest essentials. They would be required to list everything so that some good Nazi party member could purchase their home and most of its contents in a forced sale for only a few pfennigs.

The thought of giving up his practice as well as his possessions had demoralized Fritz. To compensate, he exuded a false, almost comical bravado. Perhaps he believed that the more German he appeared and acted outwardly, the less Jewish he would seem. Poor Fritz...so smart, and yet so naïve. Lately he grew angry with little provocation. A delayed dinner, an untidy room, or even the loud scrape of a chair could inexplicably set him off on another rampage. Gisela tolerated the recent mood swings, always hoping her loving husband would wake up from the charade in which he was living and return to her. But time was running out. For the sake of the children, she would not wait too much longer. Fritz might cast a blind eye to the new Nazi pronouncements, but Gisela would not. With renewed tenacity, she once again promised herself that Klara and Ernst would leave Germany once and for all. Gisela would get her children out of this godforsaken country—if necessary, without her husband's knowledge or help. Of that she was certain.

The farther Fritz walked away from the house, the more his self-assured stride began to falter. Anyone watching him now would have noticed his slumped shoulders and furtive glances. He had never felt this way before, so helpless, anxious, and vulnerable. He was resolute in his determination not to let his comportment betray his overwhelming dread of the future and further feed Gisela's intense fears. He tried to convince her that the restrictions were only temporary, a craziness that would quietly disappear as soon as fair-minded, logical Germans came to their senses, but it was becoming harder to do so with each passing day, and each passing directive. Fritz knew that he needed to act, but he felt so paralyzed by his own indecisiveness that he ended up doing nothing at all. This impotence occupied his every thought, gnawing at his conscience. He ached to confide his feelings to Gisela, but every time he tried, his shame was too great and the words would not come.

As Fritz continued on to his office, he reflected on the utter absurdity of his situation. At six feet two, the blond-haired, blue-eyed doctor looked more Aryan than most of Hitler's Brownshirts. Only a small gap between his two front teeth marred his otherwise perfect features. This fact alone almost brought a smile to his lips. *My family has been in Germany for six generations! Why, I'm more German than that maniacal Austrian with his ridiculous mustache,* he mused. A psychopath and his gang of criminals were systematically destroying Fritz's Germany, the country he loved, and there was not one damn thing he could do about it.

THREE

"She's waking, Dr. Compton. I'm certain of it. Her vital signs are good and she's beginning to stir."

"Excellent. Call me as soon as she's able to communicate. It's remarkable she's still alive. They say an American soldier found her when he saw movement near one of the mounds of bodies about to be buried," said the doctor. "He brought her here, to the hospital."

"Yes. I know he visits her every day, too. He seems to have made it his personal mission to keep this one alive."

"Do we know anything about her at all?"

"A little, doctor. Her uniform was marked with a red inverted triangle."

"A political prisoner, then. Interesting," said the doctor. "She's a sick young woman, but not as malnourished as the rest. I'm guessing she was only at Buchenwald for a few weeks before the camp was liberated—just long enough to contract typhus. I think half of the prisoners here died from that dreadful disease. The Nazis didn't need gas chambers here; filth, starvation, and exposure have done the job for them."

Dr. Thomas Compton did indeed hope this young patient made it, as he felt strangely drawn to her. He hoped no one noticed him lingering at her bedside longer than he did with his other patients. But how could he not? Even in sleep she looked so vulnerable, alone, and beautiful. He would check her again when the next shift came on. She was beginning to show signs of awakening, and he desperately wanted to be there to calm her and to let her know she was finally in safe hands. Some of his patients awoke in a state of panic, screaming god knows what in any number of languages. Others awoke silently, taking in their surroundings, fearful that this was not a safe haven, but only the beginning of another nightmare. Thomas hoped for a better scenario for this young woman. He knew that the sergeant who had saved her life would come around to see her in the next few hours, too. While he should have been grateful, he felt resentful that another man seemed as enchanted with the patient as he.

Am I losing my mind? I am jealous of a man I don't know over a woman I don't know. Even malnourished and with only short sprigs of delicate blond hair growing from her scalp, she was a beauty. Thomas was entranced. Her upturned nose was marred by the smallest little bump at the top, a slight imperfection that added character to the all-too-perfect face. He already knew that her almond-shaped eyes would be blue. He couldn't envision any other color.

Lost in his own imaginings, Thomas almost failed to notice that the woman who so captivated him had once again started to stir. *Yes*, he noted, as she opened her eyes. *They are blue, just as I expected.*

"Welcome back to the land of the living. You're safe. You're in a hospital at the camp. Please don't be alarmed," said Thomas. He pointed to his white medical coat and the stethoscope that hung from his neck. Klara looked at him blankly, not yet ready to divulge that she understood every word he was saying. "I'm sorry—I don't even know if you speak English," said Thomas. Speaking louder, as if that would make her understand, Thomas said slowly, "No one is going to hurt you... not here. I promise." He took her hands in his and held them so gently. Klara had no control over the tears that started to roll down her cheeks. It had been so long since she felt a kind touch, a tender caress.

Shaken by this unexpected emotion, Klara could no longer suppress her instinct to remain quiet. In a voice so soft the doctor would never be sure if he heard or imagined it, Klara whispered, "I understand, Herr Doctor. Thank you."

FOUR

"Lookin' at your watch isn't gonna make the time go any faster, Sam. She hasn't even opened her eyes yet, and you think you're in love. What would your mama think? Doesn't she have her heart set on you marryin' Mrs. Binelli's fat daughter, Rose? By the way, you and Rose'll make a good lookin' couple."

"Don't remind me. She sent along a real cute snap of Rose in a bathin' suit in her last letter, and...well, let's just say I'm not plannin' to pin it up. Betty Grable she's not," said Sam Rosstein to his best friend, Nick Caputo. Nick and Sam were both from Cleveland, Ohio. They had grown up just two miles apart and even played in the same high school football conference, but had never met until both were sent for basic training at Fort Benning in Columbus, Georgia, about a hundred miles from Atlanta. Sam's family lived in the predominantly Jewish neighborhood around 105th street, and Nick grew up in Cleveland's Little Italy, a community recognized for its restaurants and bakeries and insulated by geography and desire from all of the other ethnic enclaves around it. Both had enlisted just days after the Japanese bombed Pearl Harbor. At Fort Benning, the recognizable Cleveland accent had first drawn the two green recruits to one another. That comfort and familiarity had developed into a bond that had lasted three years, during which they had managed by some miracle to still be alive and together.

Sam's Italian mother had fallen in love with his Jewish father after a chance meeting at a dance at Western Reserve University. The fact that two first-generation Americans had been at college in the late 1920s was unusual in itself; the fact that both Al Rosstein and Irene Aveni had ignored convention and the wishes of their families and married was downright amazing.

Sam had not been raised with much religion at all, and even thought about dropping the Stein from the end of his name. That sure as hell would have helped him avoid a lot of bloody noses over the years. But Sam loved and respected his father too much to change it, so he kept the name. It wasn't always easy being Jewish in the US Army. Despite being wounded in battle a few days after landing at Normandy, and later being decorated for valor, he was still a convenient mark for any smart-ass new recruit trying to look tough by calling him a dirty Jew, kike, or some other derogatory expletive. Each recruit only got that one chance, however, because Sam Rosstein had grown up knowing how to take care of himself. A Golden Gloves contender while in his teens, Sam could deliver a devastating punch. It didn't take him long to win over most of the guys by his tenacity and courage. They may not have liked him, but they sure as hell respected him. He and Nick had entered the service as privates, and by war's end, both had been promoted to the rank of sergeant.

"Nick, look, I think she's wakin' up. Doesn't she have the most angelic face you ever laid eyes on?"

"Oh, boy, you got it bad. I'm leavin'. I've spent enough time watchin' you moon over this broad. Hell, Sam, you don't know one thing about her," said Nick. "Stay if you want to, but I do believe I hear a card game callin' my name. I don't mind makin' a little money off of some wet-behind-the-ears replacements."

Sam was secretly glad Nick finally decided to leave. He would rather not listen to anymore of his friend's yammering while he waited for the young woman to awaken. *Is this love? I must be nuts! I'm going to end up in a hospital, too—in the psycho ward—if I'm not careful. How can you possibly love someone you don't know?* Thoughts of her consumed him, from the moment he awoke in the morning until the moment he went to sleep at night. Then, once he fell asleep, he would dream about her, and often wake up with a pounding heart and in need of a cold shower.

The dreams were so real and always the same. They were on a dance floor. The room was dark, and in the background Lena Horne was singing "Stormy Weather." The music was sultry and the two of them were molded together, arms held tightly around one another, hands moving, caressing, exploring. Her head was on his shoulder and he could feel her hot breath on the nape of his neck. From the dance floor they ended up in the bedroom, still molded together but moving together in a different dance, a slow dance, one that left him crazed with desire, needing her and wanting her more than he ever wanted anything in his entire life.

So lost was he in his own thoughts that he almost didn't notice that Klara was again beginning to stir and waken. Within minutes she had opened her eyes and was startled to see not the doctor whom she had spoken to earlier, but a soldier with an unlit cigarette dangling from his lip, a wild mop of curly dark hair, and the kindest brown eyes she had ever seen.

"Hey, beautiful, you're up," said Sam, managing to speak without ever removing the cigarette from his mouth. "I know you probably don't understand English, but I'm the one who found you. You know, brought you here to the docs. I was patrollin' the camp perimeter, and when I passed one of those piles of bodies ready for burial, I thought I heard somethin'—a moan, somethin'. So, I dunno, I walked back just to check things out, see for myself. Damn...all those bodies. It's awful...somethin' I'll remember for the rest of my life. Anyway, you were just sprawled out there like all the rest. I couldn't believe it, so many of you, all dead— but then I saw you weren't dead. You were breathin', and I...well...you know" His voiced trailed off. *Oh, just shut up, Sam, you're rambling. She probably doesn't understand anything that's coming out of your mouth.*

Sam was so caught up in his desire to make conversation that he almost missed the attentive look on Klara's face. "Hey, wait a minute. You *do* understand what I'm sayin', don't you?"

"Yes, I speak English," said Klara. "I learned many years ago, in the Volksschule in Berlin."

Sam couldn't believe he was finally hearing her voice. It was deep and warm. Her English was remarkably good, and her accent only added to her allure. "You must think me awful," Klara said, with tears once again welling up in her eyes. "You rescued me, and I cannot bring myself to thank you."

Sam gave her a puzzled look. "You...you didn't want to be saved?"

She shook her head. "You saved someone who was already dead," she said. "I died, bit by bit, one piece at a time, long ago. And then I died the rest of the way not long ago when I learned for certain of the death of my brother and mother. I have nothing left to live for. Everyone, everyone I ever loved is gone."

Sam remained quiet and gently took Klara's small, delicate hand in his large, rough one. Pulling his chair closer to her bed, he sat there for several minutes with Klara while the tears fell freely down her face.

"I don't have any great words to take away your pain. Maybe they don't exist. This war—it's almost over, at least in Europe. Did you know that? And not a minute too soon, either. From all the reports comin' in, those Nazis were not only responsible for the rape of Europe but for the murders of thousands of civilians, maybe more," said Sam. "I'm not sure we'll ever know just how many people were slaughtered. Intel from Allied forces in Germany, all across Poland— they found dozens of camps just like this one. I can't begin to imagine what you've been through, but I'd like to try to help. If you want to talk, I'm here."

"You are very kind, but I do not understand. Why do you care? We do not know each other. I do not even know your name..., and you do not know nothing about me."

"I can't explain it," Sam answered. "I really can't. I mean, I care about all the people who've been killed in this damn war, especially the ones who weren't soldiers—like the people in these camps. But there's also, somethin' about you..., I dunno. I just want to help. Maybe. Maybe I feel responsible for you since I pulled you out of that pile. You know? Like I should, finish the job I started by makin' sure you get better."

Sam stared down at his scuffed boots. Then he straightened up and held out his hand. "So, let's at least get the name thing out of the way. I'm Sam Rosstein," he said. "Now you tell me your name, and then we won't be strangers anymore, right?"

She shook his hand tentatively. "Klara. My name is Klara Werner."

"Good," Sam said. "So that makes us friends, right?"

Klara nodded and was startled when Sam bent down and quickly brushed her cheek with his lips. "I gotta go now, but I'll stop by again later, if that's all right. Is that all right, Klara?"

"Yes," she said in a voice hardly louder than a whisper. "That would be fine, Sam. I would like that."

For the first time since Klara had awakened, the hospital was quiet. It had been a very long time since she had enjoyed the luxury of a pillow, the softness of a blanket, or the clean aroma of a freshly laundered sheet. For just a moment she forced herself to think of nothing but the sheer pleasure of those long-forgotten sensations. *I have never been kissed like that, so gently*, she thought. Klara touched her cheek and felt strangely moved when she remembered how afterward Sam seemed so awkward and embarrassed.

The moment savored, it was soon gone as the reality of her life once again invaded her thoughts. *I truly am alone. Papa, Mama, Ernst—all dead, gone*, she thought. *I must decide. I have choices. Always, even after my arrest, I had choices.* Perhaps she could locate Mama's best friend, the one who immigrated to South Africa. Or Papa's estranged cousin, the one that he had not spoken to in years, the one who had fled as soon as Hitler came to power, although Klara had absolutely no idea where the cousin had gone. Papa had thought his cousin was such a fool. *Well, guess what, Papa, she was smarter than you.*

Perhaps Klara could move to the United States, and begin again in America. She knew only one thing for certain: she would never stay in Germany. *Once I leave here, I will never set foot in this country again, not ever.*

America, that is what Mama had wanted for her and Ernst. Poor Mama. She had such dreams for them. They almost made it, too. If only they had not been betrayed. Oh why had Mama been so trusting? Klara furrowed her brow. A few hours ago she had been thinking only of death. What changed? *I am actually contemplating a future.* Perhaps it was the kindness of Sam or the good doctor that was allowing her to think, even for a moment, that she might have a future. Or she was once again remembering her promise to Mama—her promise to survive no matter the cost.

But how do I get to America? I have no one there to sponsor me. I have no property, money, or papers. I will languish here in this camp...and then where? With those somber thoughts in mind, Klara turned her head to the wall and willed herself to once again fall asleep.

For the first time all day, death had taken a sabbatical. The vital signs of many of the patients were finally stabilizing. Exhausted, Thomas folded his lanky frame into the first chair he spotted, hoping that a sympathetic nurse might take pity on him and help him find a vacant bed. Lately, though, even when he had the chance, he could only sleep for a few hours before the sensations that haunted him all day intruded into his mind at night. Nothing could have ever prepared him for the horrors of Buchenwald. The images, the sounds, and especially the smells—these were things he knew would stay with him the rest of his life.

How do you explain the unexplainable? Thomas had tried to write about what he was witnessing in his weekly letter to his mother, but her responses were always void of comment and full of local gossip and country club news. Eugenia Compton, known by all her closest admirers as Genie, never missed her weekly dinner at the Piedmont Driving Club. Not even the end of the world could have prevented her from keeping up with her multitude of social commitments. Genie was like that with everything. If it didn't affect her daily schedule, then the hell with it. She reminded Thomas of a modern-day Marie Antoinette. Well, that wasn't exactly being fair; his mother did have her positive attributes. She had managed to invest his father's fortune in lucrative stocks following his premature death at the age of forty-two after a short life filled with too many vices and a heart not strong enough to keep up with them. The small fortune had grown to a much more respectable one, and unless someone was very, very stupid, no future generation of Comptons would ever have to worry about money again.

Of course, even without money the Comptons would have always been welcome members of Atlanta's social elite. After all, old granddaddy Jedediah Lapham Compton had served the Southern Confederacy bravely in the War of Northern Aggression, and Eugenia was a proud member and past president of the Atlanta chapter of the Daughters of the Confederacy. His mother had just been born during the wrong era. Hosting one of the balls following the 1939 premiere of *Gone With The Wind* at the downtown Loew's Grand Theatre had been one of her proudest moments. Eugenia had been decked out in a dress Scarlett herself would have envied, and that evening the Compton manse had been transformed into an antebellum plantation. It surprised no one that Eugenia found it difficult to return the home to its present-day décor.

Thomas was so preoccupied with his thoughts of home it took him a moment to react to the screaming coming from the direction of Klara's bed. Jumping up, he tripped over the chair, caught himself on an adjacent cabinet, and never lost stride as he raced over to her. "Klara, Klara, it's only a dream. You're safe. You're in the hospital," he said as he gently nudged her shoulder."

Klara opened her eyes and Thomas was pained by the look of terror that tortured her expression. Once again, he took her hand and gently caressed it, oblivious to the stares of the two nurses who were more than a bit bemused by the intensive care this particular patient was receiving. He spoke to her in whispers, telling her over and over again that she was safe, that no one would ever again hurt her.

His voice and touch seemed to calm her, so he continued talking, telling her about his life away from the war, as far away from Buchenwald as his words could carry her. He reminisced about Atlanta and his summers spent on his granddaddy's pecan farm in Thomasville, Georgia. He told her about the giant oak tree in the middle of the town with limbs so twisted and heavy that townsfolk talked about bracing them up so they wouldn't fall and kill any citizens. He told her that in Atlanta there were so many streets with the name Peachtree that visitors never failed to get lost. He told her about Coca-Cola, the best drink in the whole damn world. And he told her that one day, he would take her to Atlanta, right to Jacobs' Pharmacy where Coca-Cola was first served as a fountain drink, so she could try one out for herself. He didn't know if any of this was making any sense to her, but that was irrelevant. It only mattered that she no longer seemed like the terrified women who had been screaming and thrashing about just a short while earlier.

Klara liked the slow cadence of the doctor's speech. His American accent was different from the one she had heard earlier from Sam Rosstein. Two men, both so kind and, even in her brief encounters with them, so different. This doctor was also trying to heal not just her body but her mind as well. From the looks of things, it seemed like her body was on its way toward recovery. Healing her mind was quite another matter altogether. Klara knew her nightmare was not of the ordinary variety she had as a child, usually after reading one of those horrid fairy tales so popular with her school chums. No, in this nightmare she was forced to relive the horrors of the last five years, years of a hell here on earth, all beginning on November 9, 1938.

FIVE

For the last several months, Gisela had been feverishly working behind Fritz's back arranging for their emigration. She knew that Fritz had a distant cousin in America, and she had written to Jewish agencies in New York and Washington, DC, in the hopes they would be able to locate her. Gisela needed someone who would sign the all-important affidavits of support promising that she and her family would not become a burden on the United States. There were quotas limiting the number of immigrants allowed into the country, and finding someone, anyone, to sign the affidavit was the first step in the process.

Gisela knew she might have started too late, but she hoped there was still enough time for her little family to get out. In the letters to the agencies, Gisela had bared her soul, confiding to total strangers her terror of the Nazis and the daily humiliations her family was forced to endure. She hated sounding so pitiful, but that was what her missives were intended to do—arouse enough pity that the sympathetic Americans would help them get out. Thus far, she had heard nothing. She prayed nightly that there would be a letter from America in the next day's post. She wanted to have an actual affidavit in her hands before she revealed her plans to Fritz.

Gisela begged her aged parents to leave with them, but they told her that the ocean voyage would be too hard, and that they felt they were too old to start fresh. Although she was heartsick about the idea of leaving her parents behind, nothing could deter Gisela from her mission to save her children. Her parents were elderly and her father was suffering from heart failure. Perhaps even under Hitler they would be better off staying. Her father considered himself a patriot who had willingly served the Fatherland during the First World War, and he believed his war record would be enough to keep him safe. Like Fritz, Gisela's parents believed in Germany and were convinced that the good German people would soon come to their senses and throw Hitler and his Brownshirts back down into the same sewer from whence they had come. With the same impassioned vehemence that they defended Germany, they passionately loathed and feared the Nazis.

Gisela had confided nothing about Fritz's recent behavior to her parents. They adored Fritz and had treated him like a son ever since the day she married the aspiring doctor. Her marriage was good, and one that Gisela thought could weather any storms that might arise. The frequent arguments followed by uncomfortable silences had been a recent phenomenon that only began to erode their contented home life after Hitler assumed the chancellorship. Fear was the catalyst. Little by little, as more of his rights were taken away, Fritz felt less and less like a man. Eventually he began to take it out on her and the children.

When Gisela went to her parents with her plan, they willingly gave her enough money to pay for passage and a new start in America. After that, it was only a matter of time. She would keep her secret until their quota numbers were called and then reveal her subterfuge to her husband, hoping he would finally acquiesce and leave. But even though she dearly loved her husband, she was determined to get out of this godforsaken country, with or without him.

For the Werner family, as for all Jews throughout Europe, time was running out. On November 7, 1938, Herschel Grynszpan, a seventeen-year-old Polish Jew living in Paris, assassinated Ernst vom Rath, third secretary in the German embassy. After vom Rath died on November 8, sporadic rioting erupted across Germany. Gisela was painfully aware of the climate in the streets. The fear began like an insidious snake that methodically slithered into Jewish households throughout Berlin and the rest of the country, a miasma of whispers and forebodings that you could almost touch. Warnings of *be careful, close the shop early, stay indoors* were passed throughout Germany. Gisela feared for the safety of her parents and the children.

"Fritz," she implored. "Perhaps we should drive out to the country and spend a few days with the Stiners. They're Christian and we would be safe there."

"Don't be ridiculous. We are perfectly safe here at home." Fritz patted Gisela's hand as if she were a small child who needed reassurance. With a quick wave of his hand, he dismissed any notion that his family could possibly be in danger. Gisela thought but quickly rejected the idea of asking him to close his practice for the next several days. His presence might have helped her feel safer, but it would also heighten the tension in the home. Besides, his daily absence gave her additional precious hours to plan their escape.

By the evening of November 9, Gisela was convinced that the rumors of impending disaster were true. She was uncharacteristically short-tempered with Klara and Ernst. Each time the phone rang, she jumped as if the sound was tolling the hour of their doom. Yet at eight in the evening the streets were quiet and deserted. For some reason, Fritz had not yet returned home, and even for him, that was unusual. With the dishes washed, dried, and put away, and homework completed, Gisela hurried both children into the bathroom and told them to ready themselves for bed.

"But, Mama, it's so early!" pleaded Ernst.

"He's right, Mama. We never go to bed before nine," echoed Klara.

"No arguments, not tonight. Close the curtains and read in bed if you'd like, but stay in your rooms!"

Their mother rarely disciplined her children so forcefully, and Gisela was heartbroken when she saw Ernst's lower lip begin to quiver. Lately her children had received so little affection, time, and understanding from their father that whenever Gisela raised her voice, they took it to heart. Ernst, who idolized his father, was particularly affected.

"Come here, both of you." The children ran into Gisela's open embrace. Holding them tightly, she tried to reassure them. "You have done nothing wrong. Trust me. Tonight I need you both to stay in your rooms." Gisela did not want to worry them with unsubstantiated rumors.

Perhaps if everyone stayed quiet, with the lights off, they could avoid any trouble. With the children tucked safely away for the night Gisela retreated to her own bedroom, picked up her knitting, and waited for the return of her husband and for the passage of the night.

At first Gisela thought the rapping was part of her dream. It took her a few seconds to realize that she had fallen asleep sitting up. Her knitting had dropped to the floor and her glasses hung precariously from one ear. The tapping persisted, and Gisela realized it came from the window at the back of the house. *As if I wasn't nervous enough!* she thought. Without turning on any additional lights, Gisela inched her way over to the small window and slowly moved the curtains to one side. "My God, Fritz!" Her impeccably dressed husband was crouching outside the window without his outer coat, his shirt hanging untucked. Blood trickled from a large gash over his left eye.

"Go to the back door," she mouthed. Fritz disappeared from view as Gisela hurried to the rear of the house to let him in. As she unhooked the catch, Fritz pushed through the door so hard that Gisela stumbled backward, bracing herself at the last second on the nearby desk. Fritz immediately fell to the floor, crawled to the nearest corner, and began to rock and cry with his head resting in his cupped hands. "Fritz, you're bleeding. What has happened? Let me take a look at that cut."

The house was still dark. Without thinking, Gisela turned and flicked on the light to look more closely at Fritz's wound. The light startled the still-whimpering Fritz, who frantically whispered, "No, Gisela, turn it off! We're in danger. Do as I say."

Gisela did as she was ordered. "Fritz, now I can't see well enough to help. The gash looks deep."

"Gisela, please. It is nothing compared to what I've seen tonight. I've been a fool.... God forgive me...I've been such a fool."

"Fritz, please, I'm frightened. What is happening?"

"Our countrymen, our fellow citizens—they have *lists*, names of Jews to arrest and cart off to who knows where," hissed Fritz. "Leave it to the Germans: we are always so precise, so purposeful. We are such an ordered people. Sign here, go there...never do we ask why. And now the Nazis simply pull out a list, a roster, and find us all."

Gisela handed him a towel. He sat up, pressing it to his head. "You cannot believe what is going on: businesses destroyed, streets filled with glass from broken windows. I was leaving my office when one of the Brownshirts—a man who, if you can believe it, was once a loyal patient of mine!—shouted my name. I still cannot comprehend how a man who used to come to my office, who trusted me to care for his aches and pains, could point at me and call me such names. He told the others I was a Jewish doctor. He grabbed me off the sidewalk and herded me into a group of about twenty other men. We were forced to walk down the center of Elsässer Strasse. As we marched along, not knowing where we were going or why were being so brutally treated, they pushed and shoved us. Anyone who lagged behind or took a misstep was beaten. I recognized some of my old Christian patients watching as our little band stumbled through their neighborhoods. No one—not one, I tell you!—tried to intervene. A few people I used to consider friends caught my eye, and did *nothing* except look away."

Gisela sunk down beside Fritz and put her arm around her husband. "Perhaps they were afraid, too," she said. "Perhaps they are still friends?"

Fritz ignored her. His story tumbled out as though he could not stop himself from telling it. "Franz Silverberg, the tailor? You know, the one whose shop is around the corner from my office? He was standing beside me one moment and on his knees in the middle of the street the next. He must have tripped. I reached down to give him a hand, and one of the thugs beat me...with a bat. When I lost consciousness, they left me there. Perhaps they thought I was dead. When I awoke, I was alone in the middle of the street. Franz and all the others were gone. Gone, Gisela, just taken away...and for what? Silverberg must be at least seventy-five years old. What's to become of him? Earlier, when I first came in, I asked God to forgive me. Perhaps he will if I pray hard enough. But can you? Can you ever forgive me for pretending all this would go away? I was afraid that if I confessed my fears, I would be less of a man in your eyes. I am so sorry."

Unexpectedly, tears began to stream down Gisela's face. It was the first time in the past year that Fritz had let his real feelings show and acted like the man she had married. She gently cradled his head in her arms. "Fritz, you know I have never stopped loving you. I knew you were frightened. I should have done more...."

"Shhh!" Fritz mouthed, his finger to his lips. "Stay here," he whispered. Fritz crawled over to the window and slowly raised his head to peer out. The porch light had been doused earlier and Fritz could barely make anything out. As he strained to hear where the noise had come from, there was an unmistakable light rapping on the front door.

"Fritz, don't open it. It could be them," whispered Gisela.

"No, don't worry. Brownshirts would not be so polite, nor so quiet. It must be Heinz." Fritz quietly unlatched the door and Heinz Dieter slipped silently into the room.

"Keep the lights off," Dieter ordered. "I only have a few minutes."

Heinz Dieter and Fritz had been classmates. Together they had walked hand and hand with their paper cones filled with candy, a German tradition, to start Kindergarten, and had remained friends ever since. Dieter could have been the poster boy for every Aryan propaganda poster. His blond hair, blue eyes, and chiseled chin were exactly the physical traits Hitler and his lackeys wanted to see in themselves. The clubfooted Joseph Goebbels, Hitler's propaganda minister, had taken a personal interest in Dieter and was grooming him for a position as a member of his staff. As a perfect symbol of Nordic purity, Dieter had been able to move quickly through the ranks of the Nazi Party. He was outwardly 100 percent National Socialist—but he was inwardly opposed to Der Führer with every ounce of his being. To accomplish his charade, Dieter had been forced to alienate every member of his family who had vowed to never join the Nazi party. Rather than being vocally opposed from outside, Dieter forced himself to work from the inside to save his beloved country from the horrors of the Third Reich. Too many dissidents had conveniently disappeared over the last several months. It was a dangerous and lonely position he had chosen to take, but Dieter had instinctively understood that few options remained in a nation gone completely mad.

"I gave Becker—you know, that disgusting little prick who is causing such havoc in your neighborhood?—a few Reichsmarks, and he agreed to not roust you, at least for the time being. Someone accused you of treating Aryan patients, and as you know, in today's Germany that is a crime. So, my dear Fritz, time is short. Do you have any Christian neighbors who will take you in?"

"Yes, I think so," said Fritz. "One of my patients is an old and trusted friend. At least, I *think* he can still be trusted."

"Good. I don't think you have an alternative. You must leave tonight."

"Tonight? But how?"

"You will have to find a way," said Dieter. "You have no choice. Trust me; you are not safe."

From the corner, Gisela had silently watched the exchange between her husband and Heinz Dieter. *How ironic*, she thought. *Fritz is as blond as Dieter; they could be brothers. Yet, because of our different religions, he is safe, and we are persecuted, treated like common criminals.*

"Gisela," Fritz whispered. "Come, we must make plans." Snapped out of her troubled musings, Gisela crawled over to the two men.

Fritz had partially steeled himself against the horrors of the evening and was again exuding the demeanor of a man in control. If ever she and the children needed that from him, it would be tonight. Fritz reached out his hand to help Gisela up from the floor and, with uncharacteristic emotion, hugged his wife of eighteen years and gently kissed her.

"Go, wake the children. We must take only a few necessary things for our toilet. I will call my patient to make arrangements."

Gisela entered the room where the children were sleeping. For several months now, ever since they had been expelled from the Volksschule, Klara and Ernst had sought out each other's company and were generally found in the same room in the morning. To Gisela's amazement, Klara was sitting up, fully clothed, on her neatly made-up bed. Her small red-and-white cardboard suitcase was already packed with her most prized possessions, and her coat and hat lay next to her, neatly folded, waiting to be put on.

"Oh, Klara. You are almost completely grown up, aren't you?"

"Not so grown up, Mama. I am terribly frightened."

"Was Papa hurt badly? I was afraid to come out of the room. The only thing I could think of to do was to get dressed."

Gisela sat down on the bed next to Klara and gently pulled her terrified daughter toward her. "We are all frightened. These are extreme times. But we are all together. Papa knows a lot of people in the right places, and I have—how do the Americans say it in their movies?—an ace up my sleeve. Now come, let us wake your brother and tell him we are going on a surprise outing. We must do our best acting. It is enough that you know what is going on. Let's try and keep him a child for as long as possible."

Klara dutifully nodded in agreement, and went over to roust Ernst from his peaceful slumber.

SIX

The time passed quickly, and each day Klara's ravished body gained more strength. She was no longer confined to bed, but politely refused all entreaties by the nurses to venture out of the hospital. Klara could not face leaving the sterile environment of the ward for the squalor she was certain remained outside. *Ironic*, she thought. *These striped hospital pajamas are not much different from the camp uniforms we wanted never to see again.* She lay in bed for most of the day, hoping that the sleep that eluded her during the night would somehow overtake her in the daylight hours.

Most of the time, however, she enjoyed just closing her eyes and recalling the warmth of her home and the sanctuary it had once symbolized, remembering family who simply were no more. Oh, how she missed them! The strength of her father's hand, the love of her mother's embrace, and the impish grin that always marked the face of her much-loved little brother. Were the others in the nearby beds experiencing the same pain? Klara could not bring herself to ask. The daily visits from Dr. Compton and Sergeant Rosstein helped. Their company provided her respite from her more tortured memories.

Thomas told her stories of his mother's exploits in Atlanta. Klara loved to hear about the society parties made vivid by Thomas's colorful descriptions of the city's social scene. "Oh, Klara, you should see all those blue-haired ladies at the season's charity events at the Piedmont Driving Club. Mother acts as if she were the granddaughter of Robert E.

Lee himself instead of the progeny of a dirt-poor redneck pecan farmer from South Georgia."

"And this Robert E. Lee...?" Klara said. "He is someone to be revered?"

"You've got to be kidding, Klara! Why, old General Lee is just about the most sacrosanct name in all the South. Why, he—wait, you're kidding, aren't you? Well, I'll be damned. You're actually smiling."

Klara could hold it in no longer, and burst out laughing. "You were just so serious about your General Lee, I couldn't help myself. Even here we studied the American Civil War and the two opposing generals, Lee and...the other one, the one who was victorious and later became president. What was his name?"

"Grant, Klara. His name was Grant," said Thomas. "By the way, he may have been victorious, but he was also a well-known drunk—and a lousy president to boot." Thomas's irritation at the mention of the Union General brought forth more laughter, so much so that Thomas could not help but be caught up in the contagion of it. Klara laughed, first whole-heartedly and then convulsively. Thomas was not sure when exactly the mirth turned into something else, something darker.

In a few minutes it was over. Klara sat with her knees folded up into her arms and with her head bent down into them, hiding her face.

"Hey, are you in there, Klara?"

"I am too ashamed to look at you," she said. "We were having a normal moment. I made a joke, we were laughing...and then I remembered—I shouldn't be laughing! What right do I have to laugh when my entire family is gone, murdered?"

"Klara, talk to me. Tell me what happened."

"I can't. I'm too afraid. The memories are enough. I wish I could erase the past six years from my mind forever. It hurts too much. Every time I close my eyes it all comes flooding back to me," she said. "Have you ever been afraid? I mean *really* afraid? I've been terrified for so long, I'm not sure I will ever feel safe again. Do you think that's possible, to feel safe when for so long you feared every unknown footstep, every knock on the door? And the worst part is that even though I can still taste the fear, I can no longer conjure up a clear picture of my parents. Isn't that strange? Should I not remember every detail of their faces? If only I had a photograph, just one photograph." Klara was once more overcome by emotion. "Please, Thomas, no more. I cannot talk about it anymore, please." Klara once again lay down in bed, turned her head to the wall, and closed out the world.

Like Thomas, Sam continued his daily visits to Klara's bedside. He made it a point to always arrive after Klara's doctor left for rounds or to go to the hospital mess tent. The last thing he wanted was to run into his competition, and he definitely had a rival in the good doctor.

Klara had been awake for several weeks, and much of her color and strength had started to return. She was like a blossoming flower at the height of spring. Her transformation was truly remarkable. Outwardly she showed few signs of her ordeal, yet Sam knew that her emotional scars ran deep. During each visit, she divulged a little more. Perhaps today she would tell him the rest of her story.

Sam approached her bed as quietly as a six-foot, 180-pound soldier wearing mud-encrusted army boots could manage. Slipping into the chair that was always near her bedside, he waited patiently, knowing that Klara would soon sense his presence and awaken. Preoccupied with his own thoughts, he was surprised when he looked toward the bed and saw that she was indeed awake and staring at him.

"Penny for your thoughts," he said.

"No, Sam, even a penny is too much to charge. My memories are too burdensome to inflict on anyone."

"Try me. I'm a great listener," said Sam. "And I have two little sisters, and believe you me, they never stop comin' to big brother for help solvin' their problems. In my hometown, it's actually a well known fact that I give sound advice to the lovelorn." *Except in the case of my own love sickness, that is.*

"Oh, so you are an expert in the ways of the heart?"

"You bet. And your heart is right now sayin' that you'd like to spend the next hour or so with me pourin' out your troubles," said Sam with a grin. "I've got broad shoulders, Klara. Trust me, I want to help you."

"I think perhaps I am beyond help. When I am awake, I cannot stop thinking about the last six years. Sleep, when it finally comes, offers me little escape. My dreams are so real, and I relive everything each and every night," said Klara. "My nightmare always starts in 1938, in November, the night when Jews throughout Germany were rousted from their beds in the middle of the night, my family included. Thousands were arrested and sent off to Dachau or Sachsenhausen. Those camps were originally built for political prisoners, which now included the Jews. Even before then we had been subjected to so many indignities. Jews could no longer marry non-Jews; Jews could no longer attend public schools; Jewish doctors could no longer practice medicine among the Aryan population; non-Jews could no longer work for Jews. We were slowly singled out, as though we were not German citizens. Jews could not even sit on Aryan-only park benches."

"Sounds familiar. We treat Negroes like that in our country, especially in the South, and it's a damn shame," said Sam. "We Jews catch a lot of shit, too, but it's not spelled out like it is with the Negroes. I don't understand any of it. If there's one thing a war should tell people, it's that we're all the same color on the inside; we all bleed red."

"Yes, people are persecuted in many places throughout the world, I know. But this...this was taken to absurd levels! I used to love to take Ernst to the Berlin Zoo; the Nazis even prohibited that! Perhaps they thought that the animals knew the difference between pure Aryan blood and Jewish blood—and cared," said Klara. "Oh, Sam, the list goes on and on. There were so many pronouncements. We could not keep them all straight. We were afraid to do anything for fear of breaking the law."

"Klara, I can't help wonderin' why, with all that going on, your family didn't leave? I'm not judgin'—I'd hate to leave my homeland, I know that—but I guess I just don't get it. Why stay in a place, a country, where you are hated?"

Klara readjusted herself in bed. Sitting up with her legs dangling over the side, she took Sam's strong hands and held them to her chest. "Oh, Sam we were so naïve. We thought of ourselves as Germans first—Germans who also happened to be Jewish. We were a country of innocents—faithful citizens who could not bring themselves to believe the unbelievable. My father could trace his Germanic roots back to the 1600s! He found pleasure in unrolling the family tree, explaining this person and that person to my brother and me. He loved his country."

"I understand that. I do."

"Until the madness of the Third Reich, life was good in Germany, for everyone, including Jews. But when Adolf Hitler came into power, my mother was among the few who believed from the very beginning that his madness would spread, ignite everyone, and consume us all," said Klara. "She begged my father to get our papers in order. He refused to listen. My father was more German than Jewish—or so he thought. But in the end, it was not what he thought that mattered. The only thing that mattered was what the Nazis thought, what our neighbors thought. Longtime patients and even some friends saw my father only as a Jew—nothing more, nothing less. He was the same man he had always been. My father had not changed; they had. My mother tried to make him see. When he finally did, it was too late."

"What happened?"

"That night in November 1938 changed everything. My father was forced to stop burying his head in the sand. He was nearly arrested in the first sweep, and only escaped because he was beaten unconscious and left for dead. After that night, when he finally made it home, he knew that everything my mother had been telling him was true. The country he loved, the country that he would have given his life for, no longer loved nor wanted him," said Klara. "My parents had only a very short time together after that. I could tell how much they loved one another. Their bond may have been strained, but it was never broken. My parents loved us and died trying to give Ernst and me a future. I only hope they are resting in peace."

There was so much more Sam wanted to know. *Had they all been separated? When? How did she know for certain that they were all dead? Did she have any family at all left?* But it seemed that she had exhausted herself for the moment.

"Listen to me rattle on! You have been here an hour, and I have done all the talking. It is enough," she said. "Let us speak of something else. Tell me about your family."

"Well, there's really not much to say. I'm kind of an open book, no secrets. I was born and raised in Cleveland, Ohio. My mother is a short, kind of robust Italian woman who—much to my sisters' chagrin!—thinks the sun rises and sets with me. My dad is a lawyer. He's Jewish. My mom was raised Catholic. They fell for each other in a big way, and...well, what can I say? Love won out," said Sam. "From the stories I've heard, it wasn't easy. All four of my grandparents were very set in their ways and pretty religious. Surprisin'ly, though, they developed a kind of a mutual respect for one another. Or maybe it's more like a truce. Holidays are a mess, of course. You know, Passover vs. Easter, Chanukah vs. Christmas. It was really hard on us kids gettin' all those extra presents," said, Sam grinning. Klara grinned back.

"My father is pretty well known around town. He has his own firm, and hopes that when I'm discharged I'll come home, go on to law school, and join him in his practice. Cleveland's a nice town, great place to grow up, but cold as hell in winter. When I was in the Ardennes in my foxhole, hopin' my toes wouldn't turn black and fall off, I used to imagine myself on a nice beach—you know the kind I'm talkin' about? White sand, the kind that flows through your fingers when you try to hold it. The sun beatin' down on my back. I'd just be sittin' there watchin' the surf roll in and out. I kind of promised myself that if I made it out of this war alive, I'd try to never be that cold again, and Cleveland...well you just can't describe a Cleveland winter. There's this lake effect that makes it snow like crazy, and—hey, now I'm doin' all the talkin'!"

"I like it. Go on," said Klara.

"Anyway, I'm just not sure what to tell my dad. This war has changed me, the things I've seen. You know, like these damn camps. The idea of practicin' real estate law in the Midwest just doesn't seem to cut it anymore. Of course, I haven't mentioned any of this to my folks. No sense upsettin' them until I know when I'll be discharged and what I want to do."

Without warning, Klara abruptly dropped the hand she was still holding and looked once more like the frightened little girl he had first encountered. "Klara, I'm sorry. Did I say somethin' wrong?"

"No, Sam. Your stories, they are wonderful, and I especially like it when you speak of your home. It is only that I have had not thought about you leaving. You have been such a comfort to me."

"Is that all? I don't have any orders to leave this place. We're still doin' a lot of cleanup, interrogations of camp guards, and interviewin' prisoners. There are tons of guys who have way more bonus points than I have, so I don't think I'll be goin' home anytime soon. So, Klara, don't worry, I'm goin' to be around for a bit longer. Besides," Sam continued sincerely. "In case you haven't realized, comin' to see you is the best part of my day. In fact, it's the best damn thing that's happened to me in a very long time. Maybe ever. I'm not about to let a little thing like orders mess up our daily visits, now am I?"

As casually as he could, Sam scoped out the ward, and once he was assured that everyone was occupied elsewhere, he bent down and kissed Klara on the lips, first gently, and then with frantic desire when he realized Klara was welcoming his advances and holding onto him with renewed strength and longing. A clatter of bedpans from across the room startled them both and Sam and Klara reluctantly separated, each embarrassed by the spontaneous passion that had overtaken them.

"See?" Sam said. "I'm not goin' anywhere. If it were up to me, I'd sit by your bedside day and night and entertain you with my charmin' wit, but duty calls."

Klara could only shake her head in amazement, as Sam sauntered from the room, smiling brightly, oblivious to the many pairs of eyes that watched him leave.

What am I doing? thought Klara. *This is crazy. I hardly know him. But these feelings—so new, so frightening, so wonderful—Sam, you came into my life and saved me from certain death, and now you are saving my spirit as well. But in the process I fear you are stealing my heart.*

The feelings gave Klara a renewed vitality. She was eager to take a short walk, and she knew that exercise would help clear her head, but she still did not dare to venture outside, even though the sun was shining, beckoning her. She was too afraid of what she might see if she left the confines of the field hospital. Instead she opted for walking up and down the long hallway just outside the ward. The restless pacing sent her drifting back to the last night she had spent in the safety of her home, and back to the years of hiding and terror that had destroyed her family and altered the dreams of a young woman forever.

SEVEN

In the early morning hours of November 8, 1938, the Werner family left their home carrying just three small suitcases. Klara could still clearly recall with inimitable clarity their clandestine flight to the home of her father's former patient. Once there, she and Ernst were quickly spirited to bed while Fritz spoke with Josef and his wife Erica. Too frightened to sleep, Klara lay awake for hours, peering out and eavesdropping, then replaying the day's events. Fritz was so relieved to find sanctuary for his family that when his friend revealed that they would have to leave in the morning, Klara's father resorted to something she had never seen him do before: he begged.

"Josef, please, we are at your mercy—please. Think of my wife and children."

"Fritz, my friend, believe me, if it were up to me alone, you could stay indefinitely. But Erica? She is furious. I had to use all of my powers of persuasion to allow you to stay even tonight," said Josef. "She is afraid for our own safety; harboring Jews is strictly forbidden. Perhaps it is not as bad as you think, and they will only detain you for a few hours and let you go."

"Josef, we have it on good authority," said Gisela. "The Nazis are arresting Jews and sending them off to god knows where."

For the next several minutes, no one spoke. Finally, Erica could apparently no longer control her fear or her anger. "Josef!" she shrieked. "They must go! The police would not be searching for him if he were as innocent as he claims. You are putting our family at risk, and if you don't make them leave, I will call the police."

"Erica, for once in your life, keep quiet," said Josef. "The *police* no longer exist. They stand by watching Hitler's henchmen do his handiwork. Our fellow countrymen have lost their minds. I have known Fritz for over ten years, and he is no more a criminal or a threat to the Fatherland than you or I. Are you blind to what that madman is doing to our country?"

"Be careful what you say, Josef. The walls have ears," said Erica. She abruptly turned and walked into her bedroom, slamming the door behind her. Grief stricken and humiliated, Josef stood silently, shaking his head, not knowing what to do or say.

"Fritz, what can we do? Where can we go?" asked Gisela, her voice trembling. Walking over to his distraught wife, Fritz embraced her for what seemed like many minutes before once again turning to his friend.

"Josef, as much as I hate to admit it, Erica is right. You are putting your entire family at risk by harboring us. In fact, I am risking all of our lives by not turning myself in. They are only arresting men. If I leave, Gisela and the children can safely return home."

"No, Fritz, no! I will not allow it," cried an anguished Gisela. "Nothing good will come of this. I have never been so certain of anything in my entire life."

Hearing her mother's pleading, Klara flew from the room where she had been listening intently at the door and threw her arms around her father. "Papa, please," begged Klara. "We need you! Who will protect us?"

"Klara, Gisela. Josef is right," said Fritz quietly. "We don't know how long they will keep me; I could be gone only a short time." To Gisela he whispered, "Please, my darling. Let me once again be the man you married. I have been such a fool. But I've done nothing wrong. You shall see: by tomorrow morning I will be home." He shook Josef's hand solemnly. "Thank you, Josef. Until we meet again."

Josef pulled Fritz into a hug and slapped him on the back. Then he stepped back and said, in a voiced choked with emotion, "Yes, until we meet again. And may it be under far better circumstances and in a far better Germany than we see today. Good luck, my friend."

Fritz smiled bravely. "Now then, Klara, give your Papa one more big hug. Gisela, you too. Kiss Ernst for me, and call Heinz to let him know that I have turned myself in."

Tears were streaming down the faces of both Gisela and Klara as Fritz donned his scarf and coat, placed his hat on his head in his once-typical jaunty fashion, and quickly walked to the door, closing it quietly behind him.

EIGHT

Klara stood at the hallway window, so preoccupied by her memories that she did not notice the clouds that now covered the morning sun, or the light mist falling from the sky. Nor had she noticed that Sam had once more found a way to escape from whatever duty he was supposed to be on and had returned. The warmth of his breath and the soft caress of his lips on the back of her neck signaled his arrival.

"Sam, stop! You have no shame," chided Klara."

"No, Klara, I guess I don't. I really don't care who sees me nuzzling your neck," he said. "In fact, you have a very tasty neck, and I wouldn't mind taking just the smallest little bite of it. You'd hardly miss it."

Once again, Sam's company and conversation brought Klara out of her dark reveries. "You really make me smile, do you know that?"

"You looked so alone, starin' out that window like that…. I felt this overwhelmin' desire to make you smile."

"Well, mission accomplished, Sergeant."

"Were you thinkin' about your family again?"

"Yes, constantly. If you or Dr. Compton are not by my bedside, that is all I do. I was remembering the last time I saw my father," Klara said with a slight frown. "He and my mother had not been getting along, and I constantly worried about their relationship. But at the end, I realized how much they loved each other, and how much he loved us. He really was quite heroic."

"What happened?"

"After he left to turn himself in for the crime of being a Jew, we felt an unimaginable void in our lives. We were also terribly frightened. After we returned home from Josef's house, we stayed indoors for several days—waiting, hoping Papa would return. Many of the men who were taken during what turned into two horrible nights were released during the coming weeks, so we had reason to remain optimistic," said Klara. "But then Heinz Dieter, an old and trusted friend of the family, discovered that my father had been sent to Sachsenhausen, a labor camp, not very far from Berlin."

"You survived. Maybe...maybe he did too?"

"No, Sam. He was beaten to death not long after his arrival at the camp. My father was a very proud man, and I used to take some small comfort in imagining him standing up to the Nazi beasts and at least dying with his dignity. Today, I realize how ridiculous that sentiment is. What difference does it make if you die with dignity or not? I would gladly grovel before anyone if it would bring just one member of my family back."

Sam's face clearly showed his desire to say something that would lessen her heartache, but he seemed to know that words alone had lost their potency for the moment, and could not assuage her grief. Instead, he held onto her hand and continued to listen. "My father's death devastated us all, especially Ernst. He never did get over it. He was just ten—so young to lose your father. But in those days, death was still a novelty. Later, we became numb to it. After all, it was all around us."

They were both startled by the sound of footsteps. "Sergeant, I see you're off duty again," said Dr. Compton, coming upon Klara and Sam in in the hallway. "I'm surprised with the cleanup still in full swing that you manage to have so much free time."

"Yes, well, I guess I do really need to get back," muttered Sam, quickly saluting his superior.

"Klara, it's good to see you out of the ward. I was just coming by to have a few words with you when I spotted you and the sergeant over here by the window. You were so intent on your conversation, I almost hated to disturb you." Without waiting for a response, apparently expecting no answer, Thomas continued. "You're looking quite well today. I don't need my medical license to tell me that you've started to turn the corner. I do believe that you've put on a good ten pounds since you were first brought to us."

Klara said nothing. She was watching Sam at the end of the hall, blowing her a kiss.

"Klara, are you upset with me?" said Thomas. "Did I do something to offend you? You're not talking."

Klara, to her surprise, was more than a little annoyed at the way Thomas had exerted his authority over Sam. The sense of calm that she had felt with Sam by her side was gone. Turning to Thomas, the kind doctor who had done so much to ensure her recovery, Klara said, "No, Thomas, of course not. I am just a little preoccupied. I was mulling over something Sam said. As usual, he was doing his best to get my mind onto something other than the war. I think he has taken me on as his personal pet project. He told me that in some cultures, if you save someone's life, then you are forever responsible for that person."

"Klara, I could do that, too, if you let me."

"Am I a damsel in such distress that I need *two* Sir Galahads?" joked Klara, trying to keep the mood light. "Besides, you have already done so much. Why, look at me! You said it yourself. I am almost well. Because of you, I will make a full recovery, I know." Klara sensed that Thomas wanted to say more, much more than she was ready or willing to hear. "Thomas, I am tired. I probably overdid it today. Would you mind walking me back to my bed? I think I could use a short nap."

"Klara, please, not just yet. I want to tell you something. I need to tell you something."

"Oh, Thomas, please. We are good friends, and I like that very much right now. Please do not say anything now that would change that." With that gentle request, Klara placed her index finger on Thomas's lips, imploring him to say nothing more. She then walked quickly and silently back to the ward on her own.

Securely back in the familiarity of her own tiny space, Klara found that sleep was the last thing she really wanted or needed. The day had been full of surprises. No more than a child herself when the war had broken out, Klara accepted that her experiences had forced her to lose the innocence of her youth well before many girls her age. Still, it was surprising that two such attractive and kind men seem interested in her. Both had helped to save her life, and for that she would always be grateful. Yes, she did feel gratitude to both, but with each passing moment, she enjoyed the realization that she loved only one.

A brooding Thomas Compton sat quietly in his makeshift office with only the amber glow from a small metal desk lamp to light the room. Thomas was not used to defeat, and the longer he sat, the more convinced he became that he was indeed losing the first woman he had ever really cared about—and losing her to an insubordinate sergeant who, for some inexplicable reason, Klara found charming. *She is obviously misguided, confusing gratitude with love.* Removed from the chaos and sounds of the hospital, the quiet of the office allowed Thomas the time he needed to consider all the angles in this burgeoning romantic triangle. Klara was too fragile to be capable of making good decisions. After all, she was undoubtedly still traumatized from her experiences. Her emotional growth was obviously stunted by her experiences, her judgment most likely impaired. The longer Thomas sat, the more convinced he became of the rightness of his assumptions and the sincerity of his motives. *If I don't step in, who knows what might become of her?* The Allies were still trying to figure out what to do with the survivors of the war. The numbers of displaced persons needing assistance was growing daily, and it was becoming overwhelming and burdensome to the many nations so beleaguered by this war. Displaced Persons camps were being slapped up throughout Germany—that would hardly be a safe haven for someone like Klara. The conditions at the camps were appalling, and hardly an improvement in circumstances; after all they had endured, the poor unfortunates would *still* be incarcerated. It could take years for Klara to obtain the documents needed to emigrate. The sergeant certainly couldn't help her or protect her; he was a nobody. And who knew how long it would be before the sergeant was sent home? He could even be sent to the Pacific Theater. *If Klara's plan is to wait for Sam, then I must do something to change her plans and head off an obvious disaster.*

Once he made his decision, Thomas felt as though a heavy weight had been lifted from him. No longer depressed by his recent encounter with Klara, Thomas felt liberated by the renewed sense that he was not impotent. He had connections, and he would use them. He was determined to save Klara from making a tragic mistake.

"Sam, for Pete's sake—you look like a love-sick puppy. It's downright embarrassin'. I swear, the guys're beginnin' to talk. You and me—we were at Bastogne! We've got a reputation to uphold," Nick chided his unresponsive friend. "Come on, at least say somethin', anythin'. You're actin' like one of those zombies I read about in that comic book my sister sent me. Sam? Are you in there, Sam?" Nick began to rhythmically tap hello on his friend's forehead.

"Lay off, okay? Just lay off," said Sam, who finally realized he was being spoken to.

"Oh, boy, you got it bad. I can't believe it. You really love this girl, don't you?"

"I love her so much it hurts. I'm not kiddin'. When I see her, when I speak to her, my heart starts poundin', I feel all clammy, and all I want to do is wrap her in my arms and never let go."

"Keep your voice down. The guys hear you talkin' like that? We'll never hear the end of it."

"Nick, listen...I'm goin' crazy here. I don't know what to do. And what's more, I've got that doctor from Dixie always showin' up whenever I try to have a quiet few minutes with her," said Sam. "It's downright creepy, the way he always just appears. I know he's not just checkin' on her *medical condition*. I can sense it. She's so much better—she's really ready to leave the hospital—but I don't think he wants to discharge her. He's always hoverin'. I'm tellin' you, he's up to somethin'."

"Sam, come on. Maybe he's just a good doctor who's, you know, being careful."

"No! Damn it! I'm not imaginin' it. He's after her, and if I don't do somethin', I could lose her."

Apparently realizing the depth of Sam's feelings for Klara, Nick restrained himself from making any more humorous comments. He sincerely tried to offer heartfelt advice to his love-sick best friend. "Sam, look, my parents have been married for over thirty years. My mama fell for my dad the first time she ever laid eyes on him, and I swear to god, the two of them still act like a couple of kids in love. She always told me, when it's the real thing, you know it."

"So?" said Sam. "That's your sage advice: when it's the real thing, you know it? Boy, that really helps. You ever thought of writin' a column for the lovelorn?"

"Cut the sarcasm. Shut your trap for just a minute and listen. Get off your lazy butt and go over to that damn hospital and tell her you love her," said Nick. "You and me—for us, the war's not over. We could get shipped out of here tomorrow. Don't screw this up because you're too scared to tell her how you really feel."

"That's just it, Nick. I'm more than scared—I'm terrified. What if she doesn't feel the same way? Worse yet, what if she doesn't feel anythin' at all?"

"Well, then, I guess you'll just have to work a little harder. And if you're right about the doc, you're gonna have to work fast. He's a captain, and you're just a lowly sergeant. We may just have to bend the rules a little," said Nick. "I got an idea. Go get yourself cleaned up and let old Nick take care of the details."

Sam knew that Nick was right. Klara was the one; he had felt it the first time he ever laid eyes on her. Sam believed in destiny. There had to be a reason that he found her that night, had seen her breathing, when so many others had walked by, assuming that she was dead like everybody else in that pile. Sam didn't have to report for duty until 0900. It was already 1800, leaving him just a few hours to pull off the plan that he and Nick hastily threw together for the evening.

Wiping down his muddy boots, Sam was still working on composing his speech when he jumped into the jeep Nick had miraculously borrowed at a moment's notice for Sam's personal use. For a change, the hospital seemed uncharacteristically quiet, and he hoped Klara was not asleep. To his delight, her bed was empty, and after a quick search he discovered her in the corridor staring out the same window they had looked out earlier that day. Not wanting to startle her, he cleared his throat and waited.

Klara turned toward the sound. It was obvious by the broad grin on her face that she was delighted to see that it was Sam returning for another visit. "You look more gorgeous every time I see you," blurted Sam, moved by seeing Klara with the last of the afternoon sun backlighting her small frame. "Listen, do you think you could borrow a dress or somethin' from someone? I think it's about time for you to get a little air. It's a beautiful evening, and I have a jeep waiting outside. I know a spot not too far from here. It would do you good to get out of this camp, even for a short while."

"Oh, Sam, do you really? This place...so much misery.... I would love to leave it, if only for a short time. Let me go change. Just today, several boxes of clothing were delivered to the patients, and I chose a few dresses for myself. Give me a moment. I will hurry, I promise!"

Back in the ward, Klara stepped out of the striped hospital pajamas that she had grown to despise. She carefully unfolded the brightly colored floral dress she had chosen earlier that day, once again marveling at the fact that something so pretty was in her possession. The dress had short sleeves padded ever-so-slightly at the shoulders, a style that had been popular before the war. The tapered waistline had a belt made from the same cotton fabric. To Klara's delight, the dress fit perfectly. It had been many years since Klara had worn anything so close to being new, and once she slipped the dress on, she longed for a mirror to make sure she looked as good as she felt.

She needn't have worried; Sam's eyes said it all. "You're beautiful, Klara. Has anyone ever told you that you're a knockout?"

Klara wasn't sure she knew exactly what a knockout was, but she was pretty sure it was something good. Like a young schoolgirl, Klara was delighted by the compliment. She modeled the dress, turning slowly so Sam could appreciate her from all sides.

"Now, come here and let me take a closer look." Suddenly feeling shy, Klara walked slowly toward Sam and waited patiently for him to make the next move. She didn't have long to wait. Sam instinctively knew what Klara needed. He pulled her easily into his waiting embrace. Kissing her lightly on the lips, he whispered, "Your chariot awaits, m'lady."

Nonplussed, Klara said, "Thank you, kind sir," and the two of them left the confines of the hospital for what she hoped would be the first of many such evenings together.

The early night air could not have been more perfect, and the blanket that Sam brought to protect Klara from the elements remained unused in the back of the jeep. "I have never ridden in an open automobile before. The wind—it makes you feel so alive. I think if I am ever able to purchase an automobile, I will buy one just like this."

"These are army jeeps, Klara. They don't make this model for the general market. Can you just imagine housewives all over America drivin' jeeps? That would be a sight to behold," said Sam. "They do make all kinds of pretty convertibles, though—ones that are more suited to getting' around in the States."

"Well, then, I shall buy one of those. Yes, I must have a convertible so I will always remember how I felt on this night when we went driving to...no, no...don't tell me, it really does not matter where. I am enjoying the ride so much."

"Even if you begged me, I wouldn't tell you anyway. It's sort of a surprise. That place, the camp—even with the cleanup going on, it's still hell.... But I don't need to tell you that. Anyway, we're almost there."

Klara couldn't remember the last time she had felt so at peace and so safe. With Sam at her side, she felt as if nothing bad could ever happen to her again. Sitting next to him, Klara found it difficult to control the intense desire she had to reach out and touch him. His shoulder was so close; how good it would feel to simply lay her head upon it as they drove. She longed for his touch. What would he think of her if she took hold of his hand, or if she reached up to stroke her fingers through his dark curls?

Klara was so consumed by these new emotions that she hardly noticed that the car had come to a stop. There before them was a beautiful little cottage nestled in the woods, as if one of the fairy tales her mother read to her as child had come to life. The house was made of stone, and amazingly enough the dark green shutters that surrounded each window were still in fairly good shape. The window boxes were empty, but Klara could imagine them filled with wildflowers. The chimney was made of the same stone as the house and when Klara looked up she was shocked to see a soft billow of smoke escaping from the opening.

"Sam, where are we? Who lives here?"

"Shhh...no questions. Just give me a minute."

While Klara remained sitting in the front of the jeep, totally in awe of the beautiful little house before her, Sam carried a large box from the back of the jeep into the cottage. Motioning for Klara to wait just a few more minutes, Sam managed to hold the box and push open the wooden front door at the same time. For Klara, the wait seemed endless. She was about to step out of the jeep when Sam reappeared and beckoned her to join him inside. When she reached the threshold, Sam startled her by swooping her up in into his arms and carrying her into a charming little room that conjured up all sorts of romantic notions. A roaring fire blazed in the hearth at the far end of the room. In the middle of the room, on a beautiful little claw-footed, light oak table, was a delectable feast of fruit, a multitude of cheeses, and wine already poured into two metal U.S. Army mess cups.

Klara was awed into silence and did not recover her voice even after Sam gently lowered her to the sofa—the only other piece of furniture in the room.

"Klara, don't you like it? Say somethin', anythin'. We can go if this is all too much for you," said Sam. "I'm such an idiot. I just thought the change would do you good, and we could have a little time to ourselves, away from that damn camp. My buddy Nick and I ran across this place a few weeks ago, and when I mentioned that I wanted to do somethin' special for you, he thought about our little discovery. Nick was out here earlier—you know, cleanin' it up. He even charmed the mess sergeant into scavengin' together the food. I don't even want to know where he found the wine. Oh, geez, now you're cryin'. I'm so sorry."

"Oh, Sam, please don't apologize. Never, ever apologize. You are my guardian angel. Until I met you, I had no reason to live. So, no...don't apologize," said Klara. "I am crying because I sense that something very special is happening between us, and before it is too late, I need to tell you everything. I need to tell you how I survived, because when you hear it, I think you will want nothing more to do with me."

"Klara, trust me. Nothin' you could ever say would change how I feel about you."

"Wait. Listen to what I have to say, and then decide."

NINE

"After Heinz came to report the news of my father's murder, my mother was inconsolable. She blamed herself for not preventing Papa from turning himself in. Once Papa left, there was no reason for us to stay in hiding. At that point, the Sturmabteilung, the Brownshirts, were only arresting the men," said Klara. "When we heard that Papa had...perished...Mama turned inward, you know? She was with us physically, but not really there. Without her to guide us, Ernst and I were lost and terrified. We became fearful of every knock on the door, any noise outside."

Sam handed Klara one of the metal cups of wine, then sat beside her and held her hand.

"You know that feeling you get, a premonition that something awful is about to happen, but when nothing happens the feeling finally goes away? This time, it just never went away. We were always afraid. Fear—it changes you. There was no more laughter, no enjoyment in our home. We went through the motions of living, each of us dealing with the loss of Papa in different ways. Ernst grieved openly. I sought relief in taking over most of the household chores that were piling up. Mama found comfort in the solitude of her room, perhaps trying to remember life before Hitler and happier times with my father."

She sipped her wine and nibbled at a piece of cheese. "But ignoring what was happening around us did not make it go away. Finally, Heinz persuaded Mama to pull herself back together and focus on the future, and the fact that she must get us all out of Germany. She again tried to locate distant relatives in America to send us the precious affidavits, but we never heard from any of them. Thankfully, though, because of her earlier determination to emigrate, our papers were all in order. We packed up a few things and said goodbye to our homeland for what we hoped was safety in Paris."

"Hell, Klara, why France?" asked Sam. "If she spent all that time secretly gettin' all the documents together, why the hell did she pick France?"

"Oh, Sam, it is easy to have all the right answers now. It was not so clear in 1938," said Klara. "Could we possibly have known that Britain's Neville Chamberlain would hand over Czechoslovakia and Poland to the Nazis? Or that the French would run away from a fight like frightened children? Like idiots, we all believed that the famous Maginot Line would protect us. And we all believed that the good people of Germany would rise up and finally take a stand against tyranny. We were wrong. No one did a thing. Everyone just stood by and watched it happen." She stopped, her voice choked with anguish.

"Klara, you know I don't need you to go on. I don't need to know. This is too hard for you..."

"No, Sam. I need to tell you. I finally need to tell it all. After this, I hope to never speak of it again. But I know—no, I feel—that by telling you a burdensome weight is being lifted off of me. I feel safe with you, and I know that I am with the right person and this is the right time to confess."

"Confess is an odd choice of words. You were an innocent young victim—you have nothin' to confess."

"Shhh.... Listen, and reserve your judgment until I have finished," said Klara. "Life was difficult for émigrés in France. Jobs were few and far between. Mama was lucky to find employment as a domestic for a wealthy Parisian family. We lived quietly, like invisible beings, going silently about our day-to-day activities—working, going to school, listening each evening to broadcasts, clinging to the hope that we might one day be able to return to our homeland. Instead, the news became more ominous. Hitler's successes in Austria, Czechoslovakia, and Poland were frightening forebodings of what would eventually befall

France. We knew we had to leave France, but how? Without affidavits, traveling to America was impossible. Everyone had been assigned a quota number, and ours fell near the bottom of the list, so even if we had received the affidavits we would not have been able to emigrate. And where could we go? No one wanted us. The Nazis had already conquered much of Europe, and neutral countries like Switzerland would not let us in. Did you know that it was actually the Swiss who demanded that the Nazis stamp all Jewish passports with a red J so that we would be easily identified if we tried to sneak across their border?"

"No, I didn't know that. There's a lot that's gone on over here that Americans don't know, at least yet—even those of us who have been over here sloggin' through the battlefields."

"Honestly, I do not know when Mama slept. Every night she sent us off to bed, and then stayed up brooding about a solution. The French continued to boast about their Maginot Line, their impregnable defense system that of course did not prevent the German's massive military force from outflanking the strongholds and crossing through the Ardennes in Belgium and into France. The French gave up so easily! And then they were complicit in giving their Jews up as well. We had thought that perhaps in the country of *liberté, égalité,* and *fraternité* we would find refuge, but the national motto of France did not apply to us."

The fire had burnt down to a few smoking embers, and Klara realized that it was getting late. "Sam, I imagine that you have only a few hours. Please, do not take any risks for me."

"I'm fine, really," said Sam. "Give me your hand. Are you cold? You feel a little cold." He threw another log on the fire and poured some more wine.

"Sam, I am fine, too. Come sit back down. I am afraid if I stop now, I'll never have the courage to continue."

"Just one second. More warmth and little more wine will make the tellin' a lot easier." He poked at the fire and blew on the embers, and soon the fire blazed once more. He sat down again next to Klara, gently holding her small hand.

"Mama worked very hard. The Parisian family was kind. I was fairly sure that Monsieur Dubois knew we were Jews from the start, although it was not something any of us spoke about. We knew from Papa's experience that wartime was not the right time to be forthcoming with the truth. Even with the security of the job, we had to remain cautious. We behaved like frightened little mice. Yes, mice. It is an appropriate description, because we scurried about to do our tasks, always quickly and silently, and then we scurried back to our refuge. When the invasion finally began in the summer of 1940, we—like the French people—had been lulled into complacency. There had been disappointing news from America; a Jewish resettlement agency in New York had finally found a distant cousin of my mother's, but he was not willing to sign the affidavits. He was already struggling and was afraid we would be a financial burden on his family. With his refusal, we had no choice but to try to wait out Hitler's madness in France. Of course, we had heard what the Nazis had been doing to Jews in Germany. We heard horrible stories about ghettos and mass murders in Poland. Yet we were convinced that France, with England's help, would be able to withstand the Nazi onslaught. Once again we were proven horribly wrong. On May 10, 1940, the Nazis invaded France. By June 14, Paris was occupied. Can you believe it? The French could only hold out for one month. Once again we were numbed by events we could not control. Fear gripped us day and night."

When Klara shivered, Sam edged closer and put his arm around her. It felt good. "Once the Nazis entered Paris, it wasn't long before the pronouncements began. Those of us in hiding watched—*silently!*—as our people were forced to give up their property and were subjected to untold indignities. In August 1941, there was a roundup of four thousand French Jews. They were sent to Drancy, a concentration camp just outside Paris. The foreign Jews, noncitizens, fared the worst. Jews were treated like stock being prepared for the slaughterhouse. The only difference was that unlike the cows and the hogs, Jews were not fattened up for market before their final journey. As our fellow Germans had in our homeland, we remained quiet, ashamed of standing idly by and yet knowing that speaking out would mean certain death. For the next year, there were no more mass deportations, so we clung to the hope that they would not begin again. It is funny how easily one can be lulled into complacency, even as new pronouncements reminiscent of our time in Germany were being broadcast: Jews must report to the authorities and identify themselves; Jews must wear the yellow badge that said *Jude*, centered in the Star of David. *Juif*, they said in France, on a bright yellow background. Few Jews could remain invisible."

"It must've helped that you have blond hair and blue eyes, right?"

"Yes, I am ashamed to say, our Aryan looks saved us from the monsters—especially when the deportations commenced again," said Klara. "In 1942, we witnessed our people, thousands of Jews, being rounded up and herded into the Vélodrome d'Hiver, a sports arena in Paris. We heard later that they were kept there for days—men, women, and children—with no food, water, or sanitary facilities. You may ask, what did we do? We did nothing. There was nothing *to* do but continue to hope, and pray silently that we, unlike the others, could find a way out. Every night while Ernst slept, Mama and I stayed up discussing plan after plan, and discarding them one by one when we realized the infeasibility and danger of each. Should we try to escape to the unoccupied zone? Should we leave Paris for a smaller city? Should we go to the countryside or try to cross the border into Spain? As quickly as each idea was proposed, it was discarded. We knew the odds were not in our favor. Looking back, perhaps we should have chanced one of our crazy plans; maybe things would have worked out differently. Instead, we just waited. We knew it was only a matter of time. Someone would surely denounce us. Someone would ask for our documents. The papers we had purchased on the black market would have fooled no one."

"Somehow, though, you were still safe. So you must've been doin' somethin' right."

"As you said, our only advantage was our coloring. Mama, Ernst, me—we all had blond hair. According to the Nazi propaganda posters, we did not look like Jews. Then one day, Monsieur Dubois asked my mother to come to his study. Mama was terrified. Had she done something wrong? Was she being dismissed? Would he denounce us? She was trembling when she left our room to speak with him. I can still remember the look of sheer terror in her eyes. That house was our refuge! Without that job, we would be out on the streets and be picked up immediately."

"Do you need to take a break? Asked Sam, giving Klara a comforting squeeze. *How warm and strong his arm feels! I would rather just let him hold me than keep telling this story, but I must.*

"Mama told me the whole story later. She could almost hear her knees knocking together when Monsieur Dubois motioned for her to sit in the worn leather armchair facing his desk. He was finishing up some paperwork, and several minutes passed before he looked up and faced my mother. The silence was deafening. 'Gisela,' he said. 'I am sorry to have kept you waiting. Even in these terrible times, I need to attend to my business. I have known for quite some time that you and your children are Jewish. Please, please, don't be frightened. I see by the look in your face that I have handled this disclosure very poorly, but do not be alarmed. I swear on the holy bible, your secret is safe with me.' Miraculously, he had called her to his study to say that he wanted to help us escape! He said that he knew of a man, a priest at his church, who had already helped many others leave the country. The priest was willing to provide authentic-looking false papers, including baptismal certificates for the three of us. Mama stayed in his office for what seemed like an eternity. She later told me that she was so moved by his kindness she lost all control and was unable to compose herself for a very long time."

"I thought you were goin' to tell me he was turnin' you all in unless... well, I don't want to say. In exchange for...favors from your mother," said Sam, sounding relieved.

"Thankfully, no. That night, we danced in our little room. Ernst, Mama, and I held hands and for the first time in a long time we felt joyful. Unfortunately for us, our happiness was short-lived. As promised, the priest was willing to help. He told us to come back the next day, and he would give us our new papers. Oh, Sam, how carefree we were that evening! New papers would mean survival! We had been frightened for so long, not daring to dream of life after the war, not caring to speak about a future. But that night we did. I dreamed of finishing school, and one day going on to the university. Ernst only wanted the freedom to once again play outside with friends. Mama, she just listened, smiling at the two of us. We were all so happy. Safety was within our grasp."

"You were so close, you almost made it," said Sam, shaking his head.

"We all slept soundly that night. In the morning, we nervously awaited the hour of our appointment. The priest had promised to meet us by the baptismal font, but instead the church was eerily quiet. We should have known something was amiss, but we were too excited, so perhaps our senses were dulled. Suddenly, we heard horrible shouting. 'Halt! Do not move or you will be shot!' They came at us from all sides. They dragged the priest—beaten, bloody, unable to walk—and dumped him in front of us. Then they seized us by the arms, and we were all taken to Gestapo headquarters in Paris. I never saw the priest again."

"I imagine no one did, after that day."

"We were thrown into a cell. We did our best to comfort Ernst. How can someone look a child in the face and threaten to shoot him? I shudder every time I think of how Ernst spent the last few years of his childhood. It should have been carefree, no?"

"Yes, Klara, childhood should be carefree and happy. No one—not you, your mother, Ernst—should ever have to live that way. You are an amazin'ly strong woman."

"Ah, you think I am strong. Perhaps I am in some ways, but weak in others. Nevertheless, I did survive when so many others did not. I may never really know how or why. Perhaps it was a combination of luck, determination, and of course the promise that I made to my mother."

"What was that?"

"To live, no matter the cost. That is one of the many ways I occupy my time now. I think, 'Why me? How did I make it through? What part of my own humanity did I sacrifice to survive?'"

Sam turned and held Klara in his arms. She tucked her face into the comfort of his neck and continued. "While we waited to learn our fate, Mama and I tried to think of a logical lie for why we had been in the church. We were not so naïve to believe that if questioned we could protect Monsieur Dubois; two women and a little boy would never be able to withstand questioning by the Gestapo. But even with our very lives at stake, we worried for him; Monsieur Dubois had risked his own life and that of his family to protect us. After several hours, we finally heard footsteps coming down the corridor. When they stopped at our door, Ernst began to sob uncontrollably. Mama and I were falling apart as well, and could do little to comfort him. Immediately, the door was unlocked and opened. The guard ordered Mama and Ernst to remain. Though I clung to Mama, the guard grabbed me by the arm and, with a quick tug, threw me from the door into the hallway. I was so frightened I could barely stand. The guard dragged me, upright, to an office, and told me to wait."

Klara snuggled her face closer to Sam's neck, breathing in his scent for courage.

"I could immediately tell by the opulence of the room that I would be facing someone important. Such luxury! The desk was mammoth, made from beautiful inlaid mahogany. The table behind the desk was covered with photographs. Seeing those pictures of what looked like a happy family made me feel a little calmer. I remember thinking that someone who would proudly display pictures of his own family would never do anything horrible to two women and a boy. But above the desk was a picture of the Führer. I was staring at it so intently I failed to notice that the door had opened and someone was approaching."

She shuddered, and Sam patted her back. "'Fräulein,' the man said. 'I see the Führer has worked his spell on you. You seem mesmerized by his portrait.' I remained silent, waiting for his directive, not knowing what to say or do. He told me to sit down. He even said please. I lowered myself into the chair in front of his desk and waited for him to speak. 'I saw you when you were brought in this morning. Your mother and brother—are we treating them well?' he asked. At first I said nothing, afraid that any answer would be the wrong one. Finally I said, 'No one has hurt them, but we have had nothing to eat or drink since early this morning.' 'Ah, an oversight,' he told me. He rang on his intercom, and several minutes later, a tray of food was placed before me. When he saw that I was not eating, he told me that food had also been taken to Mama and Ernst, so I could eat in good conscience. I took a few bites, knowing that I would need some sustenance to continue, but I was so sick with fright, I could barely force anything down."

As she spoke, Klara found that the cheese and bread that had tasted so wonderful when she and Sam had arrived at the cottage had now turned to ashes on her tongue. She held the wine without drinking.

"The man said, 'Now that you are not so worried about your family, we can have a little chat. Your name is Klara? Very nice, a very nice name. Do not be alarmed. You will not be interrogated. We know all we need to know. We have already arrested Monsieur Dubois and the priest. We have been watching them for quite some time. You and your family had the misfortune, I'm afraid, of being caught in our little trap.' Monsieur Dubois arrested! Though the news horrified me, it still did not prepare me for what came next. He said that he could not believe I was Jewish because I was so blond, so fair. He called me beautiful, and wondered if anyone had ever told me that before. Then he said, 'I am Standartenführer Reinhardt Frank, assistant to the Oberführer in the occupied zone of France. I will be in France for quite some time, in Paris actually, and I have a proposition for you. My wife is remaining in Germany, and I need a housekeeper—someone to clean up, to perform other duties from time to time. I realize that you are no position to say no to me, but if you come willingly and perform your duties well, I will send your mother and brother to the transit camp at Drancy with specific orders that they not be deported to the East. The conditions at Drancy are tolerable. They can survive there, and you will be able to stay in touch. If you do *not* agree, I will place all three of you on the next transport to the East. Confidentially, Fräulein, no one ever returns from there. It will mean certain death for you and your loved ones. I will give you a little time to decide. Five minutes, eh? I think that is only fair.'"

"That bastard!"

"He got up from his chair leaving me—I was not even eighteen at the time—to decide the fate of my family. What choice did I have? There was no *choice*. I had to agree to his terms. When he returned, I gave him my answer, and asked only for a few moments to say goodbye."

"Oh, Klara, I'm so sorry..." said Sam. He hugged her tightly.

"Mama, too, hugged me so tightly I could barely breathe. It was then that she whispered the last words I would ever hear from her lips. 'Go and live, Klara, for all of us.' The next moment the guard tore us apart, and I never saw my mother or my brother again. Later that day, a driver arrived to take me to the home of my new master. The first few days were uneventful. I was given certain household duties to complete, and I saw very little of Standartenführer Frank. His wife arrived for a short visit, and we were all occupied with tasks relating to her stay. She was a sullen woman with a face that hardly exemplified the Aryan standard of beauty. There were several other prisoners laboring at the house, but we were warned that interaction with the guests or with each other was strictly forbidden. I worried constantly about the fate of my mother and brother and prayed that I had not been lied to."

Klara sipped her wine again. "Finally, after several weeks, I received a letter from my mother. Ernst and Mama were together, being held at Drancy. At least the Standartenführer had kept that part of the bargain! Mama tried to spare me, and wrote only briefly about the lack of food. It is hard for me to think about what they must have endured. She hoped my situation was such that I might possibly be able to send them some things. In the letter, she begged me to live, to survive at all costs. I believe she sensed that she and Ernst would not make it. You see, my mother was giving me permission to do whatever I had to do; she knew my life was more important than my so-called virtue. That letter was her gift to me. Without it I am not sure I would have continued on."

Sam sat in silence. Klara was afraid that he knew what was coming, and that he was already prepared to denounce her. But when she looked into his eyes, she saw only compassion. Heartened, she continued.

"How innocent I was! Mama was so much wiser than I. Only a few days after his wife returned to Berlin, I was summoned by the Standartenführer to his office. Right away I could tell that he had been drinking. He was uncharacteristically disheveled. When he spoke, it was slowly and deliberately, as if he had to measure or practice each word beforehand. He locked the door and motioned for me to join him on the sofa. I realized then what he had in store for me," said Klara. Speaking in a flat, passionless voice, she told Sam what happened, and how she had known from the click of the lock that she would leave the room a different person than the one who had entered it.

"I asked him what it was he needed, perhaps a warm glass of milk or some cake before he retired? But he said, 'No, I only long for a little company.' He ordered me to sit by him on the couch, and said, 'Klara, have you asked yourself why you are here? Why I chose to save you from the same fate as your family? Honestly, I should be ashamed of myself—according to the law, you should be with your family at Drancy, and then all of you sent to the East. But—you have such beauty. I could not destroy such beauty.' He said that...as though I should be grateful. He said that he personally had nothing against our people, but that orders could not be disobeyed. I tried to be a statue, a blank slate, but he saw it. He said, 'Your eyes, they give you away. You say nothing, but in your eyes I see how much you hate me. You think me a monster?' I could only stare at him, not daring to say anything, terrified but determined not to cry. While he rambled on, he grabbed for my wrist and pulled me toward him, forcing me closer to him. He said, 'Is it so hard for you to be near me? You received a letter from Drancy. Your little family is alive and well. I did not lie to you. I am an honorable man, an officer of the Third Reich.'"

"Honorable man? Tell that to the priest, and that guy Dubois. And all those people he *did* send to the East." Sam's face was red with anger.

Klara nodded. "I sat there, saying nothing, bewildered that a man who seemed intelligent could think nothing of sending a woman and a boy to a hellish place like Drancy. After a few more moments of silence, he began to stroke my cheek, my hair, and soon his hand was reaching down inside my blouse, grabbing me, twisting my nipple, hurting me. He unzipped his pants. When I resisted, he used enough force to let me know I had no choice in what was about to happen. I cried out from the pain, and he slapped me, so I bit my lip to keep silent. Finally it was over. He told me to clean up the mess and to not speak of what had happened to anyone. Before he left the room, I somehow found the courage to ask if I could please send some food to my family in Drancy. He gave a slight nod and walked out. For the next two years, I was summoned to his office almost daily. The only time I felt safe was when his wife, Gertrude, was visiting. I think she knew what was happening; she often caught my eye with a look that I interpreted as sympathy, but she never spoke to me, not one word. I used to will her to stay, but of course, my prayers were not answered. It was always worst right after she left. He terrorized me even more, perhaps to assuage his guilt. It was always the same, though. He would get intoxicated, ramble on about Jews and his duty to the Führer, and then he would rape me."

The empty cup slipped from her hand and clattered on the wooden floor. It was the only sound in the room except for the crackling fire. "So, you see, Sam, I am not just another innocent victim. I am now—how should I say it?—a fallen woman. I traded myself to that Nazi pig for the lives of my mother and brother. And you know what? He sent them to their deaths anyway. A year after I entered his house, the letters from Drancy stopped coming. I kept sending food parcels, but in my heart I knew they were gone, though I never asked. I was too afraid. I still wanted to live, and I knew if I confronted him, I would disappear as well. So I allowed it to continue."

Klara sat up straighter on the sofa and turned her body toward Sam, but she would not look up at his face. She stared at his name, stenciled over his uniform pocket, and continued. "In 1944, when the Allies landed in Normandy, everything was chaos. Standartenführer Frank was like a man possessed, destroying documents, issuing orders, and readying himself for his return to Germany. I knew then that my days were numbered. I thought of trying to escape, but honestly I had no time to figure out a plan, even if I had the courage. One day he told me to pack a small bag. I thought maybe he was taking me with him, but no. When he was sober, he always acted as if nothing had ever passed between us. I was just...convenient. And when he had to flee, I became inconvenient. So that day it was the same; he barely looked at me, and he didn't say a word as I was driven off to join one of the last transports out of Paris."

"Removin' the evidence. Cowards," spat Sam. It was the first word he'd spoken in twenty minutes or so.

"To my surprise, the documents he had sent with me identified me as a political prisoner, not a Jew. That red triangle on my uniform saved my life. I was one of the lucky ones. I was sent to a labor camp in Poland where I made parts for munitions, and was there until just a few months ago. Finally I ended up here, in Buchenwald. I imagine the Standartenführer had something to do with my new identity. Perhaps there was some small bit of honor, of humanity in him after all, or maybe he was just keeping me alive for the next Nazi who needed a housekeeper. I doubt I will ever know."

Klara stared into the fire. "The horror of the train ride to Poland will never leave me. We were packed so tightly into one car it was impossible to change position. We took turns sitting, shifting slightly to allow people a few minutes of rest. Many of the elderly died during the trip, and their bodies were not removed. They blankly stared up at the living. After two days, we no longer heard the pitiful cries of hunger from the babies and small children. Like the aged, they were either dead or too weak to voice their despair. The stench from the bucket in which we relieved ourselves in the August heat was unbearable, suffocating. Then we stopped, and suddenly there was a welcoming gush of air as the door was pulled open. Many of us fell onto the platform as the people behind pushed to get out of the train. Immediately, I was assaulted by the horrible smells of sickness and death. Nothing could have ever prepared me for the horror of that camp. We were met by guards with dogs and by prisoners in striped suits who directed us to the various satellite camps according to our status. Because of my papers, instead of being sent to the tent camp that housed all of the Jews, I was sent to work in the armaments factory. Provisions were better for political prisoners and I once again dreamed of the possibility of survival and of reuniting with Mama and Ernst. It was just a glimmer of hope. But then I learned from another prisoner that they both died at Drancy a year earlier. Ernst died first. There was just not enough food to sustain him. My mother lasted a month or two longer, but between the grief of losing Papa and Ernst and not knowing my fate, the hard work and lack of food at the camp was too much for her, and she just gave out. When the letters stopped coming, I knew in my heart something horrible must have happened, but I could not bring myself to accept it. I now know how foolish that was. The Standartenführer must have known, but he never told me, and I was too frightened, of both him and the answer, to ask."

The fire was once again dying down. The room began to grow chilly, but Klara was determined to finish her tale once and for all. "No longer caring, no longer hoping for survival, I was easy prey for the many diseases that ran rampant in the camps, including here at Buchenwald. By April, when the camp began its evacuation, I was already too sick to travel. I crawled into the pile of bodies, to hide among the corpses the Nazis no longer had time to dispose of, and that is where I am told you found me. It is hard to describe how my senses, inured to the smell of decay and the sights and sounds of the suffering, were assaulted when I awoke in the antiseptic comfort of the hospital. Once I took in my surroundings and listened to the conversations of the staff, I realized that they expected me to be *happy*. And why shouldn't I be happy? I was alive and so many others were not. But there is no joy in discovering that you are truly alone in the world and no peace imagining the horrible last few moments of your loved ones lives."

Sensing that Klara had reached her emotional limit, Sam once again reached out—first to wipe away the tears that were streaming down her face, and then to gently coax her onto his lap, as he would a small child, to give her the physical comfort he knew she needed. Finally, pulling away from him, Klara got up from the sofa and moved closer to the fire, standing with her back to the flames to warm her still-quivering body.

"Sam, thank you for everything—for your daily visits and for tonight. Especially for tonight. I will never forget your kindness," she said. "But now, now that you know the truth about me, there is no longer any reason for you to want to see me."

Sam looked at her, too dumbstruck to speak. Apparently discouraged by his silence, Klara continued. "We should get back now. I am sure you have probably been absent too long. Why are you just staring at me? Please say something!"

Shaking his head in disbelief, Sam got up from the sofa, and in two quick strides moved to the fire to face Klara. "Look at me," he ordered. "I love you. When we first got here you asked me to keep quiet, to wait until you finished. I did pretty well. But now it's my turn. Klara, you are no longer alone. You have *me*. Klara, don't ever ask anyone—not me, not anyone—to judge you again. The world that allowed this to happen should be on trial, not you. You were a good daughter and sister, and you're one of the bravest people I have ever met. I love you. I think I fell in love with you the first time I laid eyes on you. Marry me, Klara. Together, we'll make new memories—ones that will make you smile, I promise."

Klara sobbed uncontrollably. Sam withdrew a large white handkerchief from his pocket and tried to stop the tears that were streaming down her face. "You just keep on cryin' until you start to feel better. Anyone who has been through what you just described deserves to cry as much as she wants. Now blow."

Klara did as she was told, and although the tears kept coming, she let a little trace of a smile peek through. "Oh, Sam, even now you've managed to say something to make me feel better."

"Well, I aim to please, little lady," quipped Sam, offering his best John Wayne imitation. "And now that you've wiped the snot off your face, the next thing you need is a hug."

"Yes, I believe you are right; a hug would be lovely right now," Klara managed to reply. The intensity of the embrace took them both by surprise.

"I love you," whispered Sam.

"And I you," replied Klara, who had finally stopped shaking. Taking Klara's upturned face into his hands, Sam kissed her, at first gently and then harder as Klara's lips parted, meeting his desire with her own. "Sam, I need you to make love to me. I need to feel whole again. I have been so cold and empty for so long."

"Are you sure, Klara? Here? Now? Are you sure you're ready?"

"Oh, yes, Sam," said Klara. "I am very sure. I have never been more positive about anything in my entire life."

TEN

"Nurse, nurse! Where in the hell is she?"

"I'm sorry sir. She was gone when I stared my shift this morning. I'll ask around. Maybe someone saw her leave. I'm sure she's not far. Where could she possibly go?"

"Yes, do that. Go check and then get right back to me," insisted an obviously distraught Dr. Compton. Thomas had already checked most of the obvious places where Klara might have wandered, knowing in his heart he probably would not find her there. *No sense wondering where she is,* he thought. *I may not know where, but I sure as hell know with whom. What could she possibly see in him? He's a foot soldier, a nobody! Why, he'll probably finish his service and go back to wherever he came from and work in a filling station for the rest of his life.* But Klara...she was so refined, so delicate. He told himself to get a grip, that she might not even be with the sergeant. *You've got to get control of yourself. You're never going to win her over acting like an oversexed schoolboy.*

"Dr. Compton, I see her coming now," said the nurse calmly. "She's walking down the corridor as we speak. See? Nothing to worry about. We haven't lost anybody yet."

I need to compose myself. I can't let her see me this way. When Klara drew closer, Thomas called to her. "Klara, over here! I almost didn't recognize you. You look lovely. Where did you get the dress?" Klara, still basking in the glow of her evening with Sam, spun herself around several times for Thomas to get the full effect.

"Do you like it? It came in one of the packages from America. I suspect it is not the latest fashion, but it fits me quite well, no?"

"No! I mean, yes. It looks great—better than great," said Thomas. "Klara, I was worried about you. When I came in this morning and saw that you were gone—well, I hate to act like the doting physician, but I don't want you to have a relapse."

"Thomas, it is so good of you to care so much about me when you have so many patients," said Klara. "But as you can see, I have never felt better."

Thomas had to admit it; she did look healthy and, more importantly, happy. For the first time since he had seen Klara, she seemed free of the inner turmoil and sadness that weighed so heavily on her. "Can I ask where you've been? I mean, well, it's probably none of my business, but perhaps I can prescribe this little adventure of yours to some of my other patients."

Taking Thomas's hand into her own, she placed it upon her heart. "Thomas, forgive me if I am wrong, but I feel I must be totally honest with you. I am worried you might be interested in something more from me, something I am not possibly able to give you," she said. "My heart, this heart that you feel beating so quickly, it belongs to someone else."

Thomas pulled his hand back as if it were on fire. "Klara, no! Don't say anything else. Please, you're making a mistake. What can Rosstein ever give you? You deserve more!" he said. "Klara, I beg you...just give me a chance. I know I can make you happy."

Tears glittered in Klara's eyes. "Oh, Thomas, you have been like a guardian angel to me. I never wanted to hurt you, but I love him, I love Sam," said Klara. "As soon as he is discharged, we are going to be married."

Suddenly, Thomas's demeanor changed. "Klara, you don't even know, do you? Do you know he's a Jew? Is that what you want? I have nothing against those people—and I know they've been through hell—but marry one? I just think you ought to think about that long and hard before..."

"Oh, Dr. Compton, I see you found Klara," said the nurse. "Can you come to the ward? Mr. Kaplow's breathing seems a little labored. I think you'd better come and have a look."

"Klara, I'm sorry...we have to cut this short. I have to go," said Thomas. "Can I come by later so we can talk? Please think about what I'm saying. I only want what's best for you." Without waiting for an answer, Thomas quickly followed on the heels of the nurse and left a furious and equally perplexed Klara standing alone.

So Thomas has no idea that I am a Jew, that I am one of 'those people,' just like Sam. And am I so naïve to have imagined that it might be different for Jews in America? She wondered at his confusion then recalled the red badge on her uniform. *To everyone except Sam, I am a Christian girl from Berlin, and a political prisoner of the Third Reich. What arrogance! How dare he assume he knows what is best for me? And how dare he think he can love me when he knows nothing about me except that he thinks I am an Aryan beauty? Tomorrow I will tell him why Sam and I make a very suitable couple.*

Klara could not help smiling at the thought of how surprised the good doctor would be when she told him that she was Jewish. But just as suddenly, her amusement gave way to sadness. She could not bring herself to be cruel to Thomas, not after his devotion to her, his kindness. His constant attention and care had been as much a factor in her recovery as the time she spent with Sam. *A part of me will never forget him,* she thought. *Perhaps someday, when his anger subsides, he will remember these few weeks with fondness and think kindly of the young woman he helped to bring out of the darkness.*

In another part of the hospital, Thomas sat scowling at his desk, torn by his conflicting emotions. He loved Klara; of that, he was certain. Shouldn't he then be willing to let her go? She had made her choice, and he was not it. On the other hand, Thomas felt as if he had been robbed of every opportunity to make his case by the intrusive sergeant who was available all too often, and who seemed to make an appearance whenever Thomas tried to see Klara alone. And now, somehow, Sam had spirited her away to who knows where, and somehow convinced her that she should spend the rest of her life with him.

I need time, just a little, to get through to her, to make my case. The answer came to Thomas suddenly. So satisfied was he with his plan of attack that he was surprised it had eluded him for so long. He would use his connections, and his rank, to have the sergeant transferred—possibly even shipped to the Pacific front. Although he wasn't sure he could live with himself if something happened to Rosstein. *No, nothing too dangerous,* he thought. He didn't want the man hurt or, even worse, killed; he just wanted Sam sent far enough away to give Thomas the luxury of time, time that he so desperately needed. That decided, he began placing the necessary calls to Washington. For once in his life he agreed with his mother; family connections did sometimes come in handy.

The next morning Klara awoke with a renewed appreciation for the wonderful array of possibilities life could bring. It was a startling revelation. Only a few weeks earlier, she had almost succumbed to the same malaise that had contributed to the deaths of thousands of others. The news about Ernst and her mother had almost finished her. Her anguish had been indescribable, and she had been paralyzed by an insurmountable despair. Hopelessness was a complication that hastened many a death, and was endemic throughout the camp. Now, perhaps, there was a chance for her. Maybe she could start over and make a new life for herself, a life rich with promise because there was Sam.

"Why, Klara—that's something new. A smile! Keep it up; it agrees with you," commented a nurse who was passing by. Without bothering to answer, Klara brought her finger up to her lips and slowly traced her upturned mouth. *I am smiling,* she thought. Klara remembered an oft-used admonishment from her grandmother, an old wives' tale, that cautioned Klara that her mouth would forever freeze into a frown if she looked too gloomy or sullen. *You were wrong, Oma, my face didn't freeze. I can still smile.*

Klara waited all day for Sam to come by. He had promised to get away the first chance he had, but by 1500 hours, he still hadn't appeared. The waiting became intolerable; the longing for him was another new emotion that mystified her. Over and over again she replayed their lovemaking in her mind. *Was it like that for everyone?* She remembered each kiss, each touch, and every feeling that brought fulfillment and peace to both of them. Never, after all those horrible times with Standartenführer Frank, did she ever think it could be like that. When it was over, she wanted more. She hadn't wanted to leave the little cottage in the woods, and she hoped that one day she and Sam would find a way to come back to it.

Watching the clock proved torturous. When another thirty minutes painfully ticked by, Klara decided to try to find Sam herself. By the door she hesitated, realizing that the wind had picked up and it had started to drizzle. The sky looked depressingly dark, and Klara was sure the light rain would soon turn into a downpour. She knew that the possessive Dr. Compton would have her head if he found her outside in a storm, then thought, *I should go out just to spite him.* Looking around, Klara spied a raincoat and umbrella by the door and grabbed both, rushing outside before her good sense could get the better of her.

Except for her escapade with Sam, Klara had not been outside the confines of the hospital or the makeshift quarters of the camp's officers since she had been delivered into the Americans' care weeks earlier. It was all so different now. For one thing, it was hauntingly quiet. The Nazi guards were gone and the bodies finally all buried. Yet the stench lingered, and Klara could still vividly conjure up the cries and despair of the dying, and feel the collective pain and fear that had pervaded the camp.

She really didn't know where to look for Sam, so she walked slowly. Her shoes quickly soaked with water and caked with mud. With each step, Klara sunk further into the muck until she finally had to enlist the help of an able-bodied private to help her over the worst of it. She asked him where the she might find the living quarters of the GIs stationed there, and he pointed her in the direction of the barracks. As she approached, she saw dozens of men milling around, drinking coffee, waiting to go on duty. Surely, one of these soldiers would know Sam and be able to tell her where he was.

"Have you seen Sam? Sergeant Rosstein, I mean?"

"Sam, sure—about six feet, curly dark hair, blue eyes? The Sam that hangs around with Nick Caputo?"

"Yes, yes," said Klara excitedly. "That's him!"

"Well, I'm sorry to have to tell you, Fräulein, but the two of them and the rest of their unit were shipped out at 0500 hours," said one of the soldiers. "Not a word of warning. Woke the rest of us getting their gear together, cursing and slamming around. Didn't get hardly a wink a sleep after that ruckus started."

"No! Impossible...you must be mistaken. You don't understand...he would never leave without getting word to me."

"Listen, Fräulein, I don't know nothing about getting word to you," he said. "All I know is, I saw him and the rest of them boys leaving in a truck early this morning. You don't believe me, ask the base commander. He'll tell you." He pointed toward the command center.

"Yes. Yes, I'll do that. Thank you," said a shaken Klara. She headed on through the mud and rain.

Thomas read the note that had been left for Klara with Shirley, one of the nurses. The orders for Sam's unit to move out had come so quickly, Thomas was surprised Sam had managed to write anything before his departure. *The fates must be smiling upon me*, he thought. The unsuspecting nurse had seen Thomas walking toward Klara's ward and asked him to deliver Sam's note. As Thomas read it again, he once again pondered the morality of what he had done.

> *Dearest Klara,*
>
> *Word came unexpectedly in the middle of the night. My unit is moving out immediately and I don't know when I will next be able to get word to you. As usual, we don't know where we're going or for how long.*
>
> *I heard from my captain that this should be the last official assignment for our unit. The war in Europe is basically over, but I guess some of the diehards haven't gotten the message. I don't have enough points to get home immediately like some of the guys, so I don't know where they'll send me next.*
>
> *Whatever you do, don't leave the camp. I'll come back for you! I love you, and I promise to take care of you for the rest of our lives.*
>
> *Yours forever,*
> *Sam*

Thomas considered himself an honorable man. He knew that what he was contemplating was deceitful and dishonest. If he delivered the note to Klara, she would marry Sam. If he withheld it, Thomas would have to live the rest of his life knowing he was responsible for breaking Klara's heart, and altering her hopes for the future.

When a sopping wet and clearly grief stricken Klara returned to the hospital Thomas was waiting for her. He could feel the beads of sweat gathering on his brow. Sam's note was safely hidden in his pocket. For some reason, he could not bring himself to destroy it. Perhaps someday, when Klara was far removed by distance and time from this awful place, he would show it to her, and she would be grateful that he had saved her from making a horrible mistake.

Thomas had to refrain from sweeping Klara, drenched from the rain and with tears dripping down her face, up into his protective embrace. "What in the world were you doing out in this weather?" Thomas admonished. "You're just getting over typhus. You're still very susceptible to every germ flying around in this godforsaken camp. Take off that coat and sit down. I'll get you a blanket."

Klara did not utter a sound, and Thomas knew enough not to press her. As Thomas helped her out of the dripping Mackintosh, he guided her toward his office and the more comfortable of the two chairs near his desk. He pulled off her shoes and dried her sodden feet with a towel, but she drew them quickly away from his hands, curling them up under her in the chair where she had cocooned herself. Thomas opened his desk drawer and produced two small glasses that he filled with the brandy he had been saving to celebrate the war's end.

ELEVEN

For the next several days, Klara refused to speak with anyone. Once again she escaped to her bed and pretended to sleep. Sorrow eventually turned to anger, and then fear for her future. Where would she go? What would become of her? She had no one and no place to go. She knew of only two certainties: Sam had betrayed her, and she did not want to remain on German soil.

Again and again, Thomas tried to encourage her to speak. His visits were met with silence, and he was growing more and more desperate. *What have I done? She's inconsolable, and I'm responsible. I don't think I can live with my deception.* He had hidden the letter from Sam in one of his journals, and was now convinced that he needed to reveal its contents to Klara, whatever the consequences.

Walking into the ward, Thomas expected to see Klara, asleep with her head facing the wall. Instead he found her sitting up, slowly nibbling on her first piece of bread in days. "Thomas, even with my eyes closed, I can feel your presence. I also know you have been sitting here, beside my bed, just as you did when I was first brought into the hospital. Thank you for your worry. I am grateful."

"Klara," he whispered. "I need to tell you something important. Something that I should have told you days ago."

"Please, Thomas, whatever you need to say, it can wait. You once offered to help me. I am alone in a country that I despise. My few family members are dead. Do not ask me how I know, I just do," she said. "I do not want to stay here a moment longer. I want to go to America. I want to see your country and I want to start a new life. Can you help me?"

Thomas was surprised not only by Klara's request but by her demeanor. There were no tears, just a stern look of resolve. Nervously, he once again stuck his hand in his pocket, touching the note as if it were some sort of talisman. Just moments before he had been determined to set things right, to once again become a man of principle, the kind of man he always assumed he was. But now he was torn between those principles and his desire. Slowly, he withdrew his empty hand from his pocket and tenderly took hold of hers. In a voice hardly more than a whisper, Thomas answered, "Of course I'll help you. I'll get you to America."

"Thank you," said Klara. "What was it that you needed to tell me?"

"Nothing," said Thomas. "It wasn't that important after all."

In the end, getting all the paperwork in order for their departure was easier than he imagined. Within a month they would be aboard a ship. Thomas had finished his tour of duty weeks earlier and only volunteered to stay on because of Klara. He explained to her that they needed to get married; that was the only way he could quickly and safely get her into the United States. Once she agreed, it was all just a matter of signing a few documents. There was a short ceremony conducted by the army chaplain and witnessed by two nurses.

Klara easily agreed to the marriage after he explained that once they arrived in America, they could get a divorce after a year. Or, they could be married in name only, and live separately if that was what she wanted. He hoped that would give him enough time to convince Klara that the two of them were linked by fate and that destiny had brought them together. Of course, there would be some obstacles. He wasn't a fool. His mother would be difficult. Eugenia would never understand his attraction to Klara, and would never agree with his choice of a wife, a penniless, unknown foreigner with no connections.

TWELVE

Sam and Nick, along with the rest of their squadron, were mopping up and capturing the last of the hostiles who either hadn't heard that the war was over or simply refused to give up. Many of the soldiers they ran across were tired old men or scared young boys, the last of the once-powerful German Army. Most of the time Sam was so preoccupied with thoughts of Klara, Nick worried he might do something stupid and accidently get himself killed.

"Shape up, Sam," Nick yelled. "These idiots don't know you're in love, and I'm countin' on being the best man at your weddin'. My mother would never forgive you if I get killed. And if you get killed, your mother will murder me."

Sam glared at Nick.

"Don't look at me like that," Nick said. "I may not be in love, but I wanna get out of here as much as you do. Lately all I think about is gettin' home. Every time I think of my mother's home cookin', I salivate. If you're lucky, I'll invite you over for one of her specialties. Her marinara sauce could win an award, I'm not kiddin'. I just got a letter from my Uncle Sal. He says he has a job waitin' for me at his garage, and the entire cheerleadin' squad at Cathedral Latin High School is waitin' in line to go out with me, yours truly, the best-lookin' GI to come out of Cleveland. Hell, I might just be the best-looking GI in the whole damn army. Maybe I should forget Cleveland and go straight to Hollywood. I think they're gonna be lookin' for swashbucklin' leadin' men when the war's over."

"Would you just shut your trap?" Sam said. Then he grinned. "I know, you're right. I just can't stop thinkin' about her. I'm worried she didn't get my letter. Those orders to ship out came out of the blue. I handed the note over to the first nurse I came across, and she promised to get it to Klara, but you never know. As it was I barely made it back to barracks in time to ship out, but I should've risked court-martial and told Klara in person that I had to leave. She deserved that. I'm scared shitless that when she finds me gone she'll think the worst. She's so vulnerable. If she thinks I deserted her, she might just walk out of that place and disappear."

"Sam, she'll be there. But for the two of you to get married, you need to be there, too, and if you don't stop daydreamin', we're both gonna end up buried in this shithole of a country."

"You're right. Let's round up these stragglers and get..." Before Sam could finish, he toppled over, clutching his thigh. Nick dropped to the ground and crawled to his friend.

"Damn it! I told you!" Nick screamed. "Now look what you done, you got yourself shot." He grabbed Sam's fallen weapon and slung it over his shoulder, then grabbed Sam's arms. Crouching low, he hauled Sam into the heavy brush.

"You were the one yakkin' away," said Sam.

Nick ripped open the leg of Sam's fatigues. "It's...it's not too bad, buddy," he said. "Just stay low while we find out who's out there."

Nick, Sam, and two others were pinned down for several hours by a pair of snipers before someone else finally took the shooters out. During the long volley of shots, Sam drifted in and out of consciousness. Luckily the bullet had missed his femoral artery, but the wound was large, and still bled profusely. Nick could tell that it had struck Sam's femur and shattered the bone. Finally, a medic reached them and bundled Sam onto a field gurney. Lucid for a few minutes on the way to the hospital, Sam grabbed Nick's arm and begged him, made him promise, that he would make the docs save his leg.

Nick would never forget Sam's urgent pleading. For the remainder of his life he would live with the betrayal of that promise.

THIRTEEN

Miles away from Sam, a frightened but very determined new bride was boarding a plane that would take her to the coast of England. Klara would then board a naval ship that would carry her, along with her new husband and thousands of weary soldiers across the Atlantic to either resume their old lives, or as in her case, to begin a new one. The war in Europe was finally over, and although the numbers would never be absolute, the Nazis would be charged with murdering over six million Jews, three million Soviet prisoners of war, three million Polish Catholics, seventy thousand handicapped Germans, twelve thousand homosexuals, twenty-five hundred Jehovah's Witnesses, two hundred fifty thousand Roma or gypsies, and countless other innocents across Europe. Among those killed were Klara's mother, father, and brother.

Throughout the voyage to the United States, Klara stayed fairly isolated in the small quarters assigned to her and Thomas. The room, designed for officers, held single berths; Thomas, acting the perfect gentleman, never strayed from the upper bunk. Klara need not have worried. Now that she was safely aboard, Thomas was in no hurry to consummate their union. He would give her all the time she needed. There was no doubt in his mind that she would eventually come to love him, regardless of what obstacles might lay in their path. As for now he had more immediate concerns. Ever since the day she had agreed to marry him and leave for America, she had remained distant, answering his questions with only one or two words and not initiating any conversation at all.

For now, it was enough that she was with him, there to look at. Thomas knew his love was akin to an obsession. He recognized the symptoms. He constantly spoke to her while she was awake and stared at her while she slept. In the last several weeks, she had grown more beautiful, if that was even possible. Her hair, although still short, was starting to grow thicker. The flaxen color reminded him of the wheat fields he had once seen on a train trip through the Midwest. She was also beginning to gain weight and was becoming more and more rounded, more womanly, hardly the skin-and-bone, near-death woman who had been brought into the evacuation hospital those many weeks ago.

They would make port in New York in just two days time, and Thomas decided to stay in the city for another week to show Klara some of the sights before they traveled on to Atlanta. In one of their many conversations back in the hospital, she had mentioned how much she would like to one day see the Statue of Liberty. He wanted to be with Klara when she experienced her first taste of America. She also needed more rest before the overnight train trip south.

Thomas hoped that the week in New York would help them connect. He knew that in Klara's mind, the marriage was a sham; she had only agreed to it to get to America. Unless he could change her mind—and her feelings—in a year's time, she would ask for the promised divorce. Klara also needed to be in better spirits when she met his mother. The introduction would no doubt be difficult, and he wanted Klara to make a good first impression. He had purposely not wired his mother that his return was imminent. He knew that was cruel; she worried so about his well-being, and deserved to know that he was on his way home. Nevertheless, he could not bring himself to tell her he was married, and that he was returning home with what would later be dubbed a war bride, one of the thousands of European and Japanese women who, like Klara, married American soldiers—some for love, and some to escape their war-ravaged homelands.

Eugenia would not take the news well at all, of that he was very sure.

Klara was nothing like the countless numbers of sweet young things he had dated in the past. Those girls grew up coiffed, primped, and adored—Southern belles raised believing that they were destined for lives of privilege, an endless parade of social events, card games, and civic commitments, as long as their "good works" helped to support Atlanta's white-only institutions. Thomas never really thought too much about the separation of the races in Atlanta before the war. He grew up in a world governed by Jim Crow rules and regulations, those segregationist rules not in the law books but part of the unwritten code by which whites and Negroes lived. It was just the way things were. Separate drinking fountains and entrances to movie theaters, restaurants that catered to one group or the other, and even separate white and colored clinics at Grady Hospital were part of everyday life.

Thomas had grown up in a city with a significant Negro population that supported three colleges, a newspaper, and countless colored-owned businesses. But the only Negroes Thomas knew were the ones who worked for his family: the yard man, the driver, and, of course, Beulah, who had worked for his parents his entire life. She was part of the family—at least, that was the way he felt. He never thought to ask Beulah about the way she felt. Hell, he didn't even know how many kids she had or what their names were. He supposed it never interested him enough to find out. When he really thought about it, he didn't know anything about Beulah's life outside of how it affected him and his parents. She cooked all their meals, put him to bed when he was a little boy, and was there in the morning to get him up. Beulah was the one who bandaged his knees when he fell and chased the bully next door with a broom. She stayed all-day and well into the early evening. Her day wasn't over until the dishes were washed and the floor was spick-and-span, according to his mother's specifications. Only when the house sparkled would his mother finally give Beulah permission to walk to the bus stop and go home to her own family.

Thomas was bemused by how his thoughts had drifted from imagining his mother's reaction to the new Mrs. Compton to pondering the complexities of race relations in the city he called home. More importantly, he wondered which would prove more upsetting to Klara, "separate but equal" or his mother. In his mind, even segregation was a more palatable subject than thinking about Eugenia's reaction to his upcoming surprise.

Klara felt Thomas's presence before she opened her eyes. She was getting used to his hovering. It seemed as if the only time she could be alone was when she feigned sleep. She could not summon up the will to smile, to act as if she was excited to finally get out of the hellhole of postwar Europe. What she did feel was relief—relief that she would not die at the hands of the Nazis. But she wasn't sure if she would ever truly feel excited about anything again. She knew about the efforts Thomas had made to get her out quickly, about the favors he had called in to get her paperwork expedited. Yet, even after all that, his mere presence irritated her. Maybe it was because Thomas perceived her as helpless, or saw her as either naïve or stupid. Klara knew that none of those adjectives described her. No one survived five years of Nazism by being helpless, naïve or stupid.

It was obvious to Klara that Thomas thought he was in love with her and hoped their marriage would be more than in name only. He made that quite clear by his reaction to her short-lived romance with Sam and by his determination to help her leave Germany. Klara owed Thomas so much, but she had no romantic feelings for him. And there was no denying it: regardless of Sam's betrayal, she was still in love with the man, and feared she always would be. She felt so broken and lost. Klara had divulged her most personal secrets to Sam. She had told him what the Standartenführer had done to her. Klara had trusted Sam with a part of her life she had sworn never to reveal. She had been violated. She felt dirty. Why would anyone, including Sam, want her if they knew the truth?

Klara was determined to never speak of her time in Paris or her Jewish background again. She was convinced that Thomas would not have proposed marriage if she had revealed her past to him; he had made his feeling about Jews quite clear. Thomas may not have been staunchly anti-Semitic, but Klara knew that his mother certainly was. He would never knowingly bring a Jew home to Mother, especially as his wife. *My only hope for a happy new life depends on forgetting who I am—on never revealing the sordid details of my survival, and the personal details of everything and everyone I once loved.* The decision made, Klara finally opened her eyes and smiled at the man who had saved her from years at a displaced persons' camp in Europe and who knew what kind of future.

PART II

LIFE REBORN

FOURTEEN

Klara had been living in Atlanta for three weeks when she realized she was probably pregnant. She began to notice subtle body changes—thickening at the waist, soreness in her breasts. And now the nausea was overpowering her each morning, and she could barely summon the will to eat anything but the few crackers Beulah delivered to her room. Thomas attributed her lack of appetite to her adjustment to her new life, and did not push her to join him and his mother for meals. Regardless, Eugenia had yet to extend an invitation, and Thomas had not pushed the issue.

Klara had not consummated her marriage to Thomas. The thought of doing so made her equally sick to her stomach. She had hoped to find a way out of her commitment to him and somehow find the means of supporting herself. She wanted to start anew, but now that seemed even more daunting, almost impossible. Thomas had been so kind, so understanding, over the last several weeks, catering to her every whim and giving her the space she needed to think and take in her new surroundings. Thankfully, other than telling her she looked pale once or twice, he didn't seem to suspect anything. Thomas had no idea she had given herself completely to Sam, and as much as she hated Sam for his desertion, she was secretly glad she would always have a part of him with her. Klara knew she would not be able to hide her condition for long. She had to make a plan if she was going to forge a life for herself and the child she was carrying.

The introduction to Eugenia Compton had not gone well, although Thomas commented that it had been better than he expected. Eugenia had not ranted or raved, she simply gave Thomas a quick hug to welcome him home, kissed him on the cheek, and then walked stiffly out of the room. She had not even acknowledged Klara's presence.

The Compton family home was larger and statelier than Klara had imagined. There were so many rooms, it was easy for the two women to avoid each other. Klara had seen Eugenia only once or twice since her arrival, and the two of them had yet to exchange words.

Klara had been raised in comfort, so she was not in awe of the antique vases and rich oil paintings that decorated the walls. She supposed Eugenia would be surprised to know that her parents had once owned works by Monet, Manet, Cézanne, and many others. The art had been originally purchased by her grandparents, successful financiers in Berlin, and was passed down to her parents at the time of their marriage. The Nazis confiscated it all. Who knew on what walls her family's treasures now hung?

No, it was not the Comptons' art or other displays of wealth that were so daunting, but the sheer size of the Compton home that proved to be overwhelming. The house seemed so similar to the one she had read about in *Gone With the Wind*, a book she had devoured from cover to cover in the still relatively quiet days before the war. Soon after its publication in 1936, the historical romance had been released in German, and her father purchased a copy as a present for her birthday. All of her friends, one after the other, took turns reading it after she finished. She pretended to fall for the weak-willed Ashley Wilkes character while all of her other friends were mad about Rhett Butler. They all laughed at her for her choice. They could not believe that anyone, other than Melanie, would pick Ashley over the dashing Rhett. Klara never revealed to them that she was just being obstinate; if they had all chosen Ashley, she would have undoubtedly fallen for Rhett. She hoped that aspect of her personality was not a serious character flaw. It was just such fun to see their reaction, and she loved coming up with arguments as to why her choice was better.

She had always hoped to attend university. How many dreams, let alone lives, of young men and women had been destroyed by the war? In school, her friends had encouraged her to join the debate team, and perhaps if her studies had not been interrupted, she would have done just that. And now, all these years later, here she was, living at a genuine Twelve Oaks or Tara, a house complete with its own staff of brown-skinned workers, in a world as far removed as possible from the one she had known.

As Klara lounged on the small divan in her bedroom, she considered the options that would set the course for the next installment of her life, as well as that of her unborn child. She was in America, and that was far better than being left to languish in uncertainty in one of the countless displaced persons camps hastily established throughout Europe at the close of the war. Thousands of so-called stateless individuals, for the most part Jews, had been liberated and had nowhere to return to; their homes had been confiscated by the occupying Axis forces or by local collaborators, who were more than happy to move into a house still complete with furnishings but eerily devoid of all the former inhabitants.

On the train ride from New York to Atlanta, Klara tried to picture her new mother-in-law. She imagined her with Thomas's dark hair and green eyes, and slightly built like him. Klara was shocked and then amused when she saw the rather round woman waddling over to hug her son. Eugenia's blond hair, no longer natural, was done up in a tightly bound French twist that seemed to pull her face back into a permanent state of surprise. Her one similarity with her son was the opalescent green eyes that, at the moment of their introduction, were staring straight through Klara. No words were exchanged following her perfunctory hug with her son, and Klara forced herself to stifle a snicker at how hard Eugenia was trying to show her displeasure. Perhaps she thought she could intimidate her son's new wife. Little did she know that Klara had faced up to and lived through horrors beyond anything Eugenia could imagine. Compared to the Standartenführer, Eugenia was an amateur!

So far the only good thing about Klara's new situation was that while Thomas was out of the house reestablishing his medical practice, she could count on complete solitude to contemplate her future and that of her unborn child. Her only distractions were periodic soft knocks on her door by Beulah bringing in, and then an hour later removing, picked-at plates of food.

Klara knew that her options were limited. Leaving Thomas and trying to make it alone, once a real possibility, was a plan that would now have to be discarded. The baby she had in her belly was her lifeline to her parents and her brother. Through the child, a small part of them would continue to live. Klara realized the survival of the baby depended on her staying in this house with a man she did not love and with a mother-in-law who despised her. She needed to convince Thomas that the baby was his; to accomplish that, the marriage had to be consummated.

How far have I fallen! Me, the once-proper young lady of respected Jewish Berliners, she mused. I lost my innocence and principles in the service of the Standartenführer and now, not yet twenty-one years of age, I am contemplating the loveless seduction of a man who has been nothing but kind to me. The Standartenführer would be proud of me; he taught me well. She did not love Thomas, and the thought of having sex with him felt deceitful and amoral. Until her one night with Sam, the years of rape had stripped Klara bare of any sexual feeling. Until Sam, her only experience had been of systematic, brutal dehumanization, a punishment for being Jewish, and just as violent as being whipped or beaten. She never imagined that love, patience, and tenderness could change all that. And now, she, too, was preparing to use sex as a weapon, to deceive the man who had been her guardian and savior.

And it must happen soon. According to the calendar, she was six weeks pregnant. Although she was still way too thin, she would begin to fill out before too much longer. Thomas was due to arrive home any minute, and Klara resolved that this night she would not be sleeping alone.

She looked at the clock and could not believe that she had secluded herself in her room for the entire day. Here it was already four in the afternoon, and she was still in her nightgown. Her closet was filled with wonderful dresses, skirts, blouses, and silky undergarments that Thomas purchased for her on an all-day shopping spree in New York. She had yet to wear anything that was the least bit form-fitting. The only dress she really cared about was the one she had worn the night Sam had taken her to the little cottage in the woods. It was the only item of clothing she held onto from her time in the hospital, and she could not bring herself to throw it out. She periodically pulled it out of its hiding place in her lingerie drawer; by holding it close, she could remember each and every second of the night they shared in the cottage. Tonight, however, she would don one of the many dresses Thomas had purchased for her in New York, something clingy that accentuated her new curves.

What did the girl do in her room all day, day after day? In her own room at the end of the long corridor of empty guest bedrooms, Eugenia sat trying to come to terms with the war bride her son had ensconced in her home. It was obvious that Klara had been traumatized by her experiences. She was withdrawn and rarely smiled. Normally Genie would take pity on someone like Klara. It had been Genie's idea to have the Atlanta Junior League collect clothing for the thousands of homeless people displaced by the war. However, it was one thing to send donations and clothing to the dispossessed of Europe; it was quite something else to welcome a foreigner into her own home. Who knew what the girl's background really was? If Klara wasn't so fair-haired, Genie might have suspected that her son had delivered a Jew to live with them. That wouldn't do; Thomas was her only child, and she would protect him—and her family's legacy—at all costs.

Since Hitler's invasion of Poland in 1939, Genie had campaigned for America to stay out of the war, a war that by 1941 had enveloped the entire continent of Europe. She was an ardent isolationist who fervently believed that what was happening in Europe was not America's problem. She often quoted from a speech that Charles Lindbergh had delivered in September of '39, and agreed with his isolationist policies. In that speech Lindbergh issued a warning to the Jews, saying, "Instead of agitating for war, the Jewish groups in this country should be opposing it in every possible way, for they will be among the first to feel its consequences." Genie agreed. If America's young men began to be killed in a European war, the Jews would be blamed.

In general, Genie had nothing against the Jews. She knew quite a few of them. After all, she was a loyal customer at Rich's, Atlanta's largest department store, and Regenstein's, a high-fashion women's shop, both owned by Jews. Of course, the owners and she did not travel in the same social circle, but they were often thrown together at various civic and community functions. Nevertheless, she would have forever blamed them if her only son had died while trying to save Jews. She was convinced that if the Japanese had not bombed Pearl Harbor, the United States would have remained on the sidelines, and thousands of American lives would not have been lost.

After Pearl Harbor, when America declared war on Japan and then Germany, Genie tried to convince her selfless son that while dying in Europe or Japan in some nameless field hospital was indeed patriotic and commendable, he could do more good on the home front. She recalled with clarity Thomas's response. After staring at her in utter disbelief, he had simply walked out of the room. She should not have expected him to understand. He was all she had left and nothing would ever again matter to her if he did not come home. She supposed she could have secretly pulled some strings to ensure that he remained safe, but if he had discovered her treason, their relationship would have been severed forever.

But he had come home, and for that she was grateful. She supposed she should be more civil to the girl, but so many of her hopes and dreams for her son were now spoiled. Still, she needed to make an effort, or her estrangement with Thomas might never be resolved. He seemed so utterly devoted to the skinny little waif. Genie knew nothing about her, but perhaps it was time she pulled in her claws, ever so slightly, and tried to discover exactly who Klara was and the hold she had over Thomas.

Klara was in the middle of dressing for dinner when she heard a slight rap on the door, followed by a more distinct knocking. It must be Beulah again, asking for the fifth time today if she would like anything to eat. Opening the door just a crack, expecting to politely refuse Beulah's trays of nourishment, all of which were making her increasingly nauseated, Klara was shocked to see her mother-in-law standing outside.

"Klara, may I come in?" Klara opened the door without a sound and walked over to the bedside chair. She sat, staring up at Eugenia in sheer disbelief. Unlike Klara, Eugenia did not seem the least bit nervous, and in one fluid motion took hold of the small chair near the vanity table and moved it directly in front of her. Still not able to utter a sound, Klara watched as Eugenia sat down, crossed her legs in front of her, clasped her hands together on her lap, and smiled. "Klara, my dear. I suppose I owe you an apology. I have not been what you might regard as the best advertisement for 'Southern hospitality.' Here you are, a guest in my home for almost two weeks, and I still haven't formally welcomed you. Oops, I do believe I have erred again. I can't believe I just called you a guest," Eugenia said as she waved her hand in the air to signify that her choice of words had not been quite correct. "You are not a guest, you are Thomas's wife and that makes you my daughter-in-law."

Klara still sat unmoving, not speaking. She stared at her mother-in-law in shock.

"Dear, do you understand me? Am I speaking too quickly for you? Or perhaps it is just my strong Southern accent...but no, you must be accustomed to that," Eugenia said. "I mean, after all, Thomas's accent is no less Southern than my own. At any rate, you're here and my son seems head-over-heels in love with you, so I decided it was time I finally gave you a proper welcome. I do hope you understand that my avoidance of you was simply due to my shock at your appearance at my front door. I was expecting my son to return home alone, you understand. Well, it seems that the cat has still got your tongue, Oh, again, my apologies—these American expressions must seem so foreign to you. I simply mean, I never in my wildest imagination thought that.... Oh, never mind. I'm just rambling, airing my thoughts out loud, when I ought to keep them to myself. Where are my manners? We will be dining promptly at seven this evening, and I know Thomas would very much like to see you in attendance. Perhaps by then you may have found your voice. I overheard you conversing with Beulah, so I know that you speak English. Shall I expect you, then?"

Klara gave a hardly discernable nod. Eugenia promptly arose from her chair and walked brusquely out of the room.

With Eugenia gone, Klara sat there stunned, slowly feeling the tension release from her body. Her surprise at her mother-in-law's visit and unexpected invitation to dinner was quickly replaced by a feeling of satisfaction. Klara was not sure what sort of game Eugenia was playing, but at the moment that mattered little. Klara had her own plan to set in motion and tonight's dinner gave her the perfect opportunity to do so.

Dinner was still several hours away, but Klara needed all that time to prepare, to stay focused on what she must do to ensure her child's survival. She turned the water on to fill the bath, and then began to examine the clothes that had been hanging untouched in her closet. She discarded the skirts, blouses, and modest daytime dresses; that narrowed her choices to a crepe de Chine midnight blue dress, which showed just enough of her knees and cleavage to be flirtatious, and a sultry black silk with a low back that draped below her shoulder blades and left little to the imagination as to what was underneath. Klara's entire scheme was dependent on seducing Thomas that night. Each day she waited would only increase the likelihood that the baby would be born too early and her secret revealed.

Can I actually do this? I was a child when the war began, and now I am trying to be a seductress. Worse yet, in her mind, she was lying to the one man she believed had never lied to her, and whose kindness she would never truly be able to repay.

Finally deciding on the black dress and the pearl earrings, also purchased for her in New York, Klara immersed herself into the warm, soapy water and considered again what she was about to do. What would her mother say? Would she be shocked and disappointed at her daughter's treachery, or proud of the lengths to which Klara was willing to go to safeguard her child's future? What advice would she offer? And what would her parents think of her decision to reject her heritage, her religion? Was she not helping Hitler by doing away with one more Jew? Before she knew it, tears were streaming down her eyes as she once again found herself mourning her parents and brother. This child was not just her future but theirs as well. Klara thought again of her mother's last words to her—to live, to survive...no matter the cost. There was no doubt left in her mind. She would do whatever was needed to protect their legacy.

Judging by Thomas's reaction to seeing her walk into the dining room, Eugenia had not told Thomas that Klara would be joining them for dinner. His chair toppled back as he leaped up to greet her. Catching it before it fell completely to the floor, he rushed over to take her arm and escort her to the table.

"Klara, I didn't expect...my gosh, you look absolutely beautiful. When did you decide to...? Oh, never mind. You're here, and that's all that matters!" said Thomas. "Mother, look who has decided to join us! Klara, please, have a seat. Here, next to me."

It was several seconds before Klara noticed that two people she had never seen before were also sitting at the table. With Thomas's arm protectively wrapped around her shoulders, Klara let herself be led over to the seat beside his, where he made introductions. "Judge Matthew Cole, Dorthea, this is Klara. Klara, the Coles are my parents' closest friends. I've known them my entire life." The judge, already standing, acknowledged Klara with a broad smile of welcome. His wife remained seated, merely nodding hello in Klara's general direction.

"Well, Thomas, you have surprised us all—but what a wonderful surprise she is," said the judge. "Klara, you are radiant, and Dorthea and I are so pleased to be the first of Eugenia's social circle to meet you."

It was evident to Klara that Dorthea did not share the judge's enthusiasm, but Klara was beyond caring what other people thought of her. "Thank you, both of you. Thomas's mother did not mention that she was entertaining guests when she came to my room earlier today,"

Klara responded. With Thomas's arm still around her, she quietly took her seat.

Throughout the introductions, Eugenia had remained seated with an amused expression, probably enjoying everyone's discomfort. "Klara, we are so glad you are able to join us tonight," she said.

"Thank you, Mrs. Compton. I am finally feeling better and ready to assume my duties as Thomas's wife," said Klara, stealing a glance at her husband.

"Klara, please, don't be so formal. After all, I am your mother-in-law. Please, call me Eugenia or Genie. I go by both."

Klara nodded in acknowledgment and took a sip of the wine that had just been poured by Beulah. Klara now realized that the same elderly housekeeper not only cleaned the house and brought food trays but also served the dinner. "Beulah, thank you."

"You're welcome, Miz Klara."

"Beulah, please bring out the first course," said Eugenia. "There is no need for us to starve while we get to know one another."

"Yes, ma'am. Right away, ma'am."

"Now, Klara," continued the judge. "Where did the two of you meet? Genie has told us so little about you."

"You know Klara is just getting some of her energy back," said Thomas. "I think we should let her sit and enjoy the meal without bombarding her with questions."

"Yes, yes," said the judge. "I quite agree. That was quite thoughtless of me."

"Thomas, Judge Cole...really, I don't mind," said Klara. "I know your mother is also curious about our meeting. We mustn't forget that my arrival was, to say the least, unexpected. So, I shall satisfy everyone's curiosity. Thomas and I met in a United States Army field hospital in Germany, and he is responsible for saving my life, both physically and emotionally." Placing her hand on top of Thomas's and caressing it softly, Klara continued. "Yes, I was one of the lucky war survivors to have been liberated by American soldiers when they entered the Buchenwald concentration camp in April. Although I had fallen ill with typhus, I was not as sick as many of the others, but like most I *had* lost all hope. I had given up and was only waiting to die when another American soldier, not Thomas, discovered me and brought me to the field hospital. Thomas's face was one of the first I saw when I finally opened my eyes."

"And for me," Thomas added, "it was love at first sight. I know that sounds ridiculous, but I'm telling y'all the truth."

"How charming," said Eugenia, ringing for Beulah to refill her wine glass for the third time. Glaring at his mother, Thomas turned to Klara, who continued to tell the story she would repeat over and over again in the years to come to anyone who asked her about her accent, why she didn't have any family, and how she had come to live in Atlanta, Georgia.

Sticking as close to the truth as possible, and determined to not allow emotion to get the best of her, Klara told a very abbreviated and partially fabricated version of her history. "I grew up in Berlin in a progressive Christian family with my mother, father, and my little brother Ernst, who was four years younger than me. My father was a physician, my mother a homemaker. We could trace our lineage in Germany back to the 1600s. My grandparents on my father's side were members of the German intelligentsia, those in society who hosted artistic and philosophical salons in their homes where ideas, politics, and economics were discussed and debated. My father was born into this exciting postwar Germany, where famous musicians, scientists, professors, and artists were often guests in his parents' home and where freedom of expression was encouraged. I need not explain to you how all that changed when Hitler came to power. Although we were not Jewish, we watched as the Nazis took their freedoms away one by one. My parents were horrified by what was happening to their friends and neighbors and joined the resistance. They managed to avoid the Gestapo until someone within their immediate circle betrayed them. They never discovered who it was. My parents were arrested and sent to Dachau, a concentration camp very close to Munich. I never saw them again. The Nazis did not stop at punishing our parents. Ernst and I were sent to Sachsenhausen, another camp about thirty-five kilometers north of the city. After one month, Ernst died. He cried for our parents and refused to eat the meager, vermin-infested rations that were doled out to us.

The details of my odyssey after Sachsenhausen are far too horrible to discuss, and I fear that I have already said too much. I see that I have left all of you, even Thomas, speechless. Perhaps I should excuse myself?"

"Klara, we are speechless, and not because of your story, but because of my stupidity for asking you about your past. We have been reading accounts in the newspaper about what went on in those horrible camps, but I..." stammered the Judge.

"No, Judge Cole. It is my fault. I said too much," said Klara. "Everyone was curious, and I thought, better to know the truth, no? And as you can see by Thomas's expression, it is also his first time hearing some of my story. He has not pressed me for details. And now that I have revealed a little of my background, there is no longer any need to discuss it." Turning slowly in her chair to face Thomas, whose hand she was still gripping, Klara continued. "Because of my knight in shining armor...I think that is the correct expression, no?"

"Yes," said Thomas with tears forming in his eyes.

"Yes, then...because of my Thomas, who is now my husband, I never have to be afraid again. I am starting a new life, here in your wonderful city of Atlanta."

"Klara, you are one of the bravest woman I have ever had the pleasure to meet. You and Thomas deserve a toast in your honor. I believe the two of you are destined for a bright and wonderful future," gushed Judge Cole. "I only wish I could have been the one to perform the marriage ceremony. Eugenia, perhaps you should have a reception for them here at the house."

Ignoring the glare and the under-the-table kick to his ankle from his wife, Judge Cole continued, "Now, Eugenia, Dorthea, let's refill those glasses and raise them to the newlyweds."

Eugenia's glass, once again empty, was quickly refilled. With arm raised, she quietly joined in.

"Well, that was the longest two-hour dinner I have ever had the misfortune to attend," said Thomas in hopes of getting Klara to relax once they were safely out of earshot of the others and on their way back upstairs. "My mother and Dorthea were as drunk as cooter bugs." Thomas saw the corners of Klara's mouth turn up just a little. "You're thinking, 'What the hell is a cooter bug?' I actually have no idea, but my grandma used to say that whenever anyone she knew had one too many. Luckily, the judge is sober enough to drive his wife home. I'd hate to have had them spend the night. Even with makeup, Dorthea looks like she fell out of an ugly tree and hit every branch on the way down. You just laughed! I know. I heard you, Klara. Don't deny it. Well, I'm right, aren't I? She is pretty damn ugly."

Standing outside the bedroom door, Klara finally turned to face the man she had married and whom she was about to trick into believing had fathered her child. "Thomas, how many of those funny sayings do you know?"

"Klara, those sayings are part of my upbringing. Every good Southerner is born and raised with those sayings, and if I can use one to nudge a smile out of you and erase some of your sadness, I promise to keep them coming for as long as you'll have me."

"Thomas, I do not know why, but for some reason, you love me," said Klara. "Come, let us go to bed. I think I am ready to love you in return."

It took Genie a few minutes to realize she was still fully clothed and sprawled across her bedspread when the sun started to peek though the partially open blinds in her room. Was it really morning? She remembered saying goodnight to the Coles, promising to call Dorthea in the morning. She had poured herself a nightcap from the last bottle that remained of her deceased husband's favorite single malt. She had needed to steady herself after Klara's Academy Award performance at dinner, but Genie had no idea how she made it upstairs.

I'll be damned, she thought. *The girl's not stupid. I've no doubt she orchestrated the entire evening once she realized she had an audience. And Thomas? I have never seen him so entranced, so ridiculously in love. What's her game?* Genie was convinced that something about Klara's story simply didn't ring true. There was something that she could not put her finger on, but the girl was hiding something. With her head pounding and her stomach doing somersaults, Genie was in no condition to analyze the past evening's events any further. Perhaps after a nice long bath and several cups of black coffee, she would be able to see things a little more clearly, she thought. She slowly and carefully raised herself from her bed and rang for Beulah.

At the other end of the hall, Thomas was also awake. Like his mother, he was replaying the events of the previous evening. He almost believed he had conjured up their lovemaking and was worried that when he looked over toward the other half of the bed it would be empty. But there was Klara, curled up on her side, with one foot exposed over the blanket and one arm tucked beneath her head.

Thomas had vowed to be as patient as possible with Klara, to wait for as long as he must to consummate their marriage. He knew she was fragile, that she had been in love with Sam and had been terribly wounded by the sergeant's perceived betrayal—a betrayal Thomas alone was responsible for. He also realized he did not know the extent of the horror she had experienced in the camps. He was sure that what she had revealed the night before was only part of the story, an abridged version that would stop people from asking any more questions. *Would he ever know, would she ever love him enough to tell him?* The last thing he expected was the passionate kiss she gave him on the landing before they entered their room. He was dumbfounded, and couldn't move as Klara started to undress him. She hadn't rushed. There was no frenzy, only seduction. Bit by bit she removed his clothing until he stood naked before her. In his nakedness, he was once again ashamed that he had lied about Sam, but when Klara removed her blue gown and revealed nothing underneath, his deceit was immediately forgotten.

Lost in his reverie, Thomas had not noticed that Klara was beginning to stir until her hand began to move ever so slowly up his thigh. "Good morning, Dr. Compton. You look especially content this morning," cooed a smiling Klara.

"Yes, I guess I am, because something very unexpected and absolutely wonderful happened last night and I still can't figure out if I am dreaming."

As Klara's hand rose higher and higher, she asked, "Does this feel like a dream? Or this? Or, perhaps this?" continued Klara as she straddled her supine husband and continued what they had started the evening before.

Having said goodbye to Thomas hours earlier, Klara was still lying in bed, disturbed at how easy it had been for her to orchestrate the previous evening's events. She had not expected the additional guests at dinner, but the judge's questions had allowed her to spin out her fabricated story, one that could neither be checked easily nor questioned without insensitivity. Klara's family was dead, killed by the Nazis; that was true. All traces of her Jewish ancestry had been destroyed during the Allied bombing of Berlin, and Klara could easily pass herself off as Christian without worrying that her past would be discovered. The rest of her odyssey, her years with the Standartenführer and the time spent in the camps, would remain her secret.

She had trusted one man once, and she was determined to never trust another. Yes, Klara felt she had played the game she had started exceedingly well. Thomas was convinced that she had finally snapped out of her depressed state and was ready to start a life with him. Eugenia would be thwarted in all of her attempts to divide them once Klara announced that Thomas would be a father soon. She would have to time the announcement perfectly. She was already six weeks along but, having been rail thin to begin with, she didn't expect her pregnancy to be visible for quite some time. She only hoped that when the baby came, the child would have her light hair and eyes, and not the dark curly hair that she had found so appealing on Sam.

Sam. If only she could stop thinking about him! Poor Thomas. She hated deceiving him. It was only by visualizing Sam beneath her that she could summon up the passion she needed to convince Thomas that her feelings toward him had changed. Throughout the night and into the morning, she pretended to be kissing and caressing Sam. She needed to stop thinking about him. Sam was gone, out of her life, and she was just another foolish woman who had fallen for a soldier's lies and had gotten pregnant. Today was a new beginning, and Klara was determined to start building a life for the child she was carrying. Nothing else mattered. For the first time since she had been in Atlanta, she felt like getting out of bed to begin the process of discovering exactly what this new life had in store for her.

Beulah almost jumped out of her skin when Klara appeared fully dressed in the kitchen asking for a cup of coffee and if the newspaper had arrived. "Yes'm, Miz Klara, the *Atlanta Constitution* done arrived this mornin', but Miz Compton's readin' it right now. If you want, I kin give you las' night's *Journal*."

"Thank you, Beulah, that will do. I just want to become a little more familiar with where I am living," said Klara. "I really know nothing about Atlanta except what Thomas has told me. Of course, I read the book *Gone With the Wind*, which is when I first heard of your city. Have you read it?"

"No'm, Miz Klara. I ain't had much schoolin'. I heard of it, though, and some folks I know done saw the movie."

"Ah yes, the movie! As a schoolgirl, I was madly in love with Clark Gable," said Klara. "Beulah, this coffee is wonderful. Forgive me. I must seem very rude to you. Here you have been waiting on me hand and foot for weeks now, bringing me trays with all kinds of temptations, and I have not really said thank you. Please sit down and join me and we can begin to get to know each other a little better."

"Thank you, Miz Klara, but I got work to do. I can't be takin' no coffee break."

"Please, Beulah, just for five minutes. I have not spoken to anyone other than Thomas and his mother since my arrival. You have been so kind to me, and I just thought we could have a cup of coffee together."

"Miz Klara, I know you don't understan' 'cause you new here, but there won' be no gettin' to know each other—not in this house, not in this city. Miz Compton see me sittin' down on the job...at the same table as a white woman...? I'm sorry, Miz Klara, but I can' afford to lose this job, not over a cup of coffee. So don't you be askin' me again, you hear?"

"I'm sorry, I just thought..."

"Klara, what on earth did you think? Beulah has a full day of responsibilities, and those don't include socializing," Eugenia said, as she walked into the kitchen. "Beulah, I'll take my breakfast here rather than in the dining room this morning. After that, perhaps you could get started with the upstairs bedrooms now that everyone is up."

"Yes'm, Miz Compton. Right away, ma'am."

"Klara," said, Eugenia. "I do believe you need a little instruction on some of our, shall we say, our *customs* here. I hope you don't mind if I join you." Without waiting for a reply, Eugenia took the seat across from Klara. "We—and by we I mean you, Thomas, and of course me—we do not, under any circumstances, fraternize with the help. Beulah is not your friend, nor will she ever be, and the sooner you are clear on that, the better."

Klara stared at her mother-in-law, shocked by the patronizing tone in Eugenia's voice. Her mother-in-law spoke as though Beulah were not right there in the room with them, pouring coffee and dishing up eggs and slices of buttered toast.

"Here in Atlanta, we respect our colored population and respect our differences. They have their own restaurants, and we have ours. They have their own drinking fountains, and we have ours. They sit in the back of our buses, and we sit in the front. They live in one part of the city, and we live in another. Am I making myself clear?" said Eugenia. "Now that you are married to my son, and carry the Compton family name, I expect you to conform to, not rebel against, our customs and traditions. Do not embarrass me or my friends. Now that I know you can speak, do you have any questions?"

"No. Not a question, only an observation. In Germany, we also had rules. The Third Reich issued many proclamations. Jews could not go to the same schools as Aryans. Jews could not sit on park benches. Jewish doctors could not have Aryan patients. Jews could not work in many of the professions. Eventually there were so many rules that the Jews could do almost nothing except stay in their homes to avoid being arrested. So many rules, they could not keep track of them all," said Klara. "And then, to keep Jews separate from Aryan, Christian Germans, we needed to be able to recognize a Jew, so Jews were forced to wear badges, yellow stars, on their clothing—just in case they happened to look Aryan. So, you see, Mrs. Compton, I am very used to these types of social *customs*. The only difference that I can see is that Beulah and her people do not have to wear identification badges. The color of their skin is all that is needed to give them away." Klara waited for her mother-in-law's response, but it was not immediate. "I see that perhaps now the cat has your tongue."

For several minutes more Eugenia and Klara sat in complete silence, each studying the other with renewed intensity. "Klara, you do have gumption, I'll give you that. There are not many people who dare stand up to me," Eugenia said, her eyes narrowing and her hands gripping the table. "However, Atlanta, Georgia is nothing like Berlin, Germany. We don't go around putting our colored citizens in concentration camps, nor do we murder them in gas chambers. We take care of them! We let them work in our homes. We provide them with their own schools, hospitals, and various public accommodations. For god's sake, we trust them to raise up and care for our children. Beulah's been with this family for over thirty years. You're new here, so you need to mind your manners and be a good wife to my son. Then, perhaps at least for Thomas's sake, you and I might try to at least tolerate one another. And please stop calling me Mrs. Compton. It makes me feel old. Eugenia or Genie will do. Do you think you could manage that?"

"For Thomas's sake, I will try," said Klara. "I will also try not to embarrass you, but do not expect me to agree with you."

Acknowledging their détente with a nod of her head, Eugenia offered Klara the use of the family car and driver if she wanted to acquaint herself with Atlanta. After Eugenia left the table, Klara remained seated for a few more minutes as she tried to absorb and analyze exactly what had just occurred between her and her mother-in-law. Were they calling a truce? Their feelings for one another certainly had not changed, but perhaps they could peacefully coexist. After all, they both wanted Thomas to be happy, and if Klara could convince Eugenia that the baby was indeed her grandson, then perhaps everything would work out after all.

Taking Eugenia up on her offer, Klara went out to the garage and asked Lloyd, Eugenia's driver, to take her on a sightseeing tour around Atlanta. "Miz Compton told me you might be comin' by and asked me to drive you wherever you want."

"Well, Lloyd, I am at a loss. I have no idea where to start. How about just a short drive downtown?"

"Yes, ma'am. We kin ride right down Peachtree and you can see a few of the sights." As Klara started to get into the front seat, Lloyd nearly tripped over his own feet as he rushed to step in front of her. "Ma'am, you don' never ride in the front seat. That'd get me in a heap of trouble. You jus' get yourself all settled in the back, and we be on our way."

Shaking her head in disbelief, Klara complied, and Lloyd started out on Peachtree Street toward Atlanta's downtown. "On this road, 'cept for some churches, there's not much to see until we get a ways south. Over here on the right is the Episcopal church," Lloyd said. "And over here on the lef', well, that one's Presbyterian. And a ways up, we'll be passin' it in a minute, is the Jewish church."

"The Jewish church?"

"Well, some folks call it The Temple, but I jus' calls it the Jewish church."

"Lloyd, when we get there, would you mind terribly much if I take a closer look?"

"No, ma'am. I kin pull up to the curb so you kin take a look, or you kin get out an' walk around if you like." He stopped the car in front of the synagogue.

"No, I do not think I will get out, but if we could sit here a moment, that would be wonderful."

Klara wasn't sure why she wanted to stare at the beautiful synagogue, situated on a rise on one of Atlanta's most prestigious streets. She had not been near a house of worship since before Kristallnacht all those years ago. She had always loved going to services, and had wonderful memories of celebrating the holidays with her family. Although not deeply religious, her mother had always prepared special foods and decorations for each and every festival. Was Klara really never going to enter a synagogue again? Was she ready to deny her own heritage to her unborn child and live as a Christian for the rest of her life? Would she be able to keep up the charade?

Seeing the building brought so many questions to the surface, and she was more troubled about her future than she had been since she made the decision to keep her past a secret. She realized, too, how lucky she'd been that no one had asked the night before which denomination of Christian she had been in Berlin. There were so many here! And was Atlanta so very different than Berlin? If the Negro people were forced to obey both written and unwritten laws to keep them segregated, could not the same thing happen to Jews? Might it not happen again to her or, more tragically, to her child?

Klara thought about Eugenia's reaction to her attempt to have a simple conversation with Beulah. The white and colored races did not mix in the American South, and Klara wondered if they ever would. "Lloyd, we can go now. I have been here long enough. Oh, and Lloyd, please don't tell Mrs. Compton that I asked you to stop here."

"Ma'am, me and Miz Compton, we don' have what you call conversations. You don' have to worry none about that."

FIFTEEN

Klara went into labor in the early morning hours of November 9, 1946, eight years to the day from what people called the Night of Broken Glass, *Kristallnacht*—the day her world had begun to unravel. The irony did not escape her. Six hours later, Thomas Compton III was born at Piedmont Hospital in Atlanta. Klara had been thrilled when, according to her own calculations, the baby was almost two weeks past her true due date, and therefore only a few weeks earlier than Thomas and his mother expected. Her doctor may have had his suspicions, but fortunately never voiced them out loud.

Klara was not at all surprised that the baby was a boy. Somehow she had always believed that she was carrying Sam's son. Her connection with the new baby was immediate and intense. She was unprepared for the depth of emotion she would feel toward the tiny little boy.

"How's my girl doing?" Thomas asked as he walked into her room.

"Oh, Thomas, have you seen him yet? Is he not beautiful?"

"How could he be anything but beautiful with you as his mother? And yes, I just saw him, and he looks just like you."

Klara had thought so, too, and had already breathed a sigh of relief. So far, the baby showed nothing of Sam.

"Mother is coming by a little later. I held her off for as long as I could. She wants to give her personal stamp of approval to her progeny," Thomas said. "I promise I'll stay with you throughout her entire visit so she won't have an opportunity to upset you. I know she was pleased by our choice of names, so at least for now she's relatively content."

"Thank you, Thomas, I appreciate that. Seeing your mother alone right now would be more than I could deal with."

As Thomas made himself comfortable in the bedside chair, Klara closed her eyes to prepare for Eugenia's pending visit. Throughout the pregnancy, Eugenia had made several snide comments about how quickly Klara had conceived and how fast she was showing, but Klara wasn't sure if she suspected anything or if she was simply being nasty. Klara took comfort knowing that Eugenia could not prove anything, and that Eugenia would not dare to speak of it in front of Thomas for fear of further alienating him. Thomas loved Klara unconditionally, and rarely sided with his mother when disputes arose in the household. Klara felt relatively secure in the knowledge that her secret was safe.

Just as Thomas warned, two hours later Eugenia marched into Klara's room, deposited herself in the chair Thomas had just risen from, and handed Klara a beautifully wrapped box. "Now, don't look so shocked, Klara. The gift is not for you. What kind of grandmother would I be if I didn't bring a present to my first grandchild? Now, go ahead, open it."

The box was wrapped so beautifully that Klara hated to tear the paper. She proceeded slowly, untying the ribbon gently, then opening the lid. Inside was a beautiful, white baby gown, hand smocked across the chest and sleeves, with tiny blue ducks embroidered on the collar and cuffs. "It's for his christening," Eugenia said. "I've already spoken to Reverend Clay at First Presbyterian, and when I leave here I have an appointment at Rich's department store to order the invitations and announcements. Klara, please look at the wording. I've written everything out, you know...Dr. Thomas Compton II and Clara Werner Compton are pleased to announce the birth of their son, Thomas Compton III...Well, here, read it for yourselves. I hope I haven't overstepped, but with you being so new here, you hardly need one more thing to have to worry about. And, of course, you are unfamiliar with how we do things."

While Klara stared at the handwritten draft of the announcement, Thomas turned to his mother. "Whoa, there, Mother. You need to pull up your reins for just a minute. Klara and I haven't even discussed the christening with each other," he said. "Don't you think the two of us need to be in on this conversation?"

"Why yes, of course, if you want to. I'll tell Reverend Clay to pencil in the date, and when Klara and the baby come home, we can firm up the plans. How's that sound? Now, if the two of you don't mind, I would like Thomas to escort me to the nursery to introduce Thomas Compton III to his grandmother."

"Eugenia, wait!"

"Yes, Klara?"

"My name—you have spelled it incorrectly. My name it is Klara, Klara with a K."

"How utterly charming, and so European! I'll make the change," Eugenia said as she exited the room.

Thomas and Klara joined Eugenia in the nursery. Once the nurses handed the freshly diapered and swaddled Thomas III to Eugenia, and she settled herself in one of the nursery rockers, she seemed to lose herself in the joy of holding her first grandchild. It was the first time Klara could detect a hint of a softer side to her mother-in-law. As she watched Eugenia, Klara thought again of the implications of her deceit. Her child was Jewish. Could she allow him to be baptized into a Christian church? There were so many aspects of her deception she had not considered. Like a pyramid, one lie was layered on top of another and each one complicated the one that lay below. Would she be able to carry off this charade? She dared not think of her parents. Klara's mother once told her that she was capable of anything if it would save her children. At the time Klara was too young to comprehend what her mother was implying. Perhaps, she thought, her mother would understand.

Later that evening, when Thomas and Klara were alone, Thomas apologized for his mother's latest intrusion. "She's like a damn bulldozer. I'm so sorry. Would you mind terribly if we did have Reverend Clay perform the christening? I know we've never really spoken about religion, or how we would raise Tommy, but I know it would mean the world to mother to baptize him into her church. And I guess, if I really think about it, it would mean a lot to me as well."

Klara had thought of nothing else since opening Eugenia's present to discover the beautiful gown beneath the tissue. "Thomas, I hope you understand what I am about to say. I gave up religion a long time ago. I can no longer believe in a god that allowed so many horrible atrocities to be committed to so many innocent people," said Klara. "Where was God when the Gestapo came to take away my parents? Why did God not provide nourishment to my sweet brother Ernst when he was starving and withering away to nothing? And where was God at Buchenwald? He was noticeably absent amid the misery and suffering that you yourself witnessed."

"Klara, my darling, Klara. I am no theologian, but I don't believe we can ever truly understand God's plan. You are right; everything you say is true," said Thomas. "But I believe, I have to believe, that God's hand was also involved in saving you and bringing you into my life."

"Oh, Thomas, in some ways you are such an innocent. Nevertheless, if it means that much to you, the baby can wear the gown and be christened in your church," said Klara. "I, however, cannot bring myself to attend. For my sake, please try and make your mother understand."

SIXTEEN

As soon as Nick was discharged, he had headed back to Buchenwald. Most of the military doctors and nurses had been reassigned or sent home, but Nick eventually tracked down a nurse who remembered Klara. "She got hitched, married one of the American doctors." Nick didn't have to guess which one. The nurse couldn't believe that the good-looking doctor with the adorable Southern accent had fallen for one of the former prisoners. "What a waste of an eligible American man," she said. "And that ungrateful girl didn't smile throughout the entire ceremony!"

Once Nick discovered that Klara had gone off and married the jackass from Georgia, he knew he had no choice but to tell Sam. He had lied to him once, and Sam had forgiven him for promising something that could not be delivered. Nick would not lie about Klara.

At the same moment that Thomas Compton III was taking in his first breath of life, Sam Rosstein was entering Western Reserve University as a first-year law student. After enduring six months of painful rehabilitation at the Veterans Administration Hospital, Sam was eager to have his mind occupied by the legal complexities of civil procedures, torts, and contracts.

At first, when Sam realized that Klara was okay and living in the States, he considered calling or writing to her. It wasn't as if she was hiding out. He couldn't remember how many times he had reached for the telephone, only to reconsider at the last minute. One time he even waited until someone picked up, but he couldn't bring himself to ask for her. *She didn't wait, and that was that. Even if she didn't get my note, why didn't she leave one for him? Why in the hell did she leave without a word?* No, it was better this way. A clean break. He would immerse himself in his classes and try to forge a new life.

Sam was almost glad Klara was gone. He was not the same man she had fallen for, and he didn't know if he could have mustered up the guts to face her. When he first got home, his parents had been shocked by his appearance. He had lost thirty pounds, and his suffering was clearly visible on the newly minted lines on his face. The doctors at the field hospital had tried to save his leg, but the damage had been too great. Fortunately, there was a VA facility in Cleveland, close to his family's home, so he was able to complete much of his rehab as an outpatient. The care and nurturing he received from his parents and sisters helped to heal the physical pain, but the emotional scars of losing Klara continued to haunt him. Losing her hurt worse than losing his leg.

SEVENTEEN

"Mommy, can I lick the envelopes?" asked Tommy, eager to participate in preparations for his eighth birthday party. They were celebrating the occasion at the Compton home by inviting Tommy's entire second grade class from the Westminster Schools. As a Westminster board member, Eugenia had chosen the school and, although it was affiliated with the Presbyterian church, Klara could hardly complain since Tommy was getting an excellent education and, most importantly, seemed so happy with his friends and teachers.

After eight years, Klara was still fighting Eugenia's intrusion into their lives. Thankfully, Thomas was strong enough to stand up to his mother when it really mattered. The school was a good choice regardless of the fact that her mother-in-law was advocating for it. Eugenia had attended Washington Seminary, an all-girls school that had merged with North Avenue Presbyterian to form the Westminster Schools, and she had a sentimental attachment to the exclusive academy.

"Mommy, you didn't answer. Can I please lick the envelopes?"

"Of course you may, and you may place the stamps in the corners as well," said Klara. As Klara demonstrated to Tommy where to place the stamps, she noticed how grown up her young son suddenly looked. It had been eight years since she had settled into her life with Thomas and his mother. Both he and Eugenia doted on Tommy, and Klara had grown accustomed to the daily routines of the Compton household.

As Tommy began to work on his invitations, Klara, for what seemed like the thousandth time, scrutinized her son's face, finding vestiges of her past life. The blue eyes and blond hair were much like her own, but the shape—and especially the sparkle—of the eyes reminded her so much of her beloved brother Ernst. There were times when Tommy's very actions were identical to those of Ernst, and she was simultaneously overwhelmed with a mixture of sadness and joy. Thankfully, he looked so much like Klara and her own family members that Thomas never seemed to suspect that he was not the boy's real father. Klara, though, could see traces of Sam in Tommy every time she looked at him. She supposed that Thomas barely remembered his rival, and thankfully did not associate Tommy's wavy and unmanageable hair, an adorable mop that could never be slicked down for more than a few minutes, with the young soldier who had visited her every day while she was in the hospital. As Tommy grew, Klara noticed more and more mannerisms that reminded her of Sam. A certain tilt of his head, or the way he pushed his fingers through his unruly hair, were at times all it took to remind Klara of that one night in the woods. She often wondered what had become of him—whether he ever thought of her, and what he would do if he ever discovered he had a son.

"Mommy, I'm done. Can we take a walk to the mailbox? I told everyone we were sending out the invitations today. Please, please, please—"

"Of course we can. Let's go now. I'm going to the hospital to volunteer this afternoon while Granny takes you to the club to go swimming."

In 1887, Jedediah Compton had been among the founding members of the prestigious Piedmont Driving Club, and Eugenia's entire social life revolved around her activities there. Although Klara allowed Tommy to go to the club for swimming and tennis, she herself only went occasionally and tried to avoid visiting the elitist grounds. Klara knew the club was exclusive, and that Jews were not welcome as members. Thomas wanted her to join him there for parties and dinners and Klara could not always come up with an excuse. When she told him that she didn't care for their admission policies, he agreed that the rules could use an overhaul but reminded her that most of the club members, including his mother, were already raging and worried about the ramifications of the Supreme Court decision regarding *Brown v. Board of Education*. The decision that had officially declared "separate but equal" unconstitutional was all anyone was talking about. So, he explained, it was no time to raise the question of opening up the club to Jews. Besides he noted, the Jews had their own clubs.

"I don't believe they would even be interested in joining ours," he informed Klara. When Klara reminded him that the only reason the Jews had their own clubs was because they couldn't get into his, he discontinued the conversation with a dismissive wave of his hand and walked out of the room.

EIGHTEEN

For the last several months, Klara had been volunteering in the children's ward at Grady Hospital. For the first time since before the war, she was beginning to forge a few friendships. She was drawn to one woman in particular, but thus far Klara had only spoken to her briefly, and only about the children in the ward. The woman, Lotte Bacharach, also had an accent and although Lotte's was less noticeable than her own, Klara was fairly certain that she had been born in Germany. Klara was scheduled to do volunteer work for a few hours that very afternoon, and if Lotte were also working, she would ask her to join her for a cup of coffee.

To Klara's delight, Lotte was on the ward when she arrived. "Lotte, I've noticed your accent. Very similar to mine, no?"

"Ah, I have been meaning to say the same to you. Where were you born? I think not in Dixie."

Klara could not control herself, and started laughing so hard she was doubled over. "No, not in Dixie," she finally sputtered out. "I was born in Berlin. And you?"

"Frankfurt."

"So," Klara said. "We have much in common. When did you emigrate?"

"In '38. I was one of the lucky ones. My husband had family here, a cousin in Atlanta, who signed an affidavit in support of us. Our quota numbers were low and we were able to get out," said Lotte.

"Unfortunately, my parents were not so lucky. They managed to get out of Germany to Amsterdam, but.... Well, I'm sure you can guess the rest of the story. When the Germans invaded Holland, the first ones to be deported were the non-Dutch citizens. Ah, the Dutch. They like to think they were also victims, but they did little to protect their Jewish population. I only recently found out that both of my parents were murdered in Auschwitz."

"A terrible time," said Klara, shaking her head.

"Ah, the stories we could all tell if only anyone wanted to listen. Do you agree? No one really wants to talk about what happened to us. Sometimes I think our fellow Jews, the ones lucky enough to be born in this country, are embarrassed by us. They do not want to hear about what happened in the camps. They do not want to hear that while they buried their heads in the sand, many families in Europe perished. Ah, but enough, I am talking too much and making you sad. I should be grateful. Without my husband's cousin, we, too, would have been murdered."

Klara stared at Lotte and could not summon up any words in response. After all these years of maintaining her masquerade, Klara knew she could not continue the pretense for one more minute. She longed to tell someone the truth about her past, and sensed that she could trust the person standing before her with the knowledge of her deception. With tears in her eyes, she asked Lotte to join her after their shift for a coffee at the little diner near the hospital.

Throughout Klara's story, Lotte listened, not interrupting and not judging. Klara told her about her father's arrest and the bargain she made with the Standartenführer—a bargain she had hoped would ensure the safety of her mother and brother, only to find out it was all for nothing, that they were both dead. She told Lotte about falling in love with Sam and about their night together in the cottage. She explained how she had felt betrayed and abandoned by Sam, and had then taken advantage of Thomas's obsession with her to immigrate to America, only to find that she was carrying Sam's child—which she had then deceived Thomas into believing was his own.

Only when Klara finished did Lotte reach across the table to take her hand. "Klara, thank you for trusting me with your story. I promise your secrets are safe. You are a very brave young woman. I do not know if I would have had the courage to proceed so carefully for the sake of my unborn child. You have given Tommy a good life and a family—and of that you should be very proud."

"Proud?" said Klara. "No, I am not proud. I am ashamed. I am ashamed that my marriage is based on a lie, that I have deceived the man who gave me and my son a future, that I deny who I really am every day of my life, and that as much as I try, I cannot forget Sam Rosstein and how much I loved him."

"Klara, do you think you are the only one who survived the war with secrets? We all have them. I live every day with the knowledge that I did not do more to help my parents. They wrote often, begging for me to find a way to help them emigrate," said Lotte. "Since the war ended, I have not looked at the letters; I cannot bear to. Did I ask enough people for assistance? Did I try hard enough to procure affidavits? I second-guess myself all the time...and now it is too late, of course. They are gone, and I am alive.... 'Survivor's guilt,' they call it."

"I have it, too," said Klara. "I know it's silly, but I never really imagined that there were others out there who think and feel the way I do. For the past eight years, I have felt so alone. I do not fit in. My mother-in-law's friends are polite, but I catch them looking at me, you know? Questioning, judging. I am just so different. Foreign. And German, no less—the enemy. If they knew I was a Jew.... Are there more of us, more survivors, living in Atlanta? You are the first I have met."

"Yes, we are a small but tightly knit group. Those of us who are from Germany, we have our own club," said Lotte. "Actually, it was started before the end of the war by the few of us who managed to get out before '42, but it has grown in the years since."

"A club?"

"Yes, we call it the New World Club, because all of us here in Atlanta are trying very hard to make a new world for ourselves. We meet once a month at the Jewish Educational Alliance on Washington Street. You could join us, you know."

"Oh, I couldn't. What if someone saw me? What if someone told Thomas or, worse yet, my mother-in-law?"

"Klara, who would see you? Your husband and mother-in-law do not travel in the same social circles as our members. Besides, even if you were truly Christian, you would be welcomed. You are still a survivor from Germany, no? If they ask, tell them it is a club to meet up with other postwar immigrants, and a chance to talk with others who experienced first-hand what you endured. It would be good for you. You could be honest there."

"Lotte, you have no idea how good that sounds."

Klara looked at her watch and realized that too many questions would be asked if she did not get home soon. "I really must be going, but I will think about it; I promise. Lotte, thank you for listening. I have not had a real friend in many years."

Once back at the Compton house, Klara listened with rapt attention as Tommy reported on his day at the Piedmont Driving Club. Sitting next to his beaming grandmother, Tommy recounted every point in his tennis match, and described how much fun it had been to share another day with Granny. Klara had to admit, Eugenia doted on Tommy, and for that she would be forever grateful. Klara missed her grandparents and was thankful that they had all died of natural causes before they were murdered.

"You're very quiet tonight," Thomas commented at dinner that evening.

"Am I? Sorry. I was thinking about some of the children I met today at the hospital. Some of them are so alone. Not a soul comes to visit them. I think I may devote a few more hours during the week to going over there."

"Klara, I don't see why you don't volunteer your time at Piedmont Hospital. I see patients there every day, and it's a much more pleasant environment," said Thomas. "Besides, we could fit in a lunch every now or then."

"Ah, Dr. Compton, I detect an ulterior motive...." said Klara with a smile. "And that is sweet of you, but...I think not. The patients at Piedmont do not need my help as much as the children at Grady. I love what I do there, and I enjoy the company of some of the other volunteers."

"Thomas, leave her alone," piped in Eugenia. "She's right. The patients at Piedmont have all the visitors and volunteers they need. Help is needed more at Grady."

"Genie, thank you for your support," said Klara, feigning shock.

"Don't look so stunned! When you're right, you're right. I agree with you."

"Well, I never thought I'd see this day!" said Thomas, smiling. "The two of you agreeing on something! We should mark this day on the calendar."

Thomas and Tommy excused themselves to go outside to toss a ball around while there was still daylight. "Eugenia, thank you for your support. I appreciate it, even though I am not as naïve as you apparently believe me to be."

"Why, my dear! Whatever do you mean?"

"Please do not insult me. I may be many things, but stupid is not one of them. I know you and your friends volunteer their services at Piedmont, and that you are on the board of trustees," said Klara. "Do not worry. I have no plans to change hospitals and offer my services at your prestigious institution. There will be no opportunity for a chance encounter that may embarrass you."

"Klara, I do underestimate you at times, don't I?"

"Yes, Eugenia, you do."

With Tommy safely tucked in bed and Thomas back at the hospital checking on one of his patients, Klara slipped outside to enjoy the solitude of the back porch. Ever since she had revealed the truth about herself to Lotte, Klara felt free of a great weight. *How absolutely wonderful it was to speak with someone with shared experiences!* As Klara rocked herself into a comfortable rhythm on the porch swing, she decided that the subterfuge she was about to enter into was harmless. Thomas and Eugenia had no real interest in how she spent her days, as long as it didn't affect the Comptons' social standing or good name. Joining Lotte at the New World Club would finally give Klara the chance to live honestly, at least for a few hours a month.

Over the next several years, Klara became a regular at New World Club meetings. Lotte had become very dear to her, and the meetings provided a respite from the other Klara, the *poseur* Klara who lived in the Compton family home. The heaviness in her chest had finally lifted as the horrors of her past began to fade. Her fellow survivors were a link to her parents. The members discussed recipes Klara fondly remembered from her childhood, and many members still spoke in German, evoking pleasant memories of life before the war.

Lotte was the secretary of the club and editor of their monthly newsletter. Klara wished she could bring Tommy to some of the activities they were planning. The club was a place where you could plan for the future and discuss happier times from your past. Only rarely did anyone speak of the war, and when they did it was only in the broadest terms. Members discussed the successes and failings of the Marshall Plan and the spread of communism across Europe. Some club members spoke of family still overseas—some were trapped in communist regimes in Hungary or Lithuania, unable to emigrate; others were still mired in the arduous process of trying to get reparations for homes, businesses, and possessions stolen by the Nazis.

Over the years, Klara grew increasingly disturbed that the daily indignities suffered by Atlanta's Negro citizens were never mentioned, let alone discussed at any of the meetings. When she suggested to the membership that perhaps they should, as a group, vocally oppose segregation, she was answered with a resounding "No" from all but a few. She hoped she would find an advocate in Lotte, but was shocked by her friend's stance.

"Klara," said Lotte. "Unlike our other members, you are in a unique position. Living as a Christian with a prominent Atlanta family, you are insulated from the inevitable backlash that would result if 'Jewish immigrants' were involved in calling for an end to the status quo."

"Lotte, I am sorry, but I cannot accept that as an answer. These survivors...their families were murdered because no one rallied to defend them! Entire communities stood by and watched as gas chambers and crematoria operated in proximity to their homes. In the dark of night, lifelong friends and neighbors disappeared, and no one questioned where they went!" said Klara. "Every time I see a Negro man, woman, or child drinking from a fountain marked Colored, it angers me to my core. I want to rip down the signs myself."

"Klara, enough! Stop! You have no right to judge. You of all people should know what we have been through, and what some are still enduring. Our members come here to forget—to forge friendships and to have a little fun. They are not ready, willing, or able to fight the system. They are too frightened and too fragile," said Lotte. "You consider them cowards, but think about it. They are still identifying themselves as Jews. They are still living in a city with restricted neighborhoods, clubs, and schools. I am surprised at you for judging them—you, who could not even be a legal member of your husband's club!"

Klara stared at her friend, speechless.

"You think we should speak out about the race laws. Look over in the corner, by the coffee pot. Do you see Mrs. Weiss? Perhaps you should ask her to join your protest. Ask her how it worked out for her father when he refused to step off the sidewalk to make room for one of Hitler's Brownshirts. Ask her to relive how he was shot right before her eyes, and then rolled into the street like a piece of garbage. In this place, at these meetings, you have the freedom to once again be Jewish. For them, they have to fight *every day* because they are Jewish."

Klara had never seen Lotte so angry, and she was shocked by the disappointment she could see in her friend's face.

"Klara, to tell you the truth, I am not sure I understand why, after all these years, you haven't told Thomas that you are Jewish. He loves you. Would it even matter to him at this point? You could come out of hiding, be yourself, bring Tommy to temple."

"Lotte, I cannot believe you are saying this. You know I cannot tell Thomas that I am Jewish. I have explained all this to you already. You said you understood," said Klara, her eyes wet with tears.

"Klara, please, don't cry. You know I love you. You are my dearest friend and nothing you say or do will change that, but friends need to be honest with one another, no?" said Lotte. "When we first met, you were a frightened, traumatized young woman, barely more than a child. And I truly understood. But, now.... What is stopping you now?"

Mutely, Klara stared at Lotte, ashamed to tell her the truth, afraid she might lose her only friend. In that moment, Klara realized how ridiculous and insensitive she must have sounded. What right did she have to ask her fellow survivors to compromise their security when she was not willing to compromise her own? Over the last several years, Klara's life in Atlanta had continued to grow into a pleasant routine. She and Thomas had developed a strong bond, one that many married couples would envy. Each evening, following the family dinner and bedtime ritual with Tommy, they shared a little wine and discussed the day's events. When it was warm, they often sat together on the back porch swing, a place Klara had grown to love. In the rainy cool months of winter, they snuggled together in Thomas's library, the coziest room in the house. For the first time in years she was happy and relatively content. The thought of opening old wounds and causing disruption in her life was terrifying and would accomplish nothing. Returning to her roots would not bring her parents back.

Staring into Lotte's expectant face, Klara finally answered. "You are right. I could tell him now. Thomas would understand and, in time, forgive me. But never again will I wear that star on my chest. Being Jewish brought nothing but tragedy and horror to me, my parents, Ernst. I cannot go back, Lotte, I cannot. Nor can I do that to my son."

Before parting, Lotte and Klara embraced and promised to call one another, but Klara understood that her days at the New World Club were over. Lotte would have welcomed her as always, but Klara no longer wanted to visit with her fellow survivors. For Klara to live with her shame, she needed to close that door forever.

Thomas could not have been happier or more content. His life with Klara was everything he had hoped for. His love for her had never waned, and had only grown more intense over the years. He rarely thought of the intercepted note that was still safely hidden in his old journal, the one he'd kept during the war. The guilt of his deceit, which had once weighed so heavily upon him, had long since abated. Klara was happy and their son was thriving. Thomas had wished for more children, but for whatever reason, that was not to be. Thomas was therefore that much more grateful for Tommy, a son who was doted upon by the entire family. He supposed he should get rid of the note, but for some reason he had held onto it. It was like a talisman; he worried that if he disposed of it, the world he had made for Klara and Tommy would fall apart.

Thomas did sometimes wonder what had happened to Sam. He imagined him working as a mechanic or in some other menial job. Over time, he convinced himself that he had saved Klara from a life of drudgery and sorrow.

Sam did not need to wonder what had happened to the good doctor and Klara. Much to his father's dismay, Sam had decided to forego a partnership in the family firm. Soon after finishing law school and passing the bar, Sam had accepted a position as an attorney with the Department of Justice in Washington, D.C. After the war, real estate law did not seem that exciting. Now, in 1958, thirteen years since he had first laid eyes on Klara, he still thought about her every day.

Sam worked as an attorney with the Civil Rights Division of Justice, and his work was taking him more and more often south of the Mason-Dixon line. His feelings for Klara had not diminished over the ensuing years, and to the dismay of his parents, he remained unmarried. Even Nick had finally tied the knot with someone from the old neighborhood back in Cleveland. It wasn't as if Sam wanted to be alone. He was tired of waking up each morning to an empty bed.

Sam had been engaged once. He had gone through all the motions, met the parents, bought the ring, and arranged the date, but as the wedding drew closer and closer, he had backed out, leaving a nice girl to wonder what happened and what she had done wrong. How could he begin to explain that his backing out had nothing to do with her? She was pretty, smart, and would have made a great wife and mother, but she was not Klara. No one he met ever measured up, and now, over a decade later, he was still pining away for someone he knew he could never have.

NINETEEN

Early Sunday morning on October 12, 1958, Klara was awakened by the sound of sirens as police cars and fire trucks sped down Peachtree Street. Within minutes, quiet returned and Klara pulled the blankets over her head, hoping to sleep for a few more hours before starting her day. When she heard the soft knock on the door, she thought it was Tommy. He loved hanging out at the club on Sundays, and was always in a hurry to get there. Klara was just about to tell him that it was way too early when a clearly agitated Beulah came rushing unannounced into her room.

"Miz Klara, I jus' heard on the radio that the Jewish church over on Peachtree's been bombed. You know, the place you ast Lloyd to park by but didn' want no one in this house knowin' about? And before yous start yellin' at poor old Lloyd, he only tole me. He don' discuss nothin' with this family."

As Beulah waited for a response, Klara was trying to digest the news that a building she had come to love had been bombed. "But why?" was all she could think of to ask.

"They ain't said why. I jus' now heard it on the radio, like I already done tole you."

"Does Dr. Compton know?"

"I guess he does," said Beulah. "He the one had the radio on, an' I jus' happened to be in the kitchen makin' him some eggs when it come on."

Without changing or grabbing her robe, Klara ran out of the bedroom and raced down the stairs. Thomas was so engrossed in the news that he didn't notice Klara until she spoke. "Thomas," she cried. "Is it happening again? Like in Germany? First the Nazis destroyed the synagogues and then..."

Before Klara could finish her statement, Thomas turned off the radio and walked over to embrace his trembling wife. Klara held on to Thomas for several minutes as she tried to repress memories from the war from flooding back.

"Klara, look at me," Thomas finally said. "I was going to come up in a few minutes. I'm sorry I waited, but I wanted to get all the facts before I came to see you. Yes, The Temple over on Peachtree was bombed, but it's nothing like Germany, I promise. You don't need to worry. Do you hear me? Klara, the bombers—they're segregationists, rabble-rousers. They wanted to send a message to the rabbi over there. He's made more than a few speeches directed at White Citizens' Councils and other groups of that ilk. I'm not saying he brought it on himself, but in these turbulent times, well, it's best to keep those kinds of opinions to yourself."

Klara was no longer trembling from fear but from rage, and for the first time in thirteen years, she felt betrayed by her husband. "Thomas, don't you see? This is how it happened before, with people like you turning a blind eye. I am ashamed of you. After all you witnessed during the war! How can you ignore what is happening here? The rabbi is courageous and should be congratulated for standing up to these cowards who bomb without conscience under cover of night. There is an entire race of people living as second-class citizens in your precious Atlanta, and I for one will no longer stand idly by and let it continue unchallenged."

"Klara, please, calm down. You don't understand the way things are down here." Klara was already on her way back upstairs when she heard Thomas call out, "It's not the same. It's not the same at all! Klara, please, listen to me...Klara!"

Back in the bedroom Klara shared with her husband, she wondered if she really knew the man she had married. This was a side of him she had never understood and did not particularly like. Deciding to worry about Thomas later, she quickly threw on some clothes and quietly dialed Lotte's phone number. Even without the shared interest of the club, Klara and Lotte had managed to maintain their friendship by avoiding any discussion of their one and only disagreement. When Lotte answered the phone, she must have known that Klara had been as deeply affected by the morning's bombing of The Temple as she.

"Lotte, can we meet? I desperately need to see you."

"And I you, too," said Lotte. "Meet me at the Crossroads. It opens for lunch at 11:30."

"I'll be there," said Klara. She quietly slipped down the back stairs of the house to ask Lloyd for a ride.

As a result of an investigation by state and federal authorities, five members of the National States Rights Party were indicted for the bombing on October 17, only five days after the crime. Sam was already in Birmingham to investigate the attempted bombing of Temple Beth-El in April and Bethel Baptist church in June. The department asked Sam to drive to Atlanta to help with the investigation and indictments. The authorities in Birmingham were fairly certain that the NSRP was responsible for multiple crimes as well. The Birmingham temple had been luckier than the one in Atlanta; heavy rains had doused the burning fuses on the fifty-six sticks of dynamite. At the Baptist church, church guards had discovered a paint can with a burning fuse connected to a dozen sticks of dynamite and carried it a short distance away from the church, although the blast in the ditch still blew out the windows of the church and nearby homes.

During the two-hour travel time from Birmingham to Atlanta, all Sam thought about was Klara. He didn't want to disrupt her life, but damn it, he was still angry. He wanted answers. Why hadn't she waited for him? He didn't think he would ever find happiness if he didn't address the questions from his past. The closer he got to Atlanta, the more anxious he became. It was such a visceral feeling, knowing she was in reach. He was simultaneously terrified and excited. Sam was so consumed with all the conflicting emotions that before he knew it he had arrived at the police station for his meeting with Atlanta's chief of police, Herbert Jenkins.

The meeting with Lotte on the Sunday of the bombing had galvanized Klara into action. With Lotte at her side, she joined the Southern Regional Council, and Klara began to openly advocate for changes in segregation policies. If she didn't have the courage to be true to herself, at least she could speak out for others.

"How could you? How could you join the Southern Regional Council!" screamed Eugenia. "All of my friends are talking about you! Klara, do you understand that group's agenda? They want to destroy our way of life."

"Klara," said Thomas. "You joined that organization? Are you aware that they are in favor of integrating the schools—and everything else, for that matter?"

"Yes, Thomas, I know exactly what they are in favor of, and that is *why* I joined. I stand behind them 100 percent."

"Klara, I understand how you feel personally, but Atlanta's just not ready for that much change. There's talk of closing the schools...and where will that leave all the Negro students? The whites will go off to private schools, and then where will the Negroes be?"

"Oh, shut up, the both of you," interjected Eugenia. "If we integrate the schools, it will lead to white girls dating Negro boys, and eventually to Negro doctors being able to examine white women. Is that really what you want?"

"Yes, Eugenia, that is exactly what I want," said Klara. "I don't see how you can look at yourself in the mirror! The Civil War is long since over and these people, people like Beulah and Lloyd who have worked for your family for decades, deserve to sit next to you at a diner or in a movie theater."

"Mom, why are you yelling at Gran? Stop it!" shouted Tommy, as he raced to Eugenia's side. Thomas's pleading eyes looked at both Klara and his mother, silently begging them to stop the argument that had clearly been loud enough to bring Tommy down from upstairs. He had often said that in the matter of race relations there were no easy answers. He acknowledged that his wife and his mother were clearly on opposing ends of the segregation debate, but his own position was less clear. He usually staked out his ground somewhere in the middle, and claimed he was still looking for a reasonable way out of the remnants of the peculiar institution of slavery that was the South's tragic legacy.

"Tommy, I am sorry," said Klara. "Gran and I were just having a discussion that got a little too loud. Were we not, Eugenia?"

"Yes, that's right," said Eugenia, still glaring at her daughter-in-law. Flaunting their closeness, Eugenia pulled Tommy toward her. "Come on, Tommy, let's go into the kitchen. I had Beulah make your favorite cookies. If my nose is not deceiving me, I do believe the first batch has just come out of the oven." Without even a nod in the direction of her son and daughter-in-law, she and Tommy left the room.

"He's very protective of her, you know," said Thomas, as Klara's eyes followed the two of them as they walked past.

"Yes, I am well aware of the influence your mother has over our son. It is something that has concerned me for quite some time. I should have been more involved with his activities of late, but your mother was so anxious to take him to the club for all of his lessons—and, well, you know how uncomfortable I feel over there."

"Klara, let's leave our conversation about Tommy's relationship with my mother for another day. Come on, let's go out to our porch swing and discuss your involvement with that rabble-rousing Rabbi Rothschild over at The Temple and that subversive Southern Regional Council," he said with a wink. "Maybe, if you use all of your powers of persuasion, you'll win me over. *I* should have been paying more attention to what *you've* been up to, and more importantly, to what you have been trying to tell me."

Klara's conversation with Thomas went well. He was not exactly ready to join her at meetings, but he seemed to understand and support her passion for the issues involved in the battle for racial equality. He did express concern, however, that the city he loved would become violently embroiled in racial strife. He said that unless level heads prevailed, the situation would not be resolved peacefully, and he worried about Klara's safety.

Klara confessed to Thomas that since joining the council, she had felt energized. For the first time in years, she believed she was actively doing something that would make her parents proud. She forced herself not to think about how disheartened they would have been by her decision to deny her heritage and to let Tommy be raised as a Christian. She almost felt sorry for Eugenia. If her mother-in-law knew the truth about Tommy, would she still love him? The lies had been a part of Klara's life for so long, she sometimes almost believed that Thomas was the father of her son. But then, Tommy would move a certain way or offer her one of his lopsided grins, and the reality of what she had done would all come surging back at her in a torrent of shame.

Since her confrontation with Lotte at the New World Club, Klara was having a harder time looking at herself in the mirror. Worst of all, of late, she felt as if she was no longer the main influence in her son's life. While she had been busy at club meetings and now with her work with the Southern Regional Council, Eugenia had easily slipped into the role of Tommy's primary caretaker and adult companion. Klara guiltily had to admit that at first it was a relief to not have to socialize with some of Tommy's friends' mothers, or to pretend she was comfortable over at the Driving Club. No matter how stylishly she dressed or how much she tried to fit in, the moment they heard her German accent, she felt diminished in their eyes. Eugenia, however, was an accepted fixture there, and Tommy seemed relieved when it was his grandmother accompanying him to the club and not his mother.

Klara knew that she was partly to blame. The only person outside of her two Toms that she could really be herself with was Lotte. It was just so hard to seem interested in conversations about gardening and bridge games when the white power structure of Atlanta was threatening to close the schools rather than integrate, or when hate groups were planting bombs at houses of worship. Determined to wrest control of her son back from Eugenia's fearsome grip, Klara realized that his tennis lesson was starting soon, and it was time to let Eugenia know Klara would be taking him.

Two days after the scene with Eugenia, Klara convinced Thomas to accompany her to the next meeting of the Southern Leadership

Council. They would be discussing the integration of Atlanta's schools, and Klara hoped to introduce Thomas to some of the council's more persuasive members. To Thomas's surprise, the meeting was being held at First Presbyterian, his own church.

"Klara, I had no idea there would be so many members of our church in attendance," he said. "Mother would be shocked…and not the least bit happy."

"You see, Thomas? The council is more mainstream than you thought. I hope that the level-headed leaders in our community will win the day. Now hurry, the meeting is about to start."

Kent Burrows, a prominent Atlanta architect and SLC president, was just coming to the podium as Klara and Thomas moved to seats near the front. Leaning over to her husband, Klara whispered, "The meetings generally begin with an update from the president, followed by reports from committee chairmen and then discussion."

"Shush," the woman seated behind them admonished. Klara whispered a polite apology and waited for the program to start.

"My fellow SLC members, here in Atlanta we are being faced with a real crisis—a crisis that threatens our entire pubic school system. This is a real contest between the voices of reason and the segregationists in our community who are threatening to close our schools if the law of the land is followed. There are those in our community who would rather bar the doors to all public institutions than sit next to a person of color. I say No to the segregationists and Yes to integration."

Murmurs of support rippled though the audience.

"Tonight we are very fortunate. We have a guest speaker who has worked as an attorney with the Justice Department for the last twelve years. He is a recognized authority on the new federal law demanding the immediate integration of our nation's schools. A native of Cleveland, Ohio, our speaker attended law school at Western Reserve University. He moved to our nation's capital soon after passing the bar exams in Ohio and in D.C. For the past six months, he has traveled extensively throughout Alabama, Mississippi, and Georgia, and he graciously offered to come before us tonight to report some of his findings. So, without further ado, please welcome tonight's guest speaker, Mr. Sam Rosstein."

The loud applause reverberated in Klara's ears as she and Thomas sat in stunned silence. Immediately, Thomas searched for Klara's hands, hoping to hide the fact that his own were shaking. Klara did not think Sam had seen her—at least not yet, but she knew that if she stood up now and headed for the exit, that would cause everyone else in her row to have to stand as well, and the noise alone would make Sam look directly toward her. She kept her eyes downcast, too shaken to plan her next move. By the look of Thomas and his grip on her hands, he was as distressed as she.

Thomas's reaction was something she would have to think about later; for now it was the least of her worries. Even after all these years, the sound of Sam's voice was enough to take her back to that one night in a small little cottage in the woods. She wondered again if he ever thought about her and, without thinking, dropped Thomas's hand to pin back the loose strands of hair that had fallen from her bun.

"Klara," Thomas whispered. "We should go."

"We cannot get up now! It would cause a scene."

"I don't want you to upset yourself," Thomas said. "There's no need to resurrect the past. Come on, I mean it. Let's get out of here."

"Shush," the lady seated behind Thomas whispered again. Klara motioned to Thomas to stay seated and to keep quiet.

By this time, Klara and Thomas attracted the notice not only of those seated near them, but of the guest speaker. Sam faltered slightly, but knew his speech well enough that he was able to carry on with only a short pause before regaining his outward composure. He looked surprised when he reached the end, as if the applause had awakened him from talking in his sleep.

By the end of the speech, Klara knew Sam had seen her. No one else seemed to detect the pause in his cadence, but she did. He was as shocked to see her in the audience as she was to find him at the podium. The applause after the speech gave Klara and Thomas a chance to leave before the questions started, and Thomas nearly pulled Klara out of the pew in his race to the door. By the time they reached the exit, the questions and discussion had started. Without thinking, Klara shook Thomas's arm from around her waist and for just one moment, turned to look at the man she had not seen in over a dozen years, hoping he was also searching for her. Sorrow enveloped her as she realized he had immersed himself in the discussion, seemingly unmoved by the chance encounter.

The car ride home was shrouded in silence. Neither Thomas nor Klara was anxious to start a conversation destined to dig up long-buried layers of lies and manipulations as well as unfulfilled dreams. Ten minutes after they had pulled out of the church parking lot, Klara's heart was still pounding. Sam had looked the same, yet different, too—a few more lines on his face, perhaps a little heavier than when they had first met—but the sight of him still had a visceral effect on her. Once Sam had started speaking, Klara had become entranced by the sound of his voice. She had felt glued to the pew and might still be there if Thomas had not pulled her to her feet.

Over the years Klara had fantasized about running into Sam, hoping it would happen but knowing it never should. *What could I possibly say to him? Oh, by the way you have a son! He's thirteen years old, and I never tried to find you to let you know.* She had long since forgiven him for leaving the camp without a word. His abandonment did not compare to her deception. At the time, she had not seen any other way out. She had to get out of Germany, and Thomas was her only immediate option. Thomas...what about Thomas? Over the years, Klara had grown to love him. Not in the way she had loved Sam, but they had a good marriage, a comfortable life, and a son Thomas believed was his. Her husband of thirteen years had done nothing wrong. He was the only selfless and innocent one in the threesome.

"Klara," Thomas finally said. "We're home." Klara had not noticed that they had pulled into the driveway until Thomas's voice broke through her reverie.

Thomas knew that Klara was expecting him to say something, anything, about seeing Sam at the meeting, or about their mad escape to the car. What could he possibly say? *I didn't want you to have a conversation with the man you thought you were going to marry, because you might have found out that thirteen years ago, I intercepted a letter he left for you, and then I convinced you to marry me instead. I wonder what you would think of me then, my darling?*

Instead, Thomas went over to the liquor cabinet poured himself and Klara each a stiff drink. He led her outside to the back porch swing. "Well, that was a bit of a shock," Thomas began. "I never expected to see our old friend Sam delivering a speech at a Southern Leadership Council meeting. An attorney for the Justice Department—who would've thought?"

"Oh, I always knew he would become a lawyer. His father had a firm in Cleveland, and he talked about joining his practice."

"Oh, I didn't realize," said Thomas. "I remember thinking he would end up in some blue-collar job, and wouldn't amount to much. I guess I was wrong. Him and that friend of his."

"Nick," Klara said reflexively. "I always assumed he would stay in Cleveland, so I was as shocked as you to see him there. And I was surprised you wanted to leave so quickly. I know why I did not want to face him; in a way, he left me standing at the altar. But you, Thomas, why didn't you want to see him? After all, you took home the bride."

"I guess...I suppose I was afraid you would be hurt again. I didn't know what you were thinking, so I acted on impulse and got us the hell out of there."

"Well, at least I know for sure he is still alive," said Klara. "When he did not return in the weeks before we left the hospital, I thought he might have been killed—although somehow I believed he was still alive somewhere."

"Do you want to see him?" asked Thomas.

"I am not sure. I imagine if he had wanted to find me, he would have found a way. He is obviously very much alive and I would guess that with his government connections, it would probably not have been too difficult to track me down."

"Do you still have feelings for him?"

"Oh, Thomas, do not be silly. I have not laid eyes on the man in over thirteen years. How could I possibly still have feelings for him? It was just such an unbelievable shock to see him again...just...so unbelievable. Come, Thomas, let's finish our drinks and go to bed."

"You go ahead. I'll be up in a minute."

Thomas lingered by the staircase as Klara disappeared down the corridor to their room. Since the day he had seen her, he couldn't keep his eyes off her. Whenever she asked why he was staring at her, he would always answer, truthfully, "I just love looking at you." After pouring himself a second drink, Thomas retreated to the library, his eyes drawn to the bookshelves. There nestled among his collection of military histories were his journals from his time in the army. Thomas knew exactly which volume he wanted, and once it was in his hands, he sat down to look at the evidence of his deception. There it was, tucked between the pages, the note that could destroy everything. *The evidence of my crime.* He knew he should have burnt it long ago, but somehow could never bring himself to do it. Over the years, he had quietly laid the last months of the war to rest. He and Klara had a good life. Tommy was happy and for the most part even Eugenia had accepted Klara. The reappearance of Sam didn't change anything. Klara loved him, and Sam was but a distant memory. Thomas trusted and believed her. Slipping the note back between the pages of the journal, Thomas reshelved the book and slowly walked upstairs.

It had been several hours since Thomas had come to bed, and Klara had still not fallen asleep. The chance encounter at the council meeting had paralyzed her with indecision. She wanted to believe that what she had told Thomas was true—that she rarely thought of Sam, and that she had no desire to speak with him—but in her heart she knew differently. She was desperate to speak with Sam. She needed to know what had happened to him after he disappeared. *I have a right to know. His actions changed the course of my life, and of our child, forever.* Klara resolved to try and see him the next day. She only hoped he was still in town.

Klara awoke early the next morning to find that Thomas had already set off for his rounds at the hospital. As usual, Tommy slept through his alarm, and Klara had to poke and prod him to get out of bed. The school bus never waited more than a minute, and Klara was determined that Tommy would be on it. She needed this one day to herself, and she did not want Lloyd to be tied up taking Tommy to school. Once he was off, Klara returned to her bedroom to try and find out the name of Sam's hotel. It would have been late when the meeting ended, so she assumed he stayed over.

Kent Burrows was a good friend. Klara had worked with him for over a year, and she did not need to offer much in the way of an explanation when she called to ask where the speaker was staying. When Klara told him she had known him during the war and wanted to reconnect, he was truly sorry to tell her that Sam had changed his plans at the last minute and headed back to Birmingham immediately after the meeting.

Sam had no idea how he got through the discussion that followed his presentation at the SLC meeting. Never in a million years had he expected to run into Klara there. Nothing could have prepared him for the intense feelings that arose when he saw her in the audience. He had only faltered once, and hoped no one noticed. He couldn't believe it, but she was even more beautiful now than he remembered. When he had last seen her, her blond hair was so short you could see her scalp. Now it looked luxurious, held back in a bun, with a few loose ringlets curling around her face.

When he first recognized her, he was so stunned that he did not immediately notice Dr. Compton in the pew next to her. But there he was, in the flesh: the man who had somehow managed to do what Sam couldn't, marry Klara. Sam's initial impulse had been to call out to her, to stop his presentation and rush over to wrap his arms around her. Thankfully, he was able to collect himself enough to finish. He was hoping to approach her after the applause had died down, but when he looked toward where she had been sitting, he saw that she was already hurrying toward the door. And then she was gone, home to her big house with the good doctor. *Well, so be it. If she doesn't want to see me, I'm not going to press it.* With that decided, Sam went out to his car and began the drive back to Birmingham.

TWENTY

Klara often thought of that SLC meeting when luck, fate—she wasn't sure what to call it—had brought her and Sam into the same room together after so many years. Fate, however, had little to do with the choice they both made to avoid one another that evening. Now, here it was 1964, six years later, and Sam still had not reached out to her in all that time. She had thought of calling him, but every time she looked at Tommy, who now preferred being called Tom or Thomas, she knew it was too late to open that particular door.

Klara's life had changed quite a bit over those six years. She had taken lessons and passed her driving exam, as a gift to herself on her last birthday. Thomas surprised her with a car of her very own, a cherry red Pontiac Tempest convertible. Thomas had overheard Klara telling Lloyd that she always wanted a convertible, ever since driving in an open-top jeep in Europe during the war, and Klara had to admit that she loved her car. No longer dependent on Lloyd or Thomas to drive her, Klara felt a new sense of freedom.

As the years passed quickly, Klara thought less and less of her early life. It was the 1960s, and America had a new young president with a beautiful wife at his side. The war known as World War II was long over and everyone seemed to believe it should be forgotten. Unfortunately, Klara's daytime resolve had no control over her nighttime demons. Periodically, current events like President Kennedy's trip to Berlin would intrude upon her determination to leave the past in the past.

After watching Kennedy deliver his *"Ich bin ein Berliner* speech" in 1962, she had seethed for days. The president might feel like a Berliner, but she knew she would never return to the godforsaken country that had killed her family. She was astonished to see that with the exception of Israel, many nations seemed conveniently to have forgotten how many people the Nazis had murdered. The arrest, trial, and conviction of Adolph Eichmann, Hitler's "Jewish Specialist" and one of the main architects of the "final solution" to rid the world of its Jewish population, once again brought the Nazis' crimes to the front pages of the press. Klara followed the proceedings closely and hoped the news would generate an international effort to locate and prosecute more of them. *Maybe now, some of these monsters will pay,* she thought, but as soon as Eichmann was executed, Nazi crimes were once again conveniently forgotten. So many murderers never brought to justice.

Klara took some solace in the Cold War that divided Germany between east and west. The Soviets hated the Germans as much as she, and Klara hoped her ex-countrymen were suffering at the hands of the Russians. Many Nazis were still young men, getting married, having children, and enjoying their lives. How old would her brother Ernst be now? She had to think for a moment, and then realized he would be thirty-five years old. He had been such a kind little boy, sensitive and oh so bright. He had wanted to grow up to become a doctor, just like Papa. But he had been robbed of everything—a wife, children, a life. Klara could not bear to think about how he had spent his last days. And where was the Standartenführer? Was he back in Germany, going to work every day, or was he holed up in Argentina as the murderer Eichmann had been? In the light of day Klara rarely thought of the monster she had traded herself to, but he still came to her at night. As the years passed, the dreams were less frequent, but when they did invade her subconscious, she would wake up screaming and in a cold sweat. Thomas was always comforting, but since she had never divulged the truth about the horrors she experienced during the war, he could not really understand how time simply did not heal all wounds.

She and Lotte remained close, and Thomas had even gone to dinner with them once or twice. He liked the woman and found her interesting, but much preferred being with his golfing and tennis buddies at the club. Thomas's practice was booming, and lately he had been talking about the two of them doing a little traveling now that Tommy was in college. Klara didn't like to travel. Being in Atlanta felt secure. This was her home, now, and she didn't need to see or go anyplace else. But Thomas really wanted to travel with her, so she agreed to look at some of the brochures he was constantly bringing home.

Eugenia, now in her seventies, had mellowed only slightly. She spent most of her days ordering Beulah and Lloyd around, working in the garden, or playing bridge with her cronies. Klara liked to imagine the look on her face if she ever found out that her daughter-in-law and grandson were Jewish. Once, when Eugenia made a reference about someone who "looked so Jewish," Klara had been tempted to confess, but self-preservation had won out and she had swallowed the urge. What bothered Klara the most was that for whatever reason, Eugenia seemed to have a closer relationship with Tommy than she did. Tommy would rather be with his grandmother than just about anyone else.

A first-year student at the University of Georgia, Tommy had joined one of the oldest fraternities on campus and clearly espoused some of his grandmother's views about integration. Three years earlier, when Tommy was still in high school, he had ranted on about how his Dad's alma mater was going to be destroyed because the university had accepted Charlayne Hunter and Hamilton Holmes, two Negroes, as students. Now that he was on campus, he remained ardently opposed to integration. Klara was beside herself. How could a son of hers oppose everything she believed in and had fought for? For years, she had tried to thwart Eugenia's influence over him, but from the time Tommy was little he seemed happiest when the two of them spent time at the club together.

Even though Thomas and Tommy got along, they seemed to have nothing in common other than tennis. Thomas loved history and the arts; Tommy could not stand to go to a museum unless it had something to do with science or math. Whenever Klara voiced her concerns about Tommy's segregationist views, all Thomas ever said was "don't worry, it's just a stage; he'll grow out of it." But Klara did worry. She wasn't sure he would grow out of it. She hated to say it, but if Tommy had been in Germany in the 1930s, he probably would have joined the Hitler Youth.

If Klara still believed in God, she might think it was her just reward for denying Tommy his heritage. She knew in her heart that it really was her fault. If she had been honest with Thomas, with everyone, from the start, Tommy would have been raised differently. Instead of living in a world filled only with country club activities and coming-out parties, he could have also gone to religious school where he might have made some Jewish friends. She was a coward who had made the deliberate decision to hide in plain sight. Thanks to his limited exposure to the world beyond Eugenia's bubble, Tommy had seen Klara as different his entire life. *She* was the one who didn't fit in, the one from the enemy country, the one with an accent, and the one unable to socialize with his friends' mothers.

But Eugenia? Well, *she* fit in just fine. Eugenia was like the other mothers; she was one of them, and Tommy felt most comfortable when his grandmother accompanied him.

And now what was Klara to do? If she revealed her secrets to him now, what would he think of her? Would he understand why she lied? She didn't think so, and in doing so, she would destroy the man she had married. Perhaps she should just try to describe the Germany of her youth—what the country had been like when Hitler came to power. She always shielded him from the truth whenever he asked any questions. She wanted to protect him from the terror she experienced as a child, but perhaps that had been a mistake. Looking at her watch, she saw that it was not even noon yet; if she hurried, she could be in Athens in about two hours. *I'll surprise him, take him out for dinner or something,* she thought, as she grabbed her handbag and made her way to the garage.

Tommy was living with his fellow Sigma Deltas. Klara had no problem locating the house on Fraternity Row, where all the plantation-type houses were located. It was only a little after two, and Klara decided to wait in the lobby until Tommy returned from his classes. Three hours later, when he was still not back, she began to worry. She knew that was ridiculous. Since he had been away, she had no idea where he was at any time of the day. Still, Klara knew his classes were over at three, and she continued to hope that he would be back soon. She had been mulling over what she wanted to say for the last several hours, and the longer she waited, the more nervous she became.

Just when she was about to get up to ask one of his fraternity brothers if he knew where Tommy might be, she spotted him and three other boys coming through the door. He hadn't yet noticed her, and Klara immediately saw that her son and his companions were staggering, obviously drunk. As the boys stumbled across the threshold, they were engaged in a loud conversation that drew the attention of everyone in the lobby.

"That'll teach 'em!"

"Y'all got that right!" yelled Tommy. "Goddamn niggers think they own the place!"

"What did you just say?" yelled a startled Klara.

"Hey, get a load of the babe! Vats vit the accent?" mocked one of the boys.

With tears streaming down her face, Klara walked over to her son, slapped him across the face, and walked out to her car.

Klara should have let Thomas know where she was going. It was getting late and he would probably be worried. After she ran to her car, she sat for a few minutes thinking Tommy might follow her out, but no one emerged from the stately house.

Klara had never laid a hand on Tommy before. Unlike other parents, she had never spanked her child. She had seen way too much brutality in her life, and believed she could discipline in other ways. But the truth of the matter was, she was not even sorry for slapping him now. He had deserved it. *Who is he?* She didn't even know how to answer that. She accepted that it was probably her fault. She had put Tommy into a world in which she herself was not comfortable. She was the one who had denied him the chance to know his real father, and to live in a community where he would not have been embarrassed by his mother's accent or the fact that she just didn't act like the other moms.

When Klara pulled into the driveway at home, she found every light on in the Compton house. A clearly agitated Thomas was pacing on the front porch with a drink in his hand. As soon as Thomas saw the lights of Klara's car, he raced over and yanked the door open before she had a chance to turn off the ignition.

"Klara, you had me so worried! I had no idea where you were until Tommy called."

"Tommy called?" asked Klara.

"Yes, of course he called. He said you had driven to Athens, and the two of you had an argument. He was worried."

"Oh, Thomas, I am so ashamed of myself. But I am even more ashamed of Tommy. We didn't really have an argument. I overheard something he said, and I slapped him across the face. Then I left."

"You did what? You slapped our son? What for?"

As they started for the house, Klara tried to explain what happened. "I was waiting for him for more than two hours in the lounge of the fraternity house. I suppose I was already a little nervous about speaking to him. I had driven up there to try and tell him about some of my experiences during the war. You know I have never really talked to him about it, even when he was young and asked, because I was always trying to protect him. But now that he is older, almost an adult, I felt that maybe if I told him about his grandparents and uncle, how they died for something they believed in, then maybe he would understand how unacceptable his views are to me. But he walked in—well, really, he staggered in—with two of his friends. They were all obviously drunk and were bragging about their ill treatment of the Negro students on campus. Thomas, he called them 'niggers'—and when I heard that word, I lost control!"

Klara finished her explanation on the walk up to the house and was approaching the front door when an irate Eugenia swung it open. "I just got off the telephone with my grandson. How dare you! He told me you slapped him across the face without any explanation, and if that wasn't enough, you did it in front of his friends," hissed Eugenia. "What kind of mother are you? Tommy's a good boy. I can't even look at you, Klara. Thomas, pour me one of whatever you're drinking," she ordered.

Before Thomas could respond, Klara moved directly in front of Eugenia. "I have had enough!" Klara yelled. "He's the way he is because of you and your lily-white friends who think you are better than everyone else. Times are changing, Eugenia. If you have not noticed, the Civil War is over, and so is slavery. I am *so* sorry your precious Magnolia Room at Rich's department store is no longer off limits to Negro diners; it must be terribly difficult for you and your friends to have your coconut cake with persons of color sitting next to you."

"How dare you speak to me that way! I have been nothing but kind to you since you invaded my home all those years ago. You don't fit in. After all these years you still just don't, and it's not only that embarrassing accent of yours that marks you as one of *them*!"

Klara sucked in her breath, but she knew Eugenia meant the Germans, not the Jews. Like many of her generation, Eugenia still despised anything German or Japanese.

Thomas, who had still not found his voice, just stared—first at his mother, and then at his wife—not believing that the peaceful cohabitation they had shared for the last nineteen years was now shattered. "Stop it, both of you!" he finally yelled. "Mother, you're drunk. Go up to your room and sleep it off. Klara, let's go upstairs. We need to talk."

Klara had never seen Thomas so angry. In all the years they were together, he rarely lost his temper. So, like an obedient wife, thinking she may have gone too far, she followed him upstairs.

"Klara, what in the hell is going on? When I went to work this morning, I never expected to come home to a missing wife, a worried and angry son, and a raging mother. I just don't get it. Whatever possessed you to drive up to Athens without telling me first? He's my son, too."

"Thomas, you are right. I should have told you, but honestly, I did not decide to visit Tommy until today. I didn't want to bother you. I know how much you hate taking calls while you are seeing patients. Besides, I thought I would make it home at a reasonable hour." As tears started to stream down Klara's face, she sat down on the bed, the exhaustion from the day's events finally too much for her. "I needed to talk to him. I wanted him to understand."

"Klara, my darling, I'm not angry. I was just so worried. What did you want to tell him?"

"I needed him to understand what the war was really like, what we endured, what his grandparents and uncle went through." Klara was

137

so tired that she was afraid if she continued to speak, she would say something she would later regret. The truth of her background, her real story, was suddenly very close to the surface, ready to reveal itself if she let her guard down for even a second. She couldn't think straight. Thankfully, Thomas, always her protector, told her to go to bed and rest. They would finish their conversation tomorrow. "Thomas, wait. Did I hear you correctly? When Tommy called, he said he was worried about me?"

"Klara, I promise, he was very concerned," said Thomas. "In fact, I need to call him, as I promised I would as soon as you got home, but then...well, things got a little out of hand."

"Yes, Thomas, go call him." Klara was still fully clothed when she crawled into bed, thinking she would rest for a few moments before changing into her nightgown. The nightmare began not too long after she drifted off. Thomas was still downstairs and must not have heard her cries. Usually he was there to hold and comfort her, but not tonight. Tonight, she was left to face her demons alone.

In the past, once Klara awoke from her nightmares she was able to calm herself and eventually fall back asleep. This time the feeling of panic kept her up most of the night and had still not abated by morning. For the first time in years, she felt a strong need to talk to Sam. Other than Lotte, he was the only one with whom she had ever been totally honest. It had been at least six years since Klara saw him at the SLC meeting, and she wondered if he was still with the Justice Department. The thought of reaching out to him calmed her immediately, and in that instant Klara finally accepted that she had never stopped loving him. With renewed determination, Klara was finally ready to place the call she knew might destroy the life she had built with Thomas, and further damage her fragile relationship with her son.

The operator at the Justice Department confirmed that Sam was still on staff, but added that he was on assignment and would not be back in D.C. for several days. Now that she had made her decision, the thought of any further delay in reaching him was almost too much to bear. As the panic from the previous night began to resurface, Klara started to write what was in her heart.

Dear Sam:

I am sure this letter will take you by surprise. After so many years of avoidance, of running away from my past and not being honest, I now know that even if you end up hating me more than you already do, I need to finally tell you the truth.

Sam, the morning you left I was devastated. I truly believed every word you had spoken to me in our little cottage in the woods. I was ready to commit the remainder of my life to you, to follow you wherever your path led. When you did not show up the next day, I ran through the camp like a woman possessed, asking everyone if they knew where you were. When I was told your unit had moved out and discovered you left without leaving word, I was wounded to the core. I was frightened and scared and knew I could not stay in Europe.

When Thomas said he would marry me so I could emigrate, I agreed. You probably think me a coward, but I was so young! Losing you was more than I could bear alone. I was terrified to stay in Germany and live the life of a displaced person with no family and no country to call my own. Thomas offered me a way out. The marriage was supposed to be in name only, one I could dissolve after a year. But once I arrived in Atlanta, I realized I was pregnant with your child. I had nowhere else to go and I decided to pretend the baby I was carrying belonged to Thomas.

Sam, I cannot describe how frightened I was. I knew that what I was doing was wrong. I was deceiving a good man into believing I was carrying his child, but at the time I did not think I had any other choice. I gave birth to a beautiful baby boy on November 9, 1946. I was almost two weeks overdue, so Thomas never suspected a thing.

Tommy, our son, has so many of your mannerisms, and now that he is just a little younger than you were when we first met, I sometimes forget for a second and think I am looking at you. I have never told Thomas the truth about my background—that I am the daughter of two Jewish Berliners who were murdered by the Nazis. I was too afraid to tell anyone I was Jewish. I am sure Thomas would not have married me back then if he knew, although he may have mellowed some over the years.

Over the years I could have told him the truth many times and did not, and for that I am most guilt ridden. The only person I have told is my dear friend Lotte, a fellow survivor. I am ashamed to say that I could not bring myself to jeopardize my own security and possibly that of my son, and that perhaps is my deepest regret. I have lied so often, at times, I confuse my real background with the one I have fabricated. Over the years I have come to love Thomas because he is a good man and has cared for me with all of his heart.

When I say love, however, I do not want you to confuse that with what I felt for you—and, now that I am finally being honest, I still feel. I love you, Sam. I always have and always will.

Life with Thomas has given me many opportunities. I live in a beautiful house, albeit with a mother-in-law who has never considered me worthy of her son, and have been given all of the tangible possessions many people use as a yardstick to measure a good and successful life. But living in Atlanta, seeing the discrimination that is carried out against an entire segment of our population, has been very difficult for me. Witnessing the daily indignities forced upon the black race is sometimes like living my own horrible history all over again. That is why you saw me at the SLC meeting. I have become involved in the movement for civil rights. I refuse to be a bystander in the struggle. Thomas accepts my involvement and supports it with donations here and there, while my mother-in-law is embarrassed and abhorred by my commitment.

You are probably wondering, why now? Why I am writing to you now, confessing all of my sins after all these years? I have so many regrets, and denying Tommy the joy of knowing you is the main one. In my defense, and I accept that I do not have much of one, I did not know what else to do. You were gone, and for years I did not even know if you had survived those last few weeks of the war. I probably could have searched for you since I remembered that you were from Cleveland, but a part of me was afraid of the answer. What if you had been killed in the war? What if you were alive and you just did not want me?

But I have still not told you why I am reaching out now. I am not really sure myself, except to tell you I had a horrible fight with Tommy yesterday. My son, or should I say our son, sees himself as a true Southerner, the descendant of Confederate heroes of the Civil War. He does not believe in equality between the races and loudly voices his segregationist point of view to anyone who will listen. I am so ashamed. I really do not know why I am revealing all of this to you. Perhaps in some way it will help to absolve me of some of my sins. I denied him his heritage and led him to believe he is Thomas's son, the descendant of generations of Georgia's "best."

Sam, please believe me. I have never stopped thinking about you. I always hoped there was a good reason why you did not leave word, but if am being foolish, if you never had any intention of coming back, then please be kind and simply do not respond.

Love,
Klara

Once the confession was addressed and sealed, Klara ran to the mailbox at the corner of her street and dropped in the letter before she could change her mind.

TWENTY ONE

Klara had no idea what to expect from Sam, but when two weeks went by without a word, she realized that her plea for absolution would not be coming. Now she had to come to terms with the fact that Sam had deliberately left her without a word, and that his pledge of commitment had been just another GI's line to lure one more naïve and innocent young woman into bed.

For days now she had moped around the house. She had still not settled anything with Tommy. She was actually afraid to confront him, fearing she would not like the outcome. And now, with this seeming dismissal by Sam...she felt so foolish. How could she have been so stupid as to contact him after all these years? Most likely, he hardly remembered her. Thomas kept asking her what was wrong, no longer believing her when she said she felt like she was coming down with a cold. Nevertheless, Klara knew it was time to come clean, to reveal her secrets regardless of the consequences. She could no long suppress the guilt.

When Lotte called and asked if she could possibly attend a New World Club meeting at the Jewish Community Center, Klara was shocked by the invitation. She had not been to a meeting in years and had no desire to explain her prolonged absence to the membership. Persistent as ever, Lotte begged Klara to come, promising her that many of the old members had dropped out, and then enticing her with the guest speaker who was coming to address the group about Nazi war criminals who were living openly in communities throughout Europe, the United States, and South America.

Klara was intrigued and she knew she needed to get out of the house, if only to get away from Eugenia's glares and Thomas's worried looks. "I'll pick you up at six," said Lotte.

"Okay, you talked me into it," said Klara. "I'll be ready."

Despite her initial reservations, once she was in Lotte's car, Klara immediately started to relax. As large as the Compton home was, the space was suffocating her. Eugenia was always hovering about, and seemed to sense which room Klara would be in and purposely make an appearance. Ever since the fight with Tommy, Eugenia had reverted to treating Klara like an intruder, and Klara was just too tired to fight back. Thomas, on the other hand, was smothering her with affection, constantly asking her what was wrong. She almost didn't know which Compton she wanted to avoid more. With Lotte, Klara could be herself.

"So who is this speaker?" Klara asked. "I did not think anyone was interested in Nazis anymore. When Eichmann was captured and tried, I was optimistic that others would also be arrested."

"Unfortunately," Lotte added, "with the exception of the Israeli government, no one seems to care. We must always remember, very few countries or individuals helped us then—and today is no different. Two days ago, I was at the post office. The man directly in front of me had a thick German accent. When he spoke to the clerk with arrogance and authority, I was amazed by my reaction—so many complex emotions: shock, anger, and yes, even hatred. I do not know why, but I sensed that he was not a survivor, and I had to stop myself from making a scene. I wanted to shout, 'Where were you during the war? How many Jews did you murder?' It's crazy, no? He could have been perfectly innocent of war crimes, just another eighteen-year-old foot soldier sent to the Russian front. Ah, but there must be so many actual Nazi murderers, now in their forties or fifties, living calm and peaceful lives among us. They will most likely never pay for their crimes."

They had pulled into the driveway at the Jewish Community Center on Peachtree Street. The building had opened in 1956, and now most of the Jewish clubs and organizations were using it for their events. At the entrance, Klara and Lotte stopped to admire the beautiful mosaic work created by famous Israeli artist Perli Pelzig that enhanced the building's exterior. Immediately after they entered the building, Lotte was pulled away by one of the other members who couldn't locate the plug for the coffee pot, leaving Klara to find a seat on her own. She saved one next to her for her friend.

She was staring up at the podium expectantly when she heard Lotte call her name. "Klara?" The meeting was about to start, but Lotte was motioning to her from the adjacent hallway. "Klara, there's someone I want to introduce you to." Embarrassed to leave her seat and possibly interrupt the speaker, who must have been about to step onto the small stage, Klara mouthed her excuses as she stepped over countless numbers of toes to get out of her row.

Exasperated by Lotte's bad timing, Klara was just about to tell her friend she would be happy to be introduced after the meeting when she realized whom it was standing with Lotte. It was Sam, only a few feet away.

"Klara, I am sorry the subterfuge. I didn't know what else to do. I had to see you, and your friend Lotte—well, she wasn't too hard to track down."

"Track down? Lotte, I do not understand. What, how did you get here? I think I may have to sit down." Lotte led Sam and Klara to an empty office and told them she would be back in about thirty minutes. Klara gratefully lowered herself into a seat.

"Klara, honestly," said Sam. "When I read your letter...well, I think I've been waiting for that letter for almost twenty years. Don't get me wrong. When I read it the first time, I was so angry, I couldn't even see straight. The realization that I have a son, and you never bothered to tell me, even after you saw me in Atlanta—when was that, about six years ago? That's what angered me the most. What is he now, nineteen years old? I missed out on his whole childhood. So after I read it the first time, I actually tore the letter to shreds. But then I spent the next twenty minutes taping it back together. And I read it a second time. And a third. And then, finally, I read it more carefully and I began to remember every detail of all you had confided in me...what you went through...how frightened you must have been to find yourself so alone. So I stopped being angry and I started to think about us, and what we promised each other. Remember, Klara, what we promised each other? That we would marry and have a life together. I've never forgotten what we said to each other that night in our cottage."

Klara sat very still, just watching him speak, listening to his voice, drinking in his words. She was afraid to say a word and possibly wake up from the dream.

"After I was shot, I asked Nick—you remember Nick, don't you, Klara?—I asked him to get word to you, but you were already gone, married to the doctor and off to America. At first, Nick couldn't bring himself to tell me. I wasn't exactly in the right state of mind to get that kind of news. I had just lost my leg; I was in no shape to learn I had lost you, too. For the first year or two, I thought about you constantly. I couldn't let it go. I hated you for not waiting, for not believing I would return to you. That morning, the one you described in your letter, when you came looking for me? My unit had been rousted from our bunks in the middle of the night, and ordered to move out. But Klara, I swear, as God is my witness, I left a letter for you with one of the nurses. She *promised* to get it to you. In that letter I asked you to wait for me, for however long it took. I promised I would come back. But then I took that damn bullet and after that it was all hospitals and rehab for me."

Sam barely looked at Klara as the words he had wanted to say for so long kept flowing out. Until now, he hadn't noticed the tears streaming down Klara's face, and the sight of her anguish immediately drew him to her. For Sam, holding her propelled him back in time and sent feelings through his body he had thought were no longer possible. Klara easily succumbed to his touch. Time meant nothing as she buried herself into his arms and he in turn enveloped her in his.

More than thirty minutes had passed since Lotte left her closest friend with a man she hardly knew. Although she had liked him from the start, remembering him from his speaking engagement years before, she worried about Klara. She quietly opened the door and peeked in. Klara and Sam were embracing each other so tightly that Lotte was sure the squeaking door hinge disturbed neither. Leaving them once again, she returned to the meeting, gratified in the small role she had played in Sam's and Klara's reunion.

Thomas Compton had always been pleasant the few times her friendship with Klara had brought them together, but there was something about him Lotte simply could not warm up to. The moment Lotte met Sam, she understood what Klara had seen in him. She never questioned his sincerity or his love for Klara, and that is why she agreed to act as a de facto matchmaker. She hoped she was helping Klara, not further complicating her life. Ever since she had confronted Klara and questioned her motives for denying her faith, Lotte had avoided bringing up the subject. It was the one aspect of Klara's character that Lotte found troubling, and she hoped that one day they could clear the air without too much pain for either one of them.

Klara was not certain how long she and Sam held their embrace, but the naturalness of it felt so incredibly right, and at the same time unsettling. For one brief moment, she thought of Thomas, and guilt suddenly overcame her. Sensing her change in mood, Sam begrudgingly opened his arms and released Klara from his grasp.

"So, Klara," Sam finally began. "What now? Where do we go from here? I still love you. I never stopped. You know, in the beginning, especially while I was still in the hospital, I thought about you every day. At night you were in my dreams so often I looked forward to sleep, but dreaded the mornings with the realization that my nighttime visits with you were nothing more than a fantasy. Over the years, the dreams began to fade, but now, seeing you again, I just don't know if I can go back to my job, my apartment, my life if you're not in it."

"Sam, what a mess I have made of everyone's lives. If only I had not been so frightened! I should have trusted you. I was just so scared of being left alone, and when Thomas offered to marry me and take me to America, I saw it as my only chance for survival."

"Yes," Sam said. "I understand that. I'm sure Compton was standing right there to pick up the pieces. Did he even once try to stop you, to tell you to wait for me? No, he understood your vulnerability—he knew how much the war had damaged you, and he knew that if I was out of the picture..."

"Sam, no, Thomas only wanted to help. And unlike you, he has never known my whole story. It was my fault. I take responsibility for leaving. It was my weakness," said Klara. "Like you, Thomas is a victim in all this—our own rendition of a Greek tragedy. I lied to him all these many years. I moved into his home and schemed and plotted so he would come to believe that my baby—our son!—was his. This disaster, our heartbreak, is my fault alone. Do you know that he still does not know I am Jewish? I never told him. And why? I was too comfortable, too settled, too scared. I am to blame, not Thomas, and certainly not you."

"Klara, my beautiful, darling Klara. You are more a victim in your so-called Greek tragedy than anyone else. Don't ever forget that I know better than anyone what you endured during the war. You are the one who lost everyone and everything, including trust, during those catastrophic years. I'm not going to waste any more of our time together trying to convince you of this, but you were manipulated. Compton was desperate to have you. I know the feeling, because I was, too. The difference is, he loved his image of you, and I loved the real you, the Klara I came to know at your bedside," said Sam. "Klara, I know in my heart that Thomas did something to change the odds in his favor. I'm not sure what, but trust me, I am going to find out. After all, I am an investigator," he said with a wink. "Klara, I promise you; now that we've started to straighten this mess out, I'm never going to let you go again."

"But Sam, I'm married to Thomas. I have been for the last nineteen years. Nothing you say can change that. I cannot deliberately hurt him. And what about Tommy? What am I supposed to do about Tommy?" The mere mention of her son caused tears to once again well up in Klara's eyes. "He already hates me and this—I think this will kill him. He loves Thomas, and he and Thomas's mother are extremely close. So close, in fact, I truly believe he feels more of a connection with her than with me. That is ironic, is it not? Our Jewish son, the grandson of people who perished in the Holocaust, identifies more with white supremacists than with me. And the worst part is, I placed him in that household, one that allowed him to believe that he is the progeny of Confederate officers. Sam, are you okay? You look..."

"Klara, I'm sorry I just can't..." And suddenly Sam started laughing so hard he was doubled over, and Klara, caught up in the ridiculousness of their situation and infected by Sam's laughter, joined in, feeling better than she had in years.

"Sam, stop my stomach hurts. This is not funny."

Gasping for breath, Sam tried to stop laughing, but every time Klara spoke, he laughed even harder. "Klara, I'm sorry, but our son is a segregationist—possibly even an anti-Semite. You, a victim orphaned by the Holocaust, have married into one of the most influential, hoity-toity, patronizing Presbyterian families in Atlanta—people who wouldn't share a table with you if they knew your real roots. And for the life of me, I don't know how we are going to figure this whole thing out."

Klara tried hard to control herself, but every time she looked at Sam, the two of them burst into laughter again. "This is absurd," she finally managed to say. Slowly the two of them were able to regain control. "Sam, our situation is ridiculous, but it is not funny. This time together—it changes nothing. I am as married now as I was yesterday."

"Marriages end all the time. He's had you all these years. I think that now it's my turn."

"Sam, that is childish. There are no 'turns' in these things," Klara said, trying to stay serious. "I cannot just walk out of here today, and go home and tell Thomas, 'By the way, after all these years, Sam has returned and I have decided to be with him instead of with you.' What kind of person would that make me? What would Tommy think?"

"Klara, trust me. I understand how complicated this is, but we are going to figure it out," said Sam softly. "And we will find a way to do it with the least amount of damage to those involved, including Tommy."

"Sam, do you really think so? Is there a way?"

"Klara, do you still love me?"

"You know I do. I am the one who got in contact with you, remember?"

"Then come here," Sam pleaded. With his arms once again enveloping her, he promised they would find a way.

Moments later, Lotte quietly opened the door and peeked inside. "I hate to pull the two of you apart, but the meeting is over and the center will be closing up in just a few minutes. Do you realize you have been in here for over an hour?"

"We're coming," Sam said. "Klara and I have started to sort some things out, but we need a little more time. Klara, can we meet again tomorrow? I'm staying at the Peachtree Manor Hotel. Do you know it?"

"Yes," Lotte and Klara answered in unison.

"It was the first hotel in Atlanta to integrate," said Klara. "Perhaps someday Tommy will appreciate the fact that it was a Jewish owner who had the courage to make it so."

Sam gave Klara's hand a quick squeeze and said quietly, "He will, Klara, you'll see. Someday he will."

"I knew I liked this man," Lotte said with a wink at her friend.

"So, Klara, tomorrow?" Sam asked again.

"Yes, but I will have to call you in the morning. I believe Eugenia, Thomas's mother, is planning to attend her garden club meeting in the morning. I can try and meet you then. Eugenia takes real pleasure prying into my comings and goings these days."

"I'll get the car," Lotte said, giving Sam and Klara a chance to be alone for a few more minutes.

"I'm nervous, Sam. You might find it ironic, since my entire existence here in Atlanta is based on one lie after another, but I hate deceiving Thomas. All these years, he has done his best to make me happy."

"Klara, I promise it will be okay. I'm going to figure it out. Now go home and try and get some sleep and call me in the morning." Giving Klara one final embrace, Sam helped her into Lotte's car and watched as the two of them drove away. Sam had taken a taxi to the Center. He wished he could walk back, but his prosthetic had been bothering him all day, and he knew the two-mile walk would be more than he could handle, so he called for another taxi and rode the short distance back to the hotel.

Not wanting to be alone, and acknowledging that he was too wound up to fall asleep, Sam found a secluded corner in the hotel's bar and ordered a much-needed Jack on the rocks. Seeing Klara again had unnerved him. It had been nineteen long years since they held each other, and while everything had changed, his love for her remained the same. Today, over and over again, he had promised her he would figure a way out of the mess they were in, convinced that his legal-eagle mind would help him find the right solution. Now, into his second drink, he still had no idea where to start.

Whenever he was this stuck with a complicated case at work, he often relied on his investigative skills to flesh out the facts and the truth. Maybe that was the answer now. Sam didn't trust Thomas Compton any more today then he had when he had first met him. He understood why Klara was grateful to him, and why she was unable to look past her husband's carefully constructed veneer. Sam wasn't sure how Thomas had done it, but he had somehow orchestrated Klara's future, including her decision to leave the camp and not wait for Sam. He needed to locate the nurse to whom he had given the long missing note. Perhaps she would remember something.

Thomas sat in his study, nursing a drink and engrossed in a magazine when Klara arrived back home. "How was your evening?" asked Thomas, barely looking up from what he was reading. Klara was relieved that Thomas was too interested in his article to notice the blush she could feel rising on her face when she answered that she could not remember enjoying a gathering at the club more.

"I'm glad, Klara, but I thought you had given up going to those get-togethers." Thomas said when he finally looked up.

"You are right. I have not been in quite some time, but now I am sorry I stayed away for so long," said Klara. "I have a connection with many of those people. By now, I would think you would understand that."

"Aren't most of them Jewish? You know, refugees?"

"Thomas, what do you think I am? I am no different from those Jews, those refugees who you speak of with such disparagement. I was only a little luckier. I met you and you brought me to America. What if I was Jewish? Would you have still married me?"

"Klara, don't be ridiculous."

"Thomas, I have never asked you this, but do Jews bother you? I mean, do they somehow repulse you? Because if you are repulsed, then perhaps I do not know you as well as I thought I did."

"Klara, how can you say that? You of all people know that's not true," said Thomas. "There are a number of Jewish doctors at the hospital, and I am very friendly with them."

"Oh, are you? Friendly. How benevolent."

"Klara, now you are putting words into my mouth. Don't be ridiculous, I have nothing against them as a people. Individually, well, some of them can really be irritating. There's this one doctor at the hospital, Phil...Kahn, or Cohen, no, it's Kahn...well, anyway, you know the type—from New York, moved down here right after the war, like so many of those people, and he's just so...in your face. He even asked if we would like to see a movie with him and his wife one weekend. Of course, I said no. I mean, what do we have to talk about? We have absolutely nothing in common."

"You are right, of course. Nothing in common...aside from being men. And doctors. And married. And living in Atlanta," said Klara. "Thomas, I am tired. I am going to go up to bed."

"I'll join you," said Thomas. "This article can wait until the morning."

"No, Thomas, I am fine. Finish your drink and read your magazine. I am exhausted and will no doubt be asleep in minutes."

"Okay, then, I'll be up within the hour. Love you, Klara."

Klara could not bring herself to respond and quietly left the room. Thomas was already back to his article, and Klara did not think he even noticed she had left. Once upstairs, she changed into her nightgown and went out through the French doors onto the small balcony where two wicker chairs sat side by side. Her encounter with Thomas had greatly diminished the earlier joy she felt during her time with Sam.

It was an odd sensation to realize that, while nineteen years had separated them, their feelings had remained the same. If anything, Klara thought, they were even more intense. Sam would be calling her in the morning, and Klara had no idea what to say to him. She knew what she *wanted* to tell him—that she would do anything to be with him, that she regretted all the lost years, and that they should not wait even one more day—but that was a far cry from what was right or honorable. Her entire marriage was based on deception. As long as she thought she was protecting Tommy, she was able to keep her regrets and guilt buried. But Tommy was almost an adult, and their relationship was so strained that Klara feared she would never be able to repair it.

The lies were destroying her, and Klara was sure of only one thing. She longed to tell Thomas the truth, but while the truth would finally free her, it could very possibly destroy the man who had saved her life. When Klara heard Thomas walking up the stairs, she was no closer to a solution. She longed for the arrival of morning when she could once again speak with Sam.

Eugenia and Klara had not spoken a word to each other since their horrible fight over Tommy and his beliefs. Thankfully for Genie, the house was big enough for her to avoid her daughter-in-law without too much trouble. She was sure Klara felt the same way, and had been doing her best to not run into her mother-in-law. They had not had dinner together in weeks, with Eugenia choosing to have her evening meal alone in her room. *Lord, how I hate her,* Genie mused. *This is my home, and she dares to make me to feel like the intruder.*

From the moment Klara had walked up to her front door all those years ago, Genie had sensed that there was something about the girl that did not ring true, and that feeling had only deepened over the ensuing years. There were too many inconsistencies in Klara's story, too many blanks. And her naïve son accepted it all. Thomas seemed happy, and of course Klara had given her Tommy, her only grandchild. For years, Genie had let it go, but now, fueled by the argument, she resolved to find out more about her daughter-in-law's complicated past.

The last thing Klara remembered was looking at the clock at four in the morning and thinking she would never fall asleep, but now it was already ten and she had just woken up. She was furious with herself because she had promised Sam she would call as soon as Thomas left for work, and that would have been two hours ago. Klara felt stupid, too, that she had forgotten to ask Sam for the number of the hotel, and now she had to go downstairs to grab a telephone book before making the call. Hopefully, Eugenia would still be hibernating in her bedroom or already on her way to her garden club meeting.

The directories were kept in a drawer by the kitchen phone and Klara had just copied the number when she realized, to her dismay, that she was not alone. "Good morning, Klara. I see you slept in this morning. As you can see, so did I," said an uncharacteristically chipper Eugenia. "What are you looking for? Perhaps I can be of assistance."

"No, I have what I need," said Klara. "I am meeting some friends for lunch and I needed the phone number to make reservations."

"Oh, how nice. Where are you going? Perhaps it's a place where I am a regular, and I can offer you some menu suggestions?"

"Thank you, Eugenia. As usual, you are too kind, but I am sure our tastes are dissimilar. I seem to have never become fond of barbecue and greens." Klara hurried back upstairs to make the call.

"Klara! I was beginning to get worried. I thought maybe you got cold feet and you were not going to call."

"Sam, I am so sorry. I tossed and turned most of the night, and did not fall asleep until early this morning. Before I knew it, it was ten...and then I had to go downstairs in search of the telephone number...and of course I ran into the wicked witch of the west, my mother-in-law... and..."

"Hey, slow down a notch. It's okay. You're on the line now, and that's all that matters. What time am I going to be able to see you?"

"Soon, I hope," said Klara. "I told Eugenia I was meeting some friends for lunch, so I only need to finish dressing."

"All right, Klara. Remember, Peachtree Manor Hotel, room 524. I'll see you soon," said Sam. "And Klara..."

"Yes?"

"Oh, never mind. I'll tell you when I see you."

"Okay, Sam. I will be there as soon as I can." Hearing Sam's voice again, Klara began to tremble, so excited she could hardly think straight. None of the dresses or skirts she pulled out of her closet seemed right. Klara wanted—no, she needed—to show Sam the woman she had become. She had been so young when they met, and all skin and bones. Now, just shy of forty, she still turned heads when she walked into a room. Before this morning, that had never mattered to her. She knew Thomas was simultaneously proud and a tad uncomfortable when someone, even a friend, flirted with her or told him what a lucky guy he was. Perhaps that, in addition to her accent and German heritage, her foreignness, was one of the reasons why many of the women at Thomas's club had never offered their friendship.

None of that mattered now. Sam was back and Klara could not wait to see him. Finally she chose an all-black shirtwaist dress with pearl buttons, a simple cut that showed off her figure. Klara slipped on her three-inch heels, grabbed her handbag, and quietly walked down the stairs and went out to her car.

How frightened she had been when she first thought about getting her driver's license! But now she loved driving, exploring the streets of Atlanta. As a passenger being chauffeured about by Lloyd, she had always felt embarrassed. At times, it had also made her a prisoner to Eugenia's schedule, whose need for the car always came first. Having her license and her own car gave Klara freedom to visit with friends, and to go places of which her family would not necessarily approve. As she backed out of the driveway, Klara was so anxious to start heading toward Sam that she did not notice Eugenia peering out at her from the living room blinds.

Eugenia could barely suppress her smirk as Klara left the kitchen. Although Klara had closed the directory before Genie had a chance to see what number Klara had been searching for, there was more than one way to see what her daughter-in-law was up to. Eugenia gave Klara a few moments to get back upstairs and place her call, then carefully picked up the receiver, hoping Klara would still be on the line. To her delight, the telephone was ringing, and to her shock as well as satisfaction, she listened as the hotel operator offered to connect Klara to Mr. Rosstein's room. Eugenia carefully placed the receiver back into the cradle, suddenly aware that she was in desperate need of a drink.

Eugenia gave Klara a few minutes to drive down the street before she summoned Lloyd to fetch the car. She was in no real hurry. She knew exactly where Klara was going.

Klara had driven only about five minutes when she noticed Eugenia's large black Lincoln Continental a few cars behind her. She thought at first it might be just an unfortunate coincidence, and kept hoping Lloyd would turn off on one of the many side streets, but after another mile or so, Klara conceded that her mother-in-law was truly following her. She could easily visualize Eugenia sitting comfortably in the back seat directing poor Lloyd to follow Klara's car.

This time, she has gone too far, Klara thought. *She must have listened in on my conversation with Sam.* Klara thought about stopping at the service station at the next corner to find a pay phone so she could tell Sam she would be delayed, but when she looked into her rearview mirror at the Lincoln, she could no longer contain the rage that had been building for years. In the next instant, without thinking, Klara picked up speed and made a sharp right onto the next street. Lloyd, whose reflexes were not what they used to be, missed the turn, and Klara gleefully sped off.

Within minutes, Lloyd was once more behind her. "Damn it!" She couldn't believe it. They must have known a cut off, and here they were again. Klara could picture Eugenia cackling in the back seat. Pressing the gas pedal, Klara sped up, determined to wipe the grin off that hateful woman's face. The Peachtree Manor Hotel was now clearly in sight, but Klara refused to give Eugenia the satisfaction of seeing her pull into the parking lot. When Lloyd slowed down his approach, Klara sped up once again, knowing that soon Sam would be getting worried about her whereabouts. Confused about what to do and desperate to lose Eugenia's car and to see Sam, Klara did not see the stop sign, or notice the large delivery truck heading toward the intersection.

"Mercy, mercy, Miz Compton! Look at what you made that poor girl do. Oh, mercy, mercy...look what you gone and done."

For several minutes, Eugenia could not find her voice. The truck driver had eased himself out of the cab and was walking unsteadily to the cherry red Pontiac Tempest. Its engine was smoking. Eugenia was tempted to stay and see if the girl was still alive, although she didn't think it possible from the look of the car. Her curiosity and dread gave way to self-preservation. She would find out about Klara's condition later.

"Lloyd, listen to me. Get a hold of yourself. Turn this car around. We're going home, and you will not breathe *one word* of this to anyone—especially my son. Do you hear me, Lloyd?"

"Yes, ma'am," Lloyd said, shaking his head.

"Good. Your job depends on it." As they drove home, Eugenia thought she was going to be sick. What had she done? She had lived in the same house with Klara for the last nineteen years, and even though she had never found the girl the least bit likeable, Klara was one of the few people who had the courage to stand up to her. The German girl had guts. Still, Eugenia never expected that Klara would have an affair, and right under Thomas's nose. After everything he had done for her! A torrent of emotions surged through her. If Klara was dead, Genie would have to live the rest of her life with the knowledge that *she* caused the accident. If Klara pulled through, would Klara tell Thomas everything? That, Genie realized, was the $64,000 question. Would Klara keep quiet?

Who in the hell was this Rosstein fellow she was going to meet, anyway? Genie supposed that she and Klara would have to come to some sort of agreement, a Mexican standoff, so to speak, in which she would keep quiet about Klara's assignation in return for Klara's silence about the accident.

"We's home, Miz Compton."

"Yes, Lloyd, I can see that," Genie snapped. "Now, remember what I told you. Today's outing never happened."

"Yes, ma'am. We never went nowhere today."

Thomas was just about to get into his car when he saw a woman racing toward him. "Dr. Compton, wait!" she yelled.

"Betty, slow down! You're going to have a heart attack. What's so all-fired important?"

She took his hand, something she had never done in her two-decade tenure as his nurse. "Your wife.... The police—they weren't sure at first...."

"Betty? Slow down. What are you trying to say?"

"Your wife, Mrs. Compton, has been in a terrible accident. She's most likely in the ER at Piedmont right now. Oh, Dr. Compton, I'm so sorry."

"Do you know anything else, anything at all?" Thomas heard himself ask in a voice so riddled with pain it was unfamiliar to even himself.

"No, nothing more. Give me your keys. I'll drive you," she said. "You're in no condition to get behind the wheel."

Thomas did as he was told, and later would recount that he had absolutely no memory of the drive to the hospital, or of Betty running after him as he jumped out of the car and raced through the doors into the ER.

"Where is she?" he demanded of the first person he encountered.

"Please, sir, calm down. Who are you looking for?"

"My wife, damn it, my wife! Klara Compton. She was brought here by ambulance," said Thomas. "I'm a doctor on staff here, and I demand to be told what's going on."

"Doctor, if I knew anything, I would surely tell you. Wait here a minute, and I'll find out what I can." The nurse disappeared through a set of swinging doors.

Betty took his arm. "Dr. Compton, do you want to sit down? Can I get you anything?"

"Please, Betty. I know you mean well, but for now, just leave me alone." The waiting was unbearable, but finally someone Thomas recognized came through the swinging doors and walked directly toward him.

"Thomas, relax. She's going to be okay. She has a broken leg, a couple of broken ribs, and numerous lacerations, but thankfully no head trauma. She's one lucky lady."

Thomas's knees nearly buckled with relief. The ever-solicitous Betty guided him into a chair. "Thank you, Phil, thank you," Thomas cried. "When can I see her?"

"She's in surgery. It was a pretty bad break, so we're looking at least at another hour or so. I'll keep checking, and I'll let you know when they take her into post-op."

"Phil, I don't know what to say."

"Thomas, she's your wife. You'd do the same for me."

"Yeah, Phil, I would. I really would."

Sam was happy he no longer smoked because he would have been on his second pack of the morning if he had still been hooked. *Where in the hell is she?* Sam didn't dare call her house, so his only option was to just keep pacing and worrying. *Damn it, Klara, where are you?*

After three hours had passed since Sam expected Klara at the hotel, he began to give up hope that she would show. When they had spoken that morning, she had seemed so eager to get there. *What the hell had happened?* Sam was looking out the window, deciding whether to pack up his suitcase and head for home or to drive over to the Compton house and demand to see her, when he was interrupted by the ringing telephone.

"Klara! I've been worried sick! Are you okay? Where are you? I expected you hours ago!"

"Sam, it's not Klara, it's Lotte. I'm afraid I have some upsetting news." Lotte told Sam as much as she knew about Klara's condition. Thomas had been considerate enough to have Betty call her, and from what she could make out from the one-sided conversation, Klara had driven through a stop sign and been struck by on an oncoming truck, just a block away from the hotel where Sam was staying. "Sam? Are you there, Sam?" said Lotte."

"Yes, I'm sorry. Oh, my god, which hospital? I have to be there for her...I have to see her."

"Sam, be sensible. You cannot go rushing over there," said Lotte. "First of all, she's probably still in surgery, and second, her entire family, including your son—and yes, I know about Tommy—is either already there or on the way. The last thing she needs when she wakes up is to see you standing there beside her husband and her child."

"Lotte, I can't just wait here and do nothing. It's my fault. She was on her way to see me."

"Nonsense," said Lotte. "It was an accident. Accidents happen every day. Stay where you are. I'll head over to Piedmont, and I promise I'll call you as soon as I know anything more," said Lotte. "Please, Sam, for the sake of Klara, just stay put."

"Okay—for now. I can't promise how I'll feel later, but you're right; I don't want to do anything that might make the situation worse for Klara."

"Good. As soon as we hang up, I will leave for the hospital. If I can find a private telephone, I will call you from there. If not, I will drive to the hotel and talk to you in person."

"Lotte, thank you. You're a good friend to our girl," said Sam. "I will never forget your kindness."

"I love her too, Sam. I'll call you or see you soon."

Sam didn't know if he could survive the waiting. It was almost too much to bear—reconnecting, having the chance of finally being together, only to have this happen. Rationally he knew that the accident was not his fault, but he still felt responsible. He had to see her. If Lotte gave him the go-ahead, he would try and sneak into the hospital after visiting hours. He was not going to lose her again.

TWENTY TWO

Eugenia had been waiting patiently back at the house when Thomas called to tell her the news. Grateful that Klara's injuries were not more serious, she was at the same time sickened by the pitiful demeanor of her son, who was actually crying with relief over the telephone. If she could have reached her hand through the receiver, she might have slapped him. Instead, Eugenia sympathized appropriately and told Thomas she would have Lloyd drive her directly to the hospital. "What about Tommy?" she asked.

"I already called him. One of his fraternity buddies is driving him here. I didn't want him getting behind the wheel. He was too shaken up."

"Okay, then," said Eugenia. "I'll see y'all at the hospital."

"Lloyd? Lloyd!" Eugenia called.

"Yes, ma'am?"

"Get the car. We're going to the hospital," she said. "It appears that your good friend Klara is going to be all right after all. And wipe that smile off your face. Remember what I told you; we never left the house this morning. Have I made myself clear?"

"Yes, ma'am."

"Good, now go and get the car."

For each of them, the waiting was excruciating. They were all there now, the most important players in the past nineteen years of Klara's life: Thomas, Eugenia, Tommy, and Lotte, sitting in a small room on the surgical floor, waiting to hear more about Klara's condition, like an ensemble cast without a common script.

Her mother-in-law was in a near panic that Klara would blurt out something about Eugenia's role in causing the accident—before Genie had time to warn her cheating daughter-in-law that she had equally damning information to share with Thomas.

As the minutes ticked by, Tommy privately weighed his relationships with his mother, and recognized that he was being given another chance to make things right with her. Tommy really didn't believe all the crap his grandmother and the rest of her blue-haired cronies espoused. He adored his grandmother, but hated the way she treated Beulah and Lloyd. He had known them his entire life and, if he really thought about it, his mother was the only one in the house who treated them with the respect they deserved. Tommy had just wanted to fit in, and his mother always made it so damn hard.

Thomas was not a religious man, but as he sat in the waiting room, he found himself thanking God over and over again for saving Klara. Was there now a debt to be paid? Had she been saved so he would have a chance to tell her the truth about his deception, the role he had played in sabotaging his rival's plans so many years ago?

Lotte had never met Eugenia or Tommy. From Klara's description, however, she would have known Eugenia anywhere. She could barely bring herself to look at the woman. Tommy was another matter. She couldn't stop staring at him. Except for his curly hair, he was a mirror image of his mother. Tommy and Klara shared many of the same physical traits, from the identical shape and color of their eyes down to the small little bump on the bridges of their respective noses. If Lotte had been a family therapist, she would have enjoyed studying the dynamic between the three Comptons. They were barely speaking to one another. Eugenia initially tried to comfort both her son and grandson, but both had politely brushed her ministrations aside. It seemed like hours, but it had been only five minutes since Lotte last checked her watch, and she was already extremely uncomfortable sitting with the family. Thomas was preoccupied with his own thoughts and had not introduced her to either Eugenia or Tommy. To help pass the time Lotte finally decided to do so herself. She asked if any of the three could use something to eat or drink. All politely refused, but at least the silence was broken.

"Lotte. Well, that's an unusual name," said Eugenia.

"Perhaps here," said Lotte, "but in Germany it is actually very common."

"I thought I recognized the accent. So, is that how you know our Klara?"

"Yes, actually, it is. Although I emigrated in the late 1930s, and Klara came here after the war, she and I met while volunteering at Grady hospital. Over the years, we have become quite close."

"How odd, then, that Klara has never had you over to our home," said Eugenia.

As Lotte was considering her response, she was interrupted by the reappearance of the doctor. "Thomas, you can finally relax. Klara came through the surgery with flying colors. She's in recovery, and will probably be transferred to her own room in about an hour. I don't have a problem with sneaking you back there now, but I'm afraid the rest of you will have to wait until she's moved."

"Phil, I don't know what to say. Thank you. Tommy, Mother...I'll be back as soon as I see for myself that she's okay," said Thomas. "Lotte, thank you for coming. I'll be sure to tell Klara you were here." Thomas followed quickly behind Dr. Kahn.

Lotte excused herself from Tommy and Eugenia as soon as she could and quickly located a pay telephone in the lobby of the hospital. A frantic Sam picked up the on the first ring and, before he even had time to ask, Lotte told him Klara was going to be okay and that the surgery went extremely well. Sam had not cried since the day he woke up from his own operation and discovered he was one more wartime amputee. Now the tears were flowing, and it took several minutes before he was able to catch his breath and thank Lotte for being such a good friend to Klara and now to him.

"When can I see her? Did you see Tommy? How long will Klara be in the hospital?"

Lotte couldn't help laughing at Sam's excitement. "Yes, I saw Tommy. First of all, he looks just like Klara; except for his curly hair, which I know came from you. He hardly spoke. He was visibly over-wrought about his mother, and so relieved when we were told she would be fine. I have no idea how long she will be in the hospital," said Lotte. "As for your other question, I know she would very much like to see you, but Sam, please do not go there. The last thing she needs in the days to come are more complications in her life."

"Lotte, you've been a good friend, and I appreciate all that you have done for me, for us, but I am not a complication," said Sam. "Please don't think of me that way. I love her, Lotte; I love her with my entire being. Thomas is the complication, not I."

"Sam, I understand that right now you are suffering, and that you need to see Klara, but for the next day or so she will probably be in no condition to speak with you or to explain to anyone who you are or why you are there. Please give me a little time to figure this out, and I promise I will get you into the hospital to see her."

"Okay. I'll have to accept that for now. In the meantime, I'll rear-range my work schedule so I can stay in Atlanta longer," said Sam. "If you see her, tell her.... No, never mind. You know what to tell her. You're a good friend. I won't ever forget this."

As Lotte hung up the telephone, she saw the elder Mrs. Compton walking briskly toward her. "May I ask to whom you were speaking?" asked Eugenia.

"I beg your pardon?"

"Oh, I suppose you think that was a rude question on my part—you know, a slap in the face of Southern gentility and all. But you see, Fräulein, I know more about your sweet little friend than you think. You just tell her to be careful, and to mind what she tells Thomas about where she was going when she ran that stop sign. I don't think he or Tommy will like the answer."

When Klara finally awoke in her room, both of her Toms were at her bedside. "Well, sleepyhead, you're finally awake," said Thomas as he gently rubbed her arm.

"Hey, fellas," Klara sighed. "Good to see you. Why are you both here? What's going on?" Suddenly, the horror of where she was and what had happened dawned on her. "Oh! I hit someone! Oh, Thomas, please tell me I didn't hurt anyone!"

"No, Klara, you didn't. You were the only one who was hurt. The driver of the truck was more concerned about you. His truck was barely damaged." Klara looked up at the two faces before her and saw it was not only Thomas who had tears of relief in his eyes but her son as well. "Klara, we were so worried, weren't we, Tommy?"

Tommy nodded in agreement, and then asked his father if he would mind giving them a few moments alone together. "Tommy, Mom's tired. Can't it wait until later?"

"No, Thomas, I'm fine. Let Tommy stay with me, please."

"Okay, I'll go get a cup of coffee, but Tommy..."

"I know, Dad, don't tire her out...don't upset her...." He flashed a grin at his father. Thomas winked back, and left the room. "Mom, first of all, I'm so glad you're okay. I know that you and I have a couple of things we need to talk about, and when I heard about the crash, I was in a panic, you know? I was worried that I might not get the chance to tell you some things I really need to say," said Tommy.

"You know I'm going to be fine, though, right?"

"Yes, but I still need to say these things. Mom, I know you're disappointed in me."

"Tommy, no! I'm—"

"Mom, please let me finish. I have to get this off my chest," he said. "I guess I mostly want to say I'm sorry. I just wanted to fit in, you know, with my friends and all? And I got caught up in some really ugly stuff. It's hard not to go along, and sometimes I just don't think I'm strong enough, you know, to stand up for what's right. These boys, they've been my friends since we were in the first grade, and if I say I don't want to go along with them when they taunt and torment the Negroes on campus...well, I may as well become a recluse. Because that's what I'll be, all alone. Stupid, huh?"

"No, it's not stupid. I know how hard it is to be the first to speak out."

"I thought you might. I should have come to you sooner, but you were so busy with all your meetings, and Gran, well, she was just there goading me on," said Tommy. "I don't know much about what happened to your family, but from what you've told me, your parents were so strong. They gave up their lives for what they believed in. I can't even stand up to my friends. I'm so sorry."

"Tommy, no, I should be the one to apologize," said Klara. "Trust me, I know first-hand how hard it can be to support an unpopular position or to deny who you really are out of fear of being alone."

"No, mom, you *always* stand up for what's right."

"No, Tommy. Not always," she whispered. Taking her son's hand, Klara could not bring herself yet to shatter the image Tommy had of her, and said only that when she got her strength back, there were a few things about her family she wanted to tell him. She apologized, saying that she knew she should have stepped in when she saw how much time he was spending with his intolerant grandmother.

"Mom, I love Gran, but let's face it, sometimes she goes a little too far."

"Well, that is an understatement, if I ever heard one."

Tommy tried to suppress his smile but, the more he looked at his mother, the wider his grin became until both of them started to giggle.

"Stop, it hurts my ribs when I laugh," she begged, folding her arms across her chest.

"Hey, what's going on in here?" asked a bemused Thomas as he reentered the room.

"Nothing, Dad. Me and Mom, well, we're sort of reconnecting."

For the rest of the night and throughout the next day, Thomas did not leave Klara's bedside. Being a doctor had its privileges, with one of them being not having to follow the rules for visiting hours. By late afternoon, Klara had finally convinced him to go home. She needed time to think, and she wanted to meet with Lotte—and to speak with Sam. Thomas's attentiveness was suffocating her.

The minute he walked out of the room, Klara dialed Lotte's number. She picked up on the first ring. "Klara, Thomas gave me strict instructions to not disturb you, but I swear if you didn't call me today I was going to break into your room and slug it out with your husband," said Lotte. "I've been so worried. Thomas said you were improving daily, but I needed to hear your voice to be sure."

"I am doing well, getting stronger by the hour, I promise. Lotte, tell me about Sam. Did he think I wasn't going to show up? Was he angry? I've thought of nothing else since my memory of that morning started coming back."

"He was understandably out of his mind with worry. At first he thought you had changed your mind and were not coming, but then, when I told him about the accident, he was like a man possessed. He wanted to race over to the hospital and see for himself that you were okay. Thankfully, I was able to reason with him, and remind him that your family was there as well."

"Oh, Lotte, as much as I want to see him, I cannot have Sam come to the hospital! Once again I have managed to make a mess of things. What was I thinking...that I could really just up and leave my husband with no repercussions? Honestly, I have betrayed Thomas each and every time we have made love over the last two decades. I *always* imagined it was Sam in bed with me. What does that say about me? I am such a fool. Thomas has not left my side even for a moment. I finally told him to go home and shower. The man saved my son and me from a life of struggle. Now what am I supposed to say to him? 'Thank you very much, but I never really loved you? And now that Sam has returned—yes, that Sam from the Evac Hospital—I have decided to leave you? And by the way, Tommy is really Sam's son.' And speaking of Tommy, what can I ever say to him? We finally spoke about our relationship, and for the first time in a long while I felt as if we connected."

"Klara, calm down. I'm coming over. I can hardly get a word in," said Lotte. "We'll talk this all through when I get there. I hope we'll have some time alone before Thomas returns. I'll be there soon."

Once Klara hung up the telephone, she slumped back down into her pillow and hoped that with the help of Lotte, she would be able to figure some way out of this mess. Lotte lived fairly close to the hospital, so she was not surprised when after fifteen minutes passed, she heard the doorknob turning. Expecting Lotte, she smiled broadly as the door opened. Her face fell.

"You expecting someone, I see," said Eugenia as she stepped into the room. "Clearly you are disappointed to see me walking through the door. I know I should have knocked and announced myself, but for once I set my good manners aside. I thought perhaps you would call for a nurse and not let me in. I have been wanting to have a few words with you in private, ever since we were given the good news that your injuries were not as severe as we were first led to believe. Fortunately, I ran into Thomas when he came home to shower. The man is so exhausted. I convinced him to take a short nap, and promised I would stay by your side until his return. Occasionally he still listens to his mother."

"Eugenia, thank you for your concern, but Lotte will be here shortly. So you can tell Thomas that I will be in her capable hands."

"Oh, I see, my darling daughter-in-law. I had hoped to exchange a few pleasantries before we got down to business, but I can see there isn't any time for pretenses," said Eugenia. "So I'll get right to the point. As you probably deduced, I *inadvertently* overheard your conversation with your lover the morning of the accident."

"Oh, really?" said Klara. "Inadvertently?"

"Well, yes, I was about to make a call myself and..."

"Stop, Eugenia. Do not bother to lie. Just get on with whatever you came here to say."

"Okay, my dear. When I realized you were going to meet a man, I asked Lloyd to follow you. And don't you be angry with Lloyd. He begged me to not make him my accomplice, but when I reminded him that jobs were hard to find, and about the number of mouths he had to feed, he readily got behind the wheel. Unfortunately for all of us, as they say on those police drama shows, you spotted your tail and sped up, causing a most unfortunate accident. Now, as much as I would love to tell my son about your indiscretions, I don't want to risk my already fragile relationship with him. If he thought I was even the slightest bit responsible for your injuries...well, I'm not sure if he would find it in his heart to forgive me. If my situation were not so sad, it would be funny. I have no doubt he would eventually forgive you playing him for a fool, but me? I think not. Therefore, I propose that neither of us say anything, and we just continue as before. Klara, did you hear anything I just said? Damn it, say something!"

Klara was trying to process everything Eugenia had revealed. In doing so, she was finally able to recall almost everything about her drive to the hotel, and the accident. "You were following me."

"Yes, of course I was. I just told you...Oh, I see. You didn't remember that, did you? Well I suppose my saying so out loud was a tad stupid on my part, then, but no matter. You would have recalled everything eventually. So what do you say, do we have a deal?"

"A deal about what?" asked Lotte, stepping into the room.

"This is between Klara and me. Family business," said Eugenia.

"Lotte, would you give us just a minute?" asked Klara.

"Are you sure?"

"Yes. Eugenia and I have an understanding. A mutual dislike of one another complicated by the fact that neither one of us wants to see either Thomas or Tommy hurt." Once Lotte walked out, Klara turned to her mother-in-law. "I have to say, Eugenia, you definitely know how to negotiate. For now, I will do as you want. I need to recuperate and get home. Then we will talk more."

"No, Klara, that's simply not going to work for me. I need to have your assurance that you won't breathe a word about my part in the accident to Thomas, or I swear he won't be the only one I tell about the affair."

"You would hurt Tommy to protect yourself?"

"Only if you push me too far. I love my grandson, but I will not lose my son."

"I see. Eugenia, you win. Now if you don't mind, I need to get some rest. You've exhausted me."

Offering Eugenia only the slightest of nods, Lotte brusquely walked by her and reentered Klara's room. "You look a lot worse than you did a few minutes ago. What did the witch say to you?"

"Lotte, for the life of me I cannot understand how such a horrible woman could have possibly given birth to a man as kind as Thomas."

"Maybe he was adopted and he just doesn't know," said Lotte with a grin.

"Usually I would find that amusing, but not today. I need you to do something for me. I need you to call Sam and tell him to go home and forget about me. I have brought nothing but heartache to him, and he is still young enough to fall in love with someone else and start a family of his own."

"Klara, what in the hell did that woman say to you?"

"Even though nothing happened that morning between us, Eugenia threatened to tell Thomas—and Tommy—that I have been having an affair. I was a fool to think I could walk away from Thomas without any damage to my son. Perhaps in a few years, I will tell him about Sam, but not now. He's too young and we have just reconnected. And if Eugenia discovers the truth about his conception? She will probably disown him, and I think that rejection could destroy him. I swear the woman is pure evil. She makes me shudder every time she walks into a room."

"Klara, please, take some time. You're making one of the biggest decisions of your life. This is your future. You're still a young woman, and perhaps you are not giving Tommy enough credit. He's probably a lot stronger than you think."

"Lotte, he's nineteen, and in his freshman year of college. How do you think he'll react if I tell him that the father who raised him, who played catch with him in the backyard, who took care of his broken bones and bloody noses, is not the man he thinks he is? I cannot destroy his life for the sake of mine and Sam's. I won't do it. I won't. Please, Lotte, go and tell Sam and make him understand. I am afraid if I see him, my resolve will weaken."

From the tears welling up in her friend's eyes, Lotte realized that the afternoon's encounter with Eugenia and her decision to stay with Thomas had clearly left Klara exhausted and agitated. Klara needed rest if she expected to continue to recuperate quickly. "All right, Klara, if you're sure."

As Klara's eyes were beginning to close, Lotte heard her whisper, "I'm sure, Lotte. I'm sure."

The conversation with Sam went pretty much as Lotte expected. He cursed for a good thirty minutes, demanded to see Klara, and then began cursing again. Lotte was not even sure she understood all of the expletives. When he stopped his tirade, he downed a small bottle of vodka from the hotel's minibar and slunk down on the one chair in the room.

Lotte asked him what he would really think of Klara if she put their happiness above that of Tommy's. "Lotte, I get it. Now, if you don't mind, would you just please leave? I am about to go down to the bar and get very, very drunk. Tell Klara I won't be coming to the hospital—or anyplace else to see her. Tell her I won't be contacting her again. It's too damn hard to see her, only to let her go. Tell her I wish she'd never written to me. Tell her I wish I didn't know about Tommy. Tell her I would have made a great dad. Tell her I love her. Oh, hell, don't tell her any of that. Just tell her good-bye. Now really, Lotte, I don't mean to shoot the messenger, but please, do us both a favor and go home."

PART III

RETRIBUTION

TWENTY THREE

Klara's recuperation from the accident was slower than anyone antici-pated. The first few weeks home, she stayed upstairs, asking that all her meals be sent up. She finally convinced Tommy to go back to school, but Thomas rarely left her, and asked his partner to cover for him at the hospital and in their private practice. Thomas constantly fretted over her, and annoyed her doctor with his daily phone calls to discuss her slow recovery.

Truth be told, Klara was feeling well enough physically to resume her daily routine, but she couldn't garner the energy emotionally. Sam was gone forever, and she was going to have to accept that she was the one who sent him away. There were moments when she truly thought her heart would break. Thankfully, Thomas just thought she was hav-ing a tough time getting her strength back. Eugenia was another matter entirely. The few times she had seen her, Eugenia made it clear she was enjoying Klara's discomfort over the scuttled affair. Luckily, Eugenia would never know the depths of Klara's feelings for the man she had planned to see on that ill-fated morning.

Klara's self-imposed isolation gave her time to think about past decisions that had shaped the course of her life. When she pondered them all, she recognized that except for Tommy, most of her life was one of regret. Hiding her Judaism from Thomas had prevented her from enjoying the traditions and rituals of her childhood. Unable to pass any of them on to her son, she had sat passively by as he was christened and baptized into a Christian church, and thus attended church instead of synagogue. By convincing Thomas he was Tommy's father, she had pushed parenthood onto a man who may have not have willingly taken on a pregnant Jewish immigrant who wanted to stay in America. Worst of all, she had denied Sam and Tommy the chance to be father and son. *Lotte tried to convince me years ago to confront my past, but I was too frightened, too settled*, she thought. *What a fool I have been.* Klara wanted to atone for her sins, and for the first time in years, she prayed she would find a way.

Leaving Atlanta with one of the worst hangovers of his entire life, Sam thought he would never survive the short flight back to D.C. Once there, he threw himself into his job with Justice, hoping the long days filled with complicated cases would help him continue on without Klara. There were so many civil rights infractions and outright racial crimes, he could have stayed at the office day and night and still not completed his workload.

In truth, Sam was just plain tired, and recognized that he was burning out at the job. He needed something new to reenergize him, to keep his mind off Klara and Tommy. So, when John Lassiter, the head of the Justice Department, asked him to work in the newly created Office of Special Investigations, Sam was initially excited about a possible change. When he learned that the primary purpose of the new department would be to chase Nazis now living in the United States, Sam had to stifle a laugh. That wasn't exactly the change he had been looking for. The last thing he wanted to do was hunt down Nazis; dredging up wartime memories would also stir up feelings and thoughts of Klara.

"Listen to me, Sam. You're going to love this job; it's right up your alley. You're a first-class investigator, and let me tell you, exposing these guys is not going to be easy," said Lassiter. "Ever since the Israelis caught Eichmann in Argentina, Justice has been thinking about doing some housekeeping of its own. You and I both know that some of these bastards are right here in the good old US of A, hiding in plain sight. Hell, we even brought some of them in ourselves, and gave them jobs in Huntsville, Alabama, to work on the space program! Unfortunately, those SOBs are off limits, but there are plenty more living right here under our noses—murderers who so far have escaped scot-free. But there's no statute of limitation on murder, and it's about time someone went after them. I figured you were due for a change, and this might be something you'd be interested in."

"Why?" asked Sam. "Does my heritage have anything to do with why you want me? I'm only half Jewish you know."

"Don't be a shmuck," said Lassiter with a twinkle in his eye. "Of course that's part of it. I thought you might want a little payback. You helped liberate some of those camps, didn't you? You saw first-hand what those monsters were capable of doing."

"Yeah, I did. A long time ago. Let me think about it."

"Don't think too long. Some of our other attorneys would jump at the chance to head up this group, but hey, no pressure."

"Right, John, no pressure. I can see that."

"Just in case you're interested, I brought along a few files on some of the people we're looking into. See if anything sparks your interest, and get back to me in the next day or so. You're a good man, Sam, and I don't want to lose you. Just promise me, if you ever decide to leave Justice, you won't become one of those high-priced attorneys in a four hundred dollar suit defending criminals."

Sam was surprised when John then handed over almost a hundred separate folders containing dossiers of suspected Nazis living in America. "You're kidding, right? You said a few."

"This *is* a few. I could have handed you twice as many."

"Okay...okay, I'll look through them."

For the next several hours, Sam pored over personal correspondence, birth certificates, passports, and travel documents issued from either the American or British zones of postwar occupied Europe, and from those individuals who were now under suspicion of falsifying those papers in order to immigrate to the United States. Within each individual's file was a detailed account of the crimes the person was suspected of committing.

The first file Sam opened detailed the case of Alex Grabowski, a Pole who had immigrated to the United States in 1947 and who was now working as a tool and die maker at one of the big auto parts manufacturers in Detroit. In order to get into the country, he had claimed that he was, himself, a victim of the Nazis, and that he had been sent to Auschwitz following his capture by the Germans during the Warsaw uprising of 1944. The investigators believed Alex Grabowski was really Alojzy Grysbowski, a camp guard at Auschwitz and at the killing centers of Treblinka and Sobibór. Although there were few survivors from Sobibór, one had recognized "Grabowski" as the guard who had bludgeoned his wife and two-year-old child to death moments after they were hauled from the cattle car that had brought them to the camp. The eyewitness account was enough for Justice to open a file, but not enough to bring formal charges. Sam put the Grabowski file in a pile to review later and opened folder number two. It was going to be a long night.

The second file contained the documents of Anslem Müller, who had taken the name of Arthur Miller. Sam marveled at the irony that the man had adopted the name of a Jewish playwright, esteemed author of *Death of a Salesman*. Regardless of his name choice, the man was suspected of having personally ordered the mass shooting of 4,273 children in Kovno, Lithuania, in the Great Action of October 29, 1941. According to one eyewitness, a woman who had survived the horror, the children from the newly born to age fourteen were gathered along with their parents in the town square. Müller ordered his German and Lithuanian troops to forcibly tear the children from their terrified mothers, fathers, and older siblings. They were then taken to the Ninth Fort in the hills above the city and systematically shot to death. The parents waiting in the square below could hear the gunfire as well as the screams. Anslem Müller had been an Obersturmbannführer in the Nazi SS, a rank similar to that of lieutenant colonel in the US Army, and was today using his particular skills as the manager of a Humane Society in Tulsa, Oklahoma. Prior to his move to Tulsa, Müller had worked for a delivery service in New York, where he had the misfortune of taking a package to the home of one of the few survivors from Kovno who remembered him shouting orders on the day of the Great Action. The shocked survivor called Justice, but as of yet, little had been done to build a case.

As Sam continued to read through the files, his frustration grew. John was right. The prosecutions would be difficult. One eyewitness account did not a case make. As much as Sam wanted to go after the bastards, he wasn't sure he could interview the survivors and listen to their stories without, somehow, losing a part of himself—and without thinking about what Klara must have endured. He looked at his watch and was shocked to discover that he had been going at it for over five hours. Stifling a yawn, he decided to divide the files by the location of where the war crimes had been committed. As he perused them, Sam was struck by how many of the crimes had been committed in countries now within the Soviet bloc; that would make it that much more difficult to locate any original papers that could document these individuals' identities.

With one last glance at his growing number of piles, Sam picked up the only file folder he had relating to crimes perpetrated in France and started to read. An hour later, Sam was still glued to his chair, wiping away tears that streamed steadily down his face. The suspected Nazi in the file was Standartenführer Reinhardt Frank, the man who had brutally raped Klara for over two years. *This animal nearly destroyed her, and he's here, right here, living in a suburb outside Washington, D.C! When I'm done with you, Reinhardt Frank, you'll wish you had been tried and hung in Germany.*

By eight the following morning, Sam had already called John to accept the job as lead attorney for the new Office of Special Investigations and was working on vetting possible candidates to work with him. He needed investigators who could navigate the complicated legal obstacles, proficient in both German and French, to dig through the documents captured by the Allies after the war and now held at the National Archives in Washington and in London. It would be difficult to get anything from the French, who continued to deny their role in the deportations of French Jews.

From the file already in his possession, Sam discovered that Reinhardt Frank had immigrated to the United States in 1949 using forged documents. Now going by the name of Ronnie Frick, Frank had invested heavily in the postwar real estate market. Today, his net worth was estimated at over six million dollars. Although he generally kept a low profile, "Frick" could be found on the boards of directors of a number of nonprofits in the Washington area. For the past ten years he had made substantial pledges to the United Jewish Appeal. Sam was sure it was not to assuage any guilt but to add substance to his bona fides as Ronnie Frick, developer and philanthropist.

Apparently, the wife Klara had met during the war years had not made it with Frank to America. That piece of the puzzle would definitely need to be investigated. The newly invented Frick, now in his late fifties, was single, and was considered one of the more eligible bachelors in the area. Filing charges against someone with means and connections would be difficult, especially given that "Frick" had the money to hire the best legal defense available, and would likely have paid for state-of-the-art forgeries when he left Germany.

Sam wasn't worried. He was confident in his own ability and, in Klara, he had the perfect person to bear witness to Standartenführer Reinhardt Frank's crimes.

TWENTY FOUR

Over the next several months, Klara fell back into a routine. Thomas had finally gone back to work and to his golf game, and Eugenia was back at the club playing bridge with her cronies. All had returned to normal, but nothing seemed right. Klara attended social engagements, saw Lotte for lunch once or twice a week, and spent some time in the garden. But she lost something in the wake of the accident. That one evening with Sam, she had felt so hopeful. The thought of finally telling the truth about her past and about Tommy, and perhaps even living with the man she loved, had actually seemed possible. She wanted—no, she *needed*—to hold onto that possibility.

Thomas was the same man he had always been, but Klara could no longer pretend that what she felt for him was enough. They had not made love since the accident, not that Thomas hadn't tried. Each time, she came up with a new ache or pain or excuse, and she knew his patience was wearing thin. She longed to contact Sam, but she couldn't bear to hear his voice and not be with him. She didn't even know if he would agree to speak to her. She had rejected him. Who would blame him for finally moving on?

Then there was Eugenia, constantly hovering, always making her presence known. Klara missed her own mother intensely, and would have welcomed a relationship with a surrogate...had Eugenia made any such effort when Klara had first arrived at her doorstep all those years ago. But from the beginning, Eugenia had made it clear that Klara was not what she wanted for her son, and her dislike of Klara had not abated over the years. In fact, ever since the accident, their relationship had worsened; the two women, each with a hold over the other, barely spoke. Dinners were awkward affairs, and Klara didn't know how much longer she could keep up with all the lies and pretenses. But every time Klara was tempted to reconnect with Sam, she remembered Eugenia's threat, and knew she was trapped...unless she could find the strength to tell the truth regardless of the consequences.

Tommy was the one bright spot in her life. He was a changed young man. The accident had been a wakeup call for both of them. After returning to school, he quit his fraternity and was now living in a dormitory with some boys he had met his first semester. He called Klara regularly, and their conversations were driven by his excitement about his courses and a girl he had met. He rarely saw his old friends from high school. Once he had made it known that his race-baiting days were over, they had grown further and further apart, and they had finally stopped calling him. She envied Tommy his courage and his resolve to forgo lifelong friendships for the sake of his principles. Klara's admiration for her son intensified her own self-loathing. She had still not found the courage to tell him the truth about herself or his parentage.

In an effort to cheer Klara up, Thomas once again began suggesting that they take a trip, just the two of them. He brought home a dozen brochures from the travel agency. Each locale was more romantic and exotic than the next. Most of the destinations were islands in the Caribbean, but he also included information on trips to Greece and to Paris.

Paris. When Klara opened the brochure describing the wonders and sights of the City of Lights, she was besieged by long-buried memories. The city where her own life had finally lost all meaning enticing a whole new generation of visitors. The brochures described the vast galleries of the Louvre, nighttime boat rides on the Seine, visits to the Eiffel Tower, or walks down the Avenue des Champs-Élysées to view the Arc de Triomphe, not the Paris *she* remembered. It was almost comical. The war ended, the Jews were gone, and everyone went on with their lives. Did any of the French ask what happened to all the women and children held at the Vélodrome d'Hiver? Where did they go? And, more importantly, why had they not returned? Did anyone remember an adorable boy who had played for a short time in the front yard of the Dubois Home? Did he just disappear?

For a moment, Klara thought she *should* go back—and take her two Toms with her. Perhaps there she could explain what had happened to her, to her family, and her husband and son would understand. But what if they couldn't live with her lies and deceit? Her honesty would be for nothing. No, she would not return to Paris. It was out of the question. For now, those memories needed to stay buried.

TWENTY FIVE

Several months after Sam accepted his new position with the Office of Special Investigations, the case against Reinhardt Frank, aka Ronnie Frick, was moving ahead slowly but steadily. The team he put together had done terrific work. They had managed to locate Frank's birth certificate, his diploma from high school, and even documentation that proved Frank had been a Nazi since the age of sixteen, when he joined the Hitler Youth. Frank had then matriculated into the Schutzstaffel, better known as the SS. The six-foot-one, blond-haired, blue-eyed Frank was the ideal candidate for Junkerschule, the SS officer training school.

The discovered documents had traced Frank's rise within the Schutzstaffel: he moved up quickly from SS-Junker to SS-Standartenoberjunker, where he was assigned to his first unit; before long he earned the rank of Untersturmführer, or second lieutenant; and finally, he was promoted to Standartenführer, the rank he had held when he was based in Paris. Frank had risen rapidly within the SS ranks; the Paris posting was a coveted assignment.

Sam's investigators had not yet unearthed any information about Frank's wife. She might prove to be a valuable corroborative witness if she could be located. Sam also hoped to find some of the other prisoners who had worked in the house. They had probably been deported to one of the death camps when Frank left Paris, but perhaps one of them had survived and could add to Klara's testimony. He would have to see if Klara remembered any of their names.

Klara. How to handle Klara? He would have to contact her eventually. He would have to renege on his promise to stay away, and would have to unsettle her life once again. No, unsettle was a benign word. He was about to upend the stability she had given Tommy, and possibly destroy her marriage. But Klara had the right to know that they had located Reinhardt Frank and hoped to get him deported to Germany where he could be prosecuted for his war crimes. Sam would present Klara with the facts of the case and let her make the choice: avenge her mother, brother, and countless other innocents deported and killed, or protect their son from the truth that could potentially be devastating to him and their relationship.

Unless some other witness appeared out of nowhere, Sam couldn't prosecute Frank without Klara. She was the key to his entire case. He had still not confided his complicated relationship with Klara to John Lassiter or to the other attorneys on his staff. Once he admitted that he had known their key witness during the war they would most likely suggest that he recuse himself. Sam decided to speak with John first, and convince his boss to keep Sam on the case. Sam was certain that he should be the one to go after Frank, and the only one capable of getting a conviction.

Sam decided to ask John to meet him outside of the office. He chose a steak house he knew his boss would enjoy. Sam arrived at the restaurant early and ordered a scotch on the rocks to fortify his resolve and frayed nerves. This would have to be the biggest sales pitch of his life so far, and he was justifiably on edge.

"What are you drinking?" asked John when he arrived. Motioning the waiter to bring over one of the same, John took a seat and settled into his chair. "So, Sam. What's so important we couldn't discuss it at the office? Not that I mind. The steaks here are out of this world. They taste even better when someone else is paying. You are paying, aren't you?"

"Yes, John, I'm paying," said Sam with a smile. The two men went way back, and Sam knew John thoroughly enjoyed a free meal. Once they had ordered and the waiter retreated to the kitchen, it was time to make his pitch. "I've chosen the first case to prosecute under the Office of Special Investigations," Sam began.

"Good, good. Tell me about it," said John, leaning back in his chair. As Sam pulled out the file on Reinhardt Frank, John motioned for the waiter to bring them another round of drinks.

"I've decided to go after a pretty big fish, and I hope you'll agree that his arrest and deportation will make the kind of headlines we need to keep this department going," said Sam. "His given name was Reinhardt Frank and he was born in 1915, in a small town near Munich. Today, he goes by the name of Ronnie Frick, and he lives right here in the D.C. area. Maybe you've heard of him?"

"You're kidding me, right?" asked John. "Ronnie Frick, the developer and real estate mogul, is really Reinhardt Frank, killer Nazi?

"Yeah, John, he is," replied Sam.

"Well, if we could nail his hide to the wall, that would really make a statement, wouldn't it?" said John. "Give me some background. How much do you have on him? If we go after someone well known like Frick, I want a conviction. This could be big news, so let's not muck it up."

"I agree. So, this is what we know." Sam briefed John about Frick's early roots, his rise through the ranks of the SS, and his posting in Paris. "Frank or Frick, whatever we end up calling him, left Paris weeks before the Allies marched into the city. He arrived in Berlin in early September '44 and, as far as we can tell, he stayed there until just before the end of the war," said Sam. "There is no way a guy like him would have stuck around to wait for our old friends the Russians to capture or kill him, so we're assuming he already had his new identity, forged documents, and travel plans in place. He immigrated to this country in 1949 under his new name, moved to the D.C. area, and started buying up real estate."

"Okay, I get it. He came here on forged documents. But why do we care? What were his crimes?" asked John.

"I'm getting to that. Just giving you a little background. Like I said, Frank arrived in Paris shortly after the French surrendered and made their deal with the Third Reich. He immediately moved into an opulent home the Nazis had confiscated in the first arrondissement, and brought in prisoners from the Drancy concentration camp to serve as maids, cooks, gardeners, and other menial workers. Frank oversaw the massive deportation of Jews from French internment camps to killing centers in the East. Most were sent to either Sobibór or Auschwitz-Birkenau, both in Poland."

"Okay, I get it," said John. "He was one bad guy, but where's the proof? What do we have on him?"

"We have an eyewitness. She was there from the beginning in 1942 and was in the house until his departure from Paris two years later. The Gestapo arrested her, along with her mother and brother, when they tried to escape into Spain using false papers. She was and still is exquisite, which is no doubt what prompted Frank to promise that he would keep her mother and brother at Drancy, and prevent their deportation east, if she agreed to work in his home as a maid. He could have forced her, so it hardly mattered whether she went willingly or not, but for some sick reason he made this bargain with her. Work for me, and your mother and brother will live; refuse, and you all die. For more than two years, he raped her nearly every day. The fact that he did not kill her before his departure is remarkable. That she lived at all is a miracle."

"When did this witness come forward?"

"Well, that's the glitch," said Sam. "She has no idea he is still alive, let alone living in the lap of luxury in the nation's capital."

"Sam, do I need another drink? What aren't you telling me?"

Taking a sip of his own cocktail, Sam said, "I know her. I know the witness. I met her during the war. Toward the end. When my unit entered Buchenwald, we were told to make an assessment of the entire camp—you know, ferret out any guards hiding as prisoners, find anyone still alive but too weak to stand. I found her unconscious, suffering from typhus, and brought her to the hospital. Her case was not as advanced as many of the others and she recovered. I felt responsible for her, you know? I found her. I wanted her to be okay."

Sam paused while the waiter delivered their meals. "I know this is going to sound crazy, John, but we fell in love. I mean really fell in love. I love her to this day. I know what she endured at the hands of Standartenführer Reinhardt Frank because she told me everything."

"Now I know why you wanted to pay for dinner," said John as he motioned the waiter for yet another round. "If your tale gets any longer, we're both going to be drunk."

"Maybe our next round should be coffee, because this could be a long night," said Sam. "Anyway, we fell for each other. She spoke English, and we just talked and talked. I visited every chance I had. She had no one left. Her entire immediate family was dead. That's the thing I've learned about survivors. Most of them cannot understand how they made it when other members of their families didn't. They are guilt ridden and, in some instances, like Klara's, ashamed of some of things they might have done to survive. Klara truly believed she was saving her mother and brother by cleaning his house during the day and acquiescing to the rapes at night. She was barely more than a child herself."

"And were they saved?"

Sam shook his head. "No. The mother and brother died at Drancy. The sporadic visits of Frank's wife, Gertrude, offered Klara brief respites from the abuse. Gertrude did not immigrate to the United States with her husband, and we are trying to determine what has become of her. At the time, Klara believed that Gertrude knew what was going on and was possibly sympathetic to her plight. Frank often talked about the roundups and deportations in front of Klara, and I think if he ever saw her again, it would be tantamount to his worst nightmare."

"Okay, I get it. She'd be a great witness," said John. "What's your relationship with her now?"

"Now...I guess I'm not sure. We lost each other in the chaos toward the end of the war." Beads of perspiration appeared on Sam's face as he dropped the last bombshell. "We had one night together before my unit unexpectedly shipped out just a few hours later. I left her a note, told her to not leave the camp under any circumstances, but she never got it," said Sam. "My new post was active duty. I got shot, lost my leg—you know that story. When I tried to find Klara at the camp, she was gone. She was alone, frightened, and thought I had ditched her without a word, so she up and married the doctor who had been taking care of her. She planned to divorce him once she got to the States—he knew she only married him to get out of Europe—but when she got to Atlanta, Klara discovered...she found out...well, she was pregnant."

"With whose baby?"

"Mine. No doubt about it. She wanted to keep the baby safe, so she stayed with the doctor. Our son is nineteen years old now, and I've never met him. I only found out about him a few months ago when Klara wrote to me. We met in Atlanta and...well, nothing came of it. I still haven't met Tommy—that's his name—and Klara asked that I not contact her again, as she doesn't want to upend Tommy's life. I planned to respect her decision and stay away, but then I found the name Reinhardt Frank in these files. I knew it was the same guy who almost destroyed her. For Klara's sake, I knew I had to do something about it."

"I'll be damned, Sam. When you said you had to discuss something too delicate to bring up at the office, you weren't kidding," said John, shaking his head. "Is that everything? Are you keeping back any information at all?"

"No, John. I swear, that's all of it, as far as I know."

"Okay, this is what we're going to do. You're going to step back and..."

"No way am I staying out of this! That is not going to happen!" shouted Sam, causing a number of other diners to look over at their table with displeasure.

"Sam, calm down and give me a minute. I've listened to you for the last two hours. Give me the same courtesy and hear me out."

"John, I'm sorry, but this man, this animal...what he did to her and her family. I have to make him pay."

"You will, Sam, but we can't do anything that will jeopardize our case. And we can't show our hand or our evidence too soon, or we'll blow it. We don't want to let the prick know he's being investigated. He might get the hell out of Dodge and disappear," said John. "We have to think this through very carefully. Once it gets going, we can't have Frick's defense team—and he will have a strong defense team—question your motives for bringing the indictment. We're also going to have to be upfront about your relationship with Klara. If we try and keep it a secret, it will be worse for us when they find out. First thing in the morning, I'll book a flight to Atlanta and try to speak discreetly to your friend Klara."

Nodding, Sam gave John the contact information for Lotte Bacharach. "She's Klara's best friend. If anyone can convince Klara to meet with you, it's her. And John, tell Lotte I'm sorry I acted like such an ass the last time we met. She'll understand."

Two days later, John Lassiter stepped off a Delta Airlines jet and swore to himself he would never again visit Atlanta in August. Washington in late summer was hot enough, but Atlanta was stickier and even more unbearable. His shirt was drenched. Luckily, he had just enough time to check in and change before the scheduled meeting.

When John walked into the coffee shop, he recognized Lotte immediately from Sam's description. He had been told to look for a tall, slim woman in her late forties with short salt-and-pepper hair and bright blue eyes. She was easy to spot and John walked toward her briskly with a smile on his face and a hand outstretched. "Miss Bacharach, Sam described you perfectly."

"And you as well," Lotte replied, with a grin on her face.

When Sam called, he told her that John looked like a giant puppy dog: soulful eyes, kind of large ears, and big paws. She would have known him anywhere. Lotte had chosen a quiet booth in the back of the restaurant and before John even sat down, she motioned for the waiter to come over with menus and a pot of coffee.

"Great, I'm starving," said John as he took a menu from the waiter's outstretched hand and slid into the booth. After ordering, John looked at Lotte. "So, what did Sam tell you?"

"Thank you for getting right to the point, Mr. Lassiter," said Lotte. "Personally, I can't stand small talk."

John laughed out loud at Lotte's directness. "I like you already," he said. "Call me John. You and I are going to get along famously." Pulling the folder from his briefcase, John opened it to a copy of a photograph showing Standartenführer Reinhardt Frank in uniform standing outside his home in Germany in 1944. "How much do you know about Klara's past, Miss Bacharach?" asked John.

"Call me Lotte. Klara told me a great deal, but I am not sure what or how much she held back," she said.

"This man is Reinhardt Frank," said John, pointing to the picture. "He is one of the monsters responsible for the roundup and deportation of the Jews in Paris. He is also the man who held your friend captive for over two years, sexually and physically abusing her on a regular basis during that same period of time."

Lotte couldn't take her eyes off the photograph.

"What is it? Are you okay?"

"Yes, I'm sorry," said Lotte. "It is just that...he looks so normal. There he is, smiling for the camera, holding a little white dog in his arms. How can a man who is holding a dog so gently separate babies from their mothers and send them to their deaths? What kind of man can do that and still be kind to a puppy?" asked Lotte?

"Like I said, he's not a man. He's a monster. He is still alive, and living in this country. With the help of your good friend Klara, we can get him deported from our country and sent back to Germany to stand trial for his crimes. Now let's get down to business."

"John, I must tell you before we get started. I love Klara like a sister. We both lost many relatives during the war, so when we find good friends, they become more like family. Do you understand?"

"Yes, of course I do."

"Then I must warn you. Klara has held onto many demons from the past. She is a very complicated woman. I think that testifying against Frank might finally set her free, and I hope she chooses to help you," said Lotte. "However, other than suggesting she meet with you, I will not try to convince Klara of anything. You must understand that if she decides to testify against Frank, it will affect her relationship with her husband and son. They really know almost nothing about Klara's past. They do not even know she is Jewish."

"I see," said John with a frown.

"As much as I hate Herr Frank, I must be grateful to him for something he did. Before Klara was deported from Paris, for reasons I do not know, he gave her papers that identified her as a Christian arrested for political crimes against the German state. Klara's American family knows that her parents and brother were murdered by the Nazis, but they do not know any of the details about what really happened to them or to her. This will not be an easy decision for Klara. She will want to avenge her family, but she will be extremely anxious about her son's reaction. She also will not want to cause pain to the man she has been married to for two decades. In other words, John, you have your work cut out for you."

"Thank you, Lotte. You've been most helpful in explaining the Compton family dynamics and Klara's concerns. I understand and appreciate your loyalty to your friend. I like you even more for that," added John with a smile. "When do you think she and I can get together?"

"I'll call Klara this evening and ask her over to my home for lunch tomorrow. If she wants to pursue this, I will call you, and you can come to my house as well. I live near your hotel and you can be there by taxi in less than ten minutes. My only concern in all this is Klara, and I will protect her and her privacy at all costs. You must promise me that if she says no, you will respect that decision and leave her alone."

"Lotte, as much as I would like to make you that promise, I can't. Frank is a bad man whose numerous crimes have gone too long unpunished. I plan on making a statement about how this country should be dealing with these bastards who took up residence on our shores," said John. "But of course, I can't force her to testify. That has to be her choice. All I promise is that I will be as sensitive to her family concerns as I am able."

"Okay, then. I appreciate your honesty. If Klara agrees, then we shall meet again tomorrow," said Lotte as she reached for the check.

"Lotte, this is on me. It has been a pleasure meeting you. A real pleasure."

Lotte called Klara that evening. She wasn't sure Klara would agree to come over for lunch. Since the accident, Klara had turned inward. To her surprise, Klara readily agreed, and actually said she was looking forward to getting out of the house and catching up. She sounded almost cheerful, and Lotte was tormented that what she was about to tell her would add more turmoil to her friend's already complicated life.

John called Sam in D.C. to give him an update. "I like Lotte. She's an interesting woman, that one," said John.

"Yes," agreed Sam. "And she's a faithful, loyal friend. So, she agreed to help us?"

"She agreed to arrange the meeting. She absolutely refused to try to persuade Klara one way or the other."

"I expected that. This will be a tough decision for Klara," said Sam. "I wish I could be there to offer my moral support. I'd especially like to be there for my son if Klara decides to tell him about me."

"Sam, I understand how you feel, but for now, for the sake of the case, you need to stay in Washington. I'll call you as soon as my discussion with her is over. Let's cross one hurdle at a time. I'm not even sure she's going to agree to see me."

"Okay," said Sam reluctantly. "I'll be at my desk waiting for your call. And John? Good luck. I'm counting on you." Sam hung up. Part of him wished that he did not have a role in this new assault on Klara's home life and happiness, as he wanted to protect her from any further pain. And another part of him wanted to go after Frank with his bare hands. Sam could call John and tell him they needed to choose another case, one in which he had no personal interest, but Klara was the one who had to decide. If she refused to testify, he would convince John to back off and would stay out of her life forever.

TWENTY SIX

Lotte was finishing setting the table when she heard Klara's car pull into her driveway. Looking out the window, she was pleased to see how well Klara was walking. As usual, Klara looked beautiful. Her long hair hung loosely down her back and Lotte marveled how young she still looked. Even without makeup, Klara managed to look radiant. Today she wore a beautiful white silk blouse ruffled in the front and tucked into black Capri pants accented by a thick black patent leather belt and black ballet slippers. Under other circumstances, in another life, Klara could have been a model.

Opening the door before Klara had a chance to knock, Lotte enveloped her friend in a warm embrace. "It is so good to see you looking so well," murmured Lotte, her eyes brimming with tears.

"Lotte, what has gotten into you? We saw each other just last week."

"I know, I know. You look so well and...oh, never mind. I've prepared your favorite salad," said Lotte. "I don't know about you, but I'm starving." The two former refugees looked at each other and burst into laughter.

Lotte had not lied to John. She hated small talk. Halfway through the meal, Lotte could not continue making routine conversation and put down her fork.

"What, full already?" asked Klara. "I thought you said you were starving."

"Klara, there's no easy way for me to tell you this. I wish with all my heart I was not the one dredging up horrible memories for you, but you have a right to know."

"Know what?" said Klara, her face pale with anticipation and dread.

"The Justice Department has located Reinhardt Frank. He's here, in America. And they are planning to try him for falsifying his immigration documents," said Lotte. "If they can prove he entered the country illegally, they can send him back. After that, it would be up to Germany to take it further and try him for war crimes."

"I thought...I hoped he was dead," said Klara, after a long silence. "How do you know this? What is your connection to Reinhardt Frank? Lotte, what in the hell is going on?"

"Please, Klara, give me a chance to explain," said Lotte. "I got a call... from Sam. About two or three months ago, he was asked to head up a new branch of the Justice Department, one that was specifically established to go after Nazis who entered the United States illegally. Sam was going through the files and recognized Reinhardt Frank's name. It's Frank, Klara. They're sure of it."

"He's really here? Where is he?"

"I don't know many of the details. Sam's boss, John Lassiter, contacted me. I met with John yesterday," said Lotte. "You should know... Sam wanted to come himself, but he didn't want to jeopardize the case. More important, he didn't want to be the one to make things more complicated for you. He asked me to be the one to tell you, to warn you that if you choose to testify..."

The look of anguish on Klara's face was so heartbreaking, Lotte couldn't continue. "Klara, I'm so sorry."

"I have to go," said Klara. She picked up her handbag from the nearby table and started walking toward the door.

"Klara, no. Please stay," said Lotte. "I am on *your* side, whatever that side turns out to be. We can talk this through. You shouldn't be alone."

"Lotte, I love you, and I know you mean well, but that's exactly what I should be right now. I need to be alone."

Klara didn't even remember the streets she took to get there but suddenly, there she was, parked in front of the beautiful synagogue atop the small knoll. How many times had she stopped here? First with Lloyd... and then, after she learned to drive. So many times.

For the first time, she got out of her car. She stood in front of the building. She walked inside the synagogue.

Klara was shaking as she entered the building. She smelled the distant but familiar scents of old prayer books and polished wood. Quietly opening a door, she entered the small chapel and took a seat in one of the pews. The sun streamed through the stained glass windows, flooding the room with a breathtaking array of color. *This is right*, she thought. *I belong here.*

She picked up one of the prayer books and saw the familiar Hebrew printed on the pages. It had been so long since she last read the ancient language. Holding the book to her heart, Klara thought about the news she had just received. Just hearing the name spoken aloud made her shudder. Reinhardt Frank could no longer hurt her physically, but he still had a terrifying hold on her. He had left indelible scars on Klara, ones that would never completely heal. He had not only abused her personally, but he had been responsible for sending her mother and brother and countless others to their deaths.

There really was no decision to make. Regardless of the collateral damage to her husband and to her son, Klara knew she had to testify.

Klara went back to Lotte's house after leaving The Temple. She knew her friend would be beside herself with worry and she wanted to reassure her that she was okay. She also needed a safe haven from which to make her telephone calls. She had no doubt Eugenia was still listening in on her conversations whenever the opportunity arose.

When she called Sam at two, he clearly expected it to be either John or Lotte telling him how Klara had taken the news.

"How did it go? Will she do it?" he said.

"Sam, it's me. Klara. I heard from Lotte that my real knight in shining armor is *still* trying to rescue me," said Klara. "Now that you have found the dragon, I am counting on you to slay him."

"I will, Klara. I swear to you, we'll get him."

Next she called John Lassiter. John was finally able to convince Klara that they had a better shot at a conviction if Sam was not involved. She arranged to meet with him the following day for lunch.

TWENTY SEVEN

After leaving Lotte's house, Klara drove around Atlanta for an hour. She wanted to put off going home as long as possible. It would be hard to see Thomas and pretend that their lives would continue as before. Tomorrow, if John convinced her that they had a strong case and could win with her testimony, she would finally tell Thomas and Tommy everything.

When Klara finally arrived home and pulled into the driveway, Lloyd was outside washing and waxing Eugenia's black Lincoln. The car was five years old and still looked as if it had just been driven out of the showroom.

Lloyd and Klara had not spoken since the accident, and Klara decided that the time had come for them to clear the air. After tomorrow, she might not have another chance. Of late, as usual, Lloyd barely looked up to acknowledge her as she approached.

"Hi, Lloyd. The car looks great," she said. "I'm sure Eugenia will be pleased."

"Thank you, Miz Klara. I 'preciate that," Lloyd said, still not stopping his polishing motion to look up.

"Lloyd, I'd like to talk to you. You know, about the morning of my accident."

"I can't talk about that Miz Klara. It would mean my job, and I got a family to feed. Ain't no time to be lookin' for work."

"Lloyd, I only wanted to let you know that I understand. I don't blame you for anything," said Klara. "Eugenia's a complicated woman, and as you know, there is no love lost between the two of us. She has disliked me from the moment I walked through her front door nineteen years ago. I have never been good enough for her son, and I know she forced you to follow me."

"Miz Klara, I will always be sorry for that," said Lloyd, finally throwing his rag into the nearby bucket. "I shoulda said no to her that morning. I shoulda just stopped the car and not driven one more minute. I know you was tryin' to get away from her, and she told me to speed up or I wouldn' be drivin' for her no more. She meant it, too. I worked for that woman near twenty-five years, and nothin' mattered to her that day but followin' you. When you hit that truck—well, I been blamin' myself all these many months. I shoulda stood up to her."

"Lloyd, I could have pulled over, too. My anger, my hatred of her, got the best of me. And I didn't want her to know where I was going," Klara said with a wink. "It was none of her damn business."

"Why, Miz Klara, I never heard you curse before!"

"Lloyd, be prepared. In the next few days, you will probably hear a lot of cursing," said Klara. "Although not all of it will be coming from me."

That night Eugenia's old friends the Coles were coming to dinner. Klara had promised Thomas that she would be there, and had no way to get out of it gracefully. It seemed fitting that she would be spending what was most likely her last night in the Compton home dining with Judge Cole and his wife Dorthea, given that they had been there at the very beginning, the night Klara first ventured out of her room to have dinner with her new husband and mother-in-law. Klara remembered how carefully she had chosen her dress for that evening, the night she had seduced Thomas, the night her real deceit began.

By tomorrow evening, Thomas would know the truth about her, and so would Tommy. She shuddered at the thought. Looking into her closet, Klara again decided to take extra pains dressing for the evening. She loved the new mod styles of the late sixties, and chose a pair of black boots and a boxy black and white dress that hit a couple inches above the knee. She was sure her mother-in-law would disapprove, but Klara was past caring what Eugenia thought. She rarely took off the pearls that Thomas bought years ago in New York, and decided they would accent her dress perfectly.

The Coles were due to arrive at seven thirty. Klara decided to fortify herself with a glass of wine before dinner with Eugenia. Thomas was already in the study sipping on his own drink, and didn't hear Klara as she approached the doorway. She was glad he didn't look up, because she wanted to remember him sitting in the room he loved, poring over a rare book or one of his wartime journals. Even if their marriage managed to survive tomorrow's confession, she recognized that their relationship would be altered forever.

For a change, Thomas wasn't reading. He was just staring at a tattered piece of paper in his hand.

"What do you have there?" asked Klara, as she walked into the room, finally making her presence known. Startled, Thomas quickly inserted the paper into the nearby journal and looked up.

"Nothing, really, just something I had stashed in one of my journals, an old notation about a patient at the Evac Hospital."

"It must have been a very complicated case. I have been standing in the doorway for about five minutes."

"No, it's nothing important, really," said Thomas. "You look beautiful, by the way. How about a drink before mother's guests arrive?"

"You read my mind. I would love one."

Thomas left the journal on the table as he walked over to the bar to pour Klara's drink. *Why haven't I destroyed that damn note? A psychiatrist would have a good time analyzing my pathology about that one*, he thought, as he walked over to hand Klara a glass of wine.

Thankfully, Klara seemed preoccupied, and the journal looked like it hadn't been disturbed. "Do you remember the first time I met the Coles?" Klara asked. "I'll give you a hint. Your mother got smashed, really sloppy drunk. Does that ring any bells?"

"No, not really, though it seems to be happening more and more frequently of late."

"What does?" asked Klara.

"My mother. She seems to be drinking a lot. Anyway, why do you ask? Did something else happen that evening?" Thomas said with a smile. He remembered the night well. It was the first time they had ever made love. He thought of the note in the journal, and his smile faded.

Klara was about to say more, to remind Thomas that they had consummated their marriage that night, when Beulah knocked on the door to tell them that the Coles had arrived.

The first time Klara had sat at the table with the judge and Dorthea, she had been six weeks pregnant with Tommy. Klara could not believe how quickly the years had passed and that she was now sitting across from her nineteen-year-old son, watching him dig enthusiastically into his first course. Tommy would be heading back to school in the morning and perhaps, if Thomas could ever find it in his heart to forgive her, the two of them could talk to Tommy together and explain why Klara had lied to everyone for so many years.

Would any of them really understand what people like me endured during the war? The horror and terror were so pervasive; they diluted people's sense of right and wrong. The only thing that had mattered then was survival for her baby. As Klara took in her son's features, she silently told him she was sorry and prayed he would forgive her.

Fortunately for everyone, the dinner passed without too much drama. Eugenia drank too much, but managed to not say anything outrageous. The judge and Dorthea made their excuses only a few minutes after finishing dessert.

"Tommy, are you all packed? Do you need any help getting your clothes together?" Klara asked.

"Sure, Mom that would be great," Tommy said. Klara was delighted that she could also leave the table early. She and Tommy headed upstairs.

"So, Thomas, how are you and Klara getting along these days?" Eugenia asked after everyone had left the dining room.

"Fine, Mother. Why do you ask? You always seem to have an ulterior motive to your questions."

"No, no reason at all. It's just...Klara seems a little distant these days. Surely you've noticed."

"Residual pain, I think, from the accident," said Thomas. "She won't admit to it, but I know she still feels it. And maybe if you were a little nicer to her.... Oh, never mind. It's too late to try and mend that particular fence. I think I'll have a nightcap in my study. Good night, Mother."

"Yes, have a good night, Thomas," said Eugenia. He left her sitting at the head of a very empty table.

Klara was already asleep by the time Thomas made his way upstairs. He had not wanted to go up too soon. Since the accident, Klara and Tommy had reconnected. They had spent countless hours together over the summer. Thomas was more than a little jealous. He loved his son, but they had so little in common. Lately he really felt like the odd man out. He was envious of the time they spent together, and was not the least bit sad that Tommy's summer break was over.

When he finally walked into the bedroom, Klara was asleep. Thomas took a moment to stare at her supine form. She looked absolutely beautiful and Thomas couldn't take his eyes off of her. He recognized that his obsession, his need to have her, had not abated over the years. For one brief moment he wondered what his life would have been like without her. Quickly, he shoved that thought aside and slipped into bed.

TWENTY EIGHT

Klara dressed early for her meeting with John. She was ready to go a full hour before they were scheduled to meet. She had chosen an out-of-the-way café never frequented by Eugenia or any of her friends.

Outside of Sam and Lotte, Klara had never discussed her wartime experiences with anyone. It would be difficult to do so with a total stranger. At the restaurant, Klara asked for a corner table in the back, hoping the location would afford them a small bit of privacy. From Sam's description, Klara recognized John immediately, and waved to him from where she was sitting. John's meaty hand was already outstretched as he made his way toward her.

"Sam wasn't kidding. You are one beautiful lady."

"Thank you," answered a blushing Klara, who really wasn't sure how to respond. This was not a social call for her. This was her chance to make Reinhardt Frank pay for the deaths of her loved ones, and she was not in the mood for small talk. "Mr. Lassiter," she began.

"John. Please call me John."

"Okay, John. I want to begin by explaining how difficult it is for me to discuss my time as Frank's prisoner. I was still in my teens. He did unspeakable things to me for over two years. I also want to say, though, that I will testify only if you truly believe you can win this case, destroy his reputation, and deport him. You may think me selfish, but...well, when my husband finds out I have lied to him all these years, he will probably divorce me. And when my son finds out I have deceived him about his parentage, I may lose him as well. He may not forgive me. So, as you can see, for me the stakes are very high."

"I understand. I'm sorry if you thought I was making light of your situation. I was trying to put you at ease, but I truly did not mean to offend you," said John. "Your courage is inspiring, and I assure you that I will do my utmost to make sure Reinhardt Frank answers for the crimes he committed. So, shall we get started?"

"I'm not sure I know where to begin," said Klara.

"Sam told me some of what you endured, but I'd like to hear the story of your experiences in your own words," said John. "Tell me everything you remember. Even something minor may prove important."

Taking a sip of water, Klara began. "My mother, brother, and I were captured by the Gestapo in Paris. Following our arrest, the French citizens who were helping with our escape were rounded up, and I never saw any of them again. My family was handed over to the SS, who took us to their headquarters on Avenue Foch and threw us into a cell. It was there that Reinhardt Frank first saw me. He, too, thought I was beautiful," Klara said, looking directly at John. "At that moment, our fates were sealed. I did not realize it at the time, but my brother and mother were already doomed. Frank brought me to his office and promised to spare my family if I came willingly to his home. I was so naïve, a child. I know now that he would have taken me regardless; I had no power, no real choice. It was all a game to him. But I thought I was saving them," added Klara, crying silently. "Stupid, I was so stupid."

Klara continued for another hour, describing in detail the beatings and sexual abuse she endured at the hands of Frank. "Finally, suddenly, it was over. The Allies were approaching Paris, and Frank had to get out. By that time, I sensed that Mama and Ernst were dead. I had not heard from them in over a year. I never asked Frank. In my heart, I already knew the answer. He and the other Nazis who worked with him scurried about, bumping into each other in their hurry to destroy any incriminating documents. We prisoners were ordered to help, and we did, even though we knew our days were numbered. And then he was gone. I never saw him again. We were—I believe there were five of us in total at the end—marched to the station and loaded onto the last transport going east."

When John was certain that Klara was finished, he described to her what the Justice Department had in evidence against Frank.

"So what it comes down to it this," John said. "Frank's forged documents are state-of-the-art. He will have his experts, and we will have ours. We have a lot of little pieces of evidence, but without your testimony, it will be difficult for us to prove he is a war criminal."

"What happens if my testimony is still not enough? Can he come after me?"

"We can protect you, of course, but I think he'd be a fool to risk it. It would be like confessing."

"But what if I testify, destroying my relationship with my husband and son, and it is still not enough?"

"Klara, I'll be honest with you. There are no guarantees. We do, however, have an ace in the hole," said John. "We think we have another credible witness. Sam is pretty sure he's located Frank's former wife. She lives pretty much off the radar in a small town near the Swiss border. She calls herself Gertrude List."

"Gertrude.... I remember, that was her given name. He used to call her Trudy. She came to visit regularly, but she never stayed long."

"Sam is on his way to Germany as we speak. He caught a flight early this morning. We have no idea how she feels about her husband or whether she'll see Sam. We don't know if she is aware that Frank is still alive, or under what circumstances they came to be separated," said John. "So, Klara. There you have it. I've told you everything I know."

"No, John, you haven't. Where is Frank living now, and what he is doing? I hope he is living a miserable life in fear and poverty."

John had hoped to avoid telling Klara, at least at the moment, about Reinhardt Frank of today. There were no adjectives to describe how unjust it was that someone responsible for the deaths of thousands of men, women, and children was living in a penthouse in the nation's capital, running a profitable business, and welcomed into the homes of powerful people. But Klara needed to know; he recognized that. He just wished he didn't have to be the one to tell her.

"Klara, there is no way I can sugarcoat this. Frank is a successful businessman. He apparently came to the United States with money, and he has done very well in the real estate market. He has not remarried, perhaps because he is still married to Gertrude and did not want to draw any attention to his legal status," said John. "He has had numerous girlfriends over the years, a few long-term relationships, but nothing has lasted more than a couple of years. He's a generous contributor to a number of charities and is invited, although he rarely attends, to all of the galas sponsored by the nonprofits he supports. He keeps a low profile."

"I would very much like to change that," said Klara. "I hope by the time we are through, his face and his crimes will be known everywhere."

John and Klara parted ways in the parking lot of the restaurant. John promised he would call Lotte as soon as he heard from Sam. Lotte would then get word to Klara. Klara made it clear that she didn't want any suspicious telephone calls coming into the Compton home until she could tell Thomas about her past. She admitted that while revealing all was now inevitable, the thought of doing so made her physically ill.

Nevertheless, John left the luncheon feeling optimistic. He was convinced Klara would make a very credible and sympathetic witness. If Sam is able to convince Gertrude Frank to testify, too…. *I shouldn't get ahead of myself*, thought John. *One step and one witness at a time.*

TWENTY NINE

The nine-hour flight from Washington to Frankfurt, Germany, was grueling. Sam had hoped to sleep, but was too wound up to catch more than a catnap. His thoughts were always about Klara. The strain she was under had to be agonizing. He yearned to be with her, to comfort her. Instead, once he landed, he had another three-hour drive to the city of Freiberg, where Gertrude Frank now lived. Sam's contact in Germany, Joseph Strauss, had spent the last several weeks keeping an eye on her.

Unlike her former husband, Gertrude was proving to be rather reclusive. She rarely had visitors and ventured out only to ride her bicycle to the market. Sam didn't want to spook her, so a nighttime surprise visit was out of the question. Besides, he was exhausted and wanted to look and feel his best when he and Joseph arrived at Frau Frank's doorstep in the morning.

When Sam finally arrived at the Zum roten Bären, Freiberg's oldest hotel, Joseph was waiting for him in the lobby. "I didn't expect you until morning," said Sam.

"Ach, I know, but I wanted to greet you and take you to dinner before you retire to your room," said Joseph. He relieved Sam of his bag and ushered him into the hotel's charming dining room. Before they were even seated, Joseph took the liberty of ordering a good German beer for both of them. He then squeezed his wide girth into one of the fragile chairs Sam hoped would not collapse under the strain. "Do not worry," Joseph said with a smile, as if reading his mind. "The chairs are stronger than they look. You should order the Schnitzel, by the way. It is excellent."

Sam was grateful and delighted that Joseph would act as translator. He was not only an affable dinner partner but as dedicated to hunting and punishing war criminals as Sam. "So, tomorrow we find out why Frau Frank no longer lives with Reinhardt."

"Yes. I will meet you for breakfast here at eight-tomorrow morning, and after that we will drive to Frau Frank's cottage. It is only a mile or so from here," said Joseph.

"Perfect. What have you learned about her?" asked Sam.

"She moved to Freiberg in the 1950s and took up residence in the small house she lives in to this day. Allied bombs destroyed Freiberg during the war, and many of the locals were surprised when a lone woman arrived and purchased one of few houses still standing. The cottage she moved into had suffered some damage, but over the years she single-handedly completed the repairs and, at least from the out-side, it is an enchanting little place—a Hansel and Gretel type of dwell-ing. The residents believe I am a tourist using Freiberg as my base for day trips into the Black Forest and surrounding attractions. I hired a guide to take me on a tour of the city. He was the one who pointed out Frau Frank's home and recounted the story of the mystery woman who moved to Freiberg after the war."

One beer with Joseph was followed by two more, and soon Sam was feeling the effects of too much alcohol and not enough sleep. "I look forward to learning more about our mystery woman," said Sam, "but for now I must admit that I am more interested in meeting my pillow."

"Of course. Until tomorrow, then, my friend," said Joseph.

After breakfast the next morning, Joseph drove them to Frau Frank's quaint cottage. He parked the car on the street a few meters away from Gertrude's home. Sam was anxious to hear her story, and hoped she would be willing to speak with them. More important, he hoped that she would be able and willing to corroborate Klara's testimony against Reinhardt.

The door opened before they had a chance to knock.

"I was looking out the window and saw you walking toward my home. Since I am the only house at the end of this road, I assumed you were coming to see me," said Gertrude Frank, speaking in very precise English.

"We're here to..." Sam began.

"I know exactly why you are here. Would you like to come in, or do you want to speak about the war crimes of Reinhardt Frank on my front stoop?"

"Yes, thank you," Sam muttered, astonished at Gertrude's directness. "We would definitely like to come in. Thank you for seeing us."

"It seems you have given me little choice in the matter, as you are already here. Come in, I believe we have much to discuss. Give me a moment to make some coffee, or do you prefer tea?"

"Coffee is fine," said Joseph and Sam in unison.

"So, where should we begin?" asked Frau Frank, once she poured the coffee and placed mouthwatering breakfast pastries in front of her guests.

"I am afraid you have us at a loss," said Sam. "Why do you think we are here?"

"Oh, don't be foolish. This is no time for games. You are here because you would like to arrest my husband for war crimes, no?"

"No. I mean yes, that is exactly why we are here, but how do you know that?"

"An American man in a suit visits me, with a translator in tow, just in case? The conclusion is logical. Let us get started. I am eager to see the bastard punished," said Frau Frank. "Where is he, by the way?"

"He's in America—Washington, D.C. to be exact."

"That is unfortunate. As with Eichmann, I had hoped his only option was Argentina. He would have hated South America," Gertrude said with a grim smile. "As soon as the war was over, he walked out on me, and I lost track of him. I have not seen nor spoken to him in twenty years. Oh, what an idiot I was! I truly loved him in the beginning. Ach, I was so young, and he was so handsome. I was a member of the Bund Deutscher Mädel, the girls' equivalent of the Hitler Youth. My parents begged me not to join, but since all of my friends were bragging about the handsome young men they were meeting, I joined without their permission. I met Reinhardt at one of our joint gatherings and was immediately smitten. He was several years older than I and seemed so sophisticated. Ah, and how dashing he looked in his uniform! Every Deutscher Mädel desired him."

"But he chose you," said Sam, to allow Frau Frank a moment to sip her coffee and take a breath. She seemed eager to continue, however.

"Ha. Yes. I should have realized he was not after me for my beauty. You see, there was a slight flaw in his lineage. He had a great-grandmother who was Jewish, but my family tree was pure Aryan, no imperfections. I was the ideal match for someone like him who hoped to continue his advancement in the Schutzstaffel. Much to my parents' chagrin, we married when I was only sixteen years old. My parents considered Hitler nothing more than a buffoon, and were passionate in their hatred of the Nazis. They never really forgave me. Perhaps, if I had been able to give them a grandchild...but unfortunately for them, and for Reinhardt's career, he and I were never able to conceive together. He hoped I would be honored with the Nazi Party's coveted Mother's Cross, awarded for producing at least five children for the Third Reich. When I could not give him even one, he grew tired of me. It never occurred to him, of course, that it might be *his* fault."

She gazed out the window, apparently lost in some memory she did not share. "He happily accepted the posting to France. After 1942, I saw him only for the short periods of time when I was allowed to visit him in Paris."

"Frau Frank?" said Sam.

"Please, call me Gertrude or Frau List. I took back my maiden name years ago."

"Gertrude, it's that time, the period of your visits to Paris, that we are most interested in hearing about just now," said Sam. "There was a girl, not quite eighteen years old, working in Frank's home when he was stationed in Paris."

"Klara," said Gertrude, in a voice barely above a whisper. "Klara," she said, louder. "Yes, I remember Klara quite well. She is one of the reasons for my penance—why I have imprisoned myself in this town, in this cottage, seeing and speaking to no one. You see, I knew what he was doing to her. I saw the bruises on her cheeks, the marks on her arms. I remember the way she looked at me for help. I did nothing for her. I have always wondered if she survived."

"Yes, Klara is very much still alive," said Sam. "She will be testifying in his trial. Klara will be asked to identify Frank as the man who sent her mother and brother to Drancy, and who perpetrated heinous acts against her own person while she worked as a prisoner in his Paris home. We need you to corroborate her identification of Frank. We need you to testify against him."

"I can do more than testify," said Gertrude. "After the war, everything was in chaos. Berlin, the city...well, you remember. Streets were no longer streets. All was in rubble. I was born in Berlin, and I would not have known how to find my own home. I was one of the fortunate few. We knew the end was near, and I found relative safety with my parents at their country house in Bavaria. Reinhardt, always the strategist, was able to stay one step ahead of the Russians, and made it out of Berlin. He arrived at my family's doorstep wearing the uniform of a private in the Werhmacht, the regular army. My parents tried to bar him from coming in, but his weapon held to my head convinced them otherwise. At our home, he changed to civilian clothing belonging to my father, stole as much jewelry, art, and silver as he could afford to ship, and left. Unfortunately, for him, he left behind the documents that he had left in my care when we were still together. I saved them, all these years, hoping that someday they might prove useful. Perhaps they will help absolve me from my complacency, for doing nothing for Klara, Reinhardt's other prisoners, and for so many others."

While Joseph studied the documents, Sam explained the legal process of bringing Frank to trial, as well as Gertrude's role in the proceedings. He was pleased. Gertrude would be a formidable witness. The documents she produced, including ones bearing the names of Gisela and Ernst Werner, had all been signed by Frank, and were proof of his culpability in the deportations of Jews from Paris. "Thank you, Frau List," said Sam, shaking Gertrude's hand. I cannot wait to see Frank's face when you walk into the courtroom."

"Nor can I," said Gertrude. "I only wish my parents had lived to see me finally accept responsibility for joining him, and for refusing to acknowledge and take responsibility for what was going on all around me."

"I'm a believer in God," said Joseph. "And I believe that even now your parents will know how you have redeemed yourself. Auf Wiedersehen, Frau List. We will be in touch."

"Yes, I expect you will."

The drive back to the hotel lasted only a few minutes. While Joseph arranged his own transportation to the United States, Sam bounded up the four flights of steps to his room, anxious to call John and Lotte to tell them the news.

"We got him!" Sam cried, the minute John picked up the telephone. "She's agreed to testify. And we've got hard evidence, documents, to back it all up!"

THIRTY

Two days after interviewing Gertrude List, Sam was back in Washington, preparing for the arrest of Reinhardt Frank for immigration violations. He had not spoken to Klara, and hoped she would call him. He knew she would need his moral support in the days ahead and feared that the toll of telling her husband about her past would prove too much for her. As Sam sat at his desk, ruminating over Klara, he glanced through the mail that had piled up while he was in Germany. Tossing all of the junk in the nearby trashcan, he almost missed it: among the fliers and advertisements was a letter, handwritten and addressed to him personally. He opened it and started to read.

> *Dear Mr. Rosstein:*
>
> *By the postmark, I see your letter came to my home several months back, and I would like to apologize for not replying sooner. Unlike most of the nurses who were discharged after the war, I chose to stay in the military. I have just returned from Vietnam following a six-month deployment, and I am finally catching up with all of my correspondence.*
>
> *I was pleasantly surprised to hear from you after all these years. I have often thought of you and Klara, the young beautiful woman who survived the camps. I hoped*

she found some peace and ended up having a good life. She was always so sad.

I clearly remember the day you gave me the letter because the next day I was reassigned, and I never had the chance to ask Klara if she received it. I understand from your letter that the note was never delivered to her. I am sorry I did not hand it to her directly but the wards were overwhelmed that day by an influx of survivors from yet another of the camps. When I spoke with Dr. Compton, he said he was on his way over to Klara's area, so I asked if he would deliver your note. He said he would be happy to deliver it for me. It's odd he forgot to give it to her. I told him it was from the soldier who had proposed to her, the one she planned to marry, and stressed how important it was that she receive it, as you had been redeployed in the middle of the night.

I hope this helps in your search for some answers as to where Klara went and why she disappeared in those chaotic few months at the end of the war.

Sincerely,

Colonel Shirley Mosley

Sam couldn't believe it. With everything going on, including the imminent arrest of Reinhardt Frank, Sam had totally forgotten about the inquiries he made months earlier. *The bastard*, he thought. *He really did orchestrate everything. He knew she loved me, and he convinced her I wasn't coming back.* Sam sat at his desk and tried to absorb the implications of what he had just discovered. He was now sure that Compton had manipulated Klara, and he suspected that the well-connected doctor had also had something to do with the unexpected orders commanding his unit to move out suddenly. Sam had lost everything because of him. He lost Klara and all those years watching his boy grow up. He had to find a way to speak to her.

It had been two days since Klara heard the good news from John. She was thrilled that Gertrude Frank had agreed to testify against Reinhardt.

She wondered what she was like, how she was getting on, and how it would feel to see her again. John had told her that Justice was ready to make an arrest, and Klara knew the dreaded conversation with Thomas would finally need to happen.

As big as it was, the Compton home offered little in the way of privacy. With Eugenia creeping about, Klara never knew what was being overheard, but she was determined to tell Thomas without her mother-in-law present. She suggested to Thomas that the two of them go out to an intimate restaurant they liked in one of Atlanta's new burgeoning suburbs. Thomas agreed immediately. It had been months since they had spent a quiet evening together.

In Washington, Sam's pacing was wearing a hole in the office carpet. He needed to speak with Klara, but he didn't dare compromise her situation by calling the Compton residence. His only option was to call Lotte. For the next ten minutes Sam dialed her number and was met by the relentless annoyance of a busy signal. Over the next half hour Lotte's number continued to ring busy, and Sam had to restrain himself from throwing the phone against the wall. *Damn it*, he thought. *In one more minute, I'm going to call the operator and have her break into her conversation.* At last, the call went through.

"Finally!" blurted out Sam.

"Excuse me, but who is this?" said Lotte.

"It's Sam! I'm sorry, Lotte. I know I sound like an ass, but you were on the phone *forever* and I have to get a hold of Klara before she discloses anything to Thomas. Do you have any idea where she is?"

"Oh, Sam. I'm afraid you're too late. They're on their way to dinner and Klara is planning to tell Thomas everything tonight."

"Lotte, I know I'm asking a lot. Hell, I've already asked you too much, but you're my only hope," said Sam. "Please, Lotte, try and find her and ask her to wait until I get there. I'm on the first flight from D.C. in the morning, and I can meet her whenever and wherever she says."

"Sam, I can't promise, but I'll try."

"Lotte, that's all I'm asking. Thank you, I'll be waiting in my office for your call."

Lotte dialed the Compton house, hoping Klara and Thomas had not yet left, but Eugenia replied curtly that they were out for the evening. Without even saying goodbye, Lotte hung up, grabbed her purse, and went straight to her car. The restaurant was located north of Atlanta in one of the new suburban areas being developed to meet the growing housing needs. It would take her at least thirty minutes to get there.

When Klara and Thomas arrived at the restaurant, their table wasn't ready. The hostess suggested they wait in the lounge. "So, reservations don't matter to your establishment," barked Thomas, glaring at the hostess.

As the startled hostess glared back, Klara apologized for her husband, then led him by the hand into the bar. "What in heaven's name has gotten into you?" Klara asked. "That was so rude. I could have sworn I heard your mother's voice coming out of your mouth."

"You're right, I'm sorry. I've just been feeling edgy lately. We've spent so little time together, and I wanted tonight to be perfect."

Shaken by Thomas's hopes for the evening, Klara was relieved when the drinks they ordered arrived, and she was able to take a couple of sips of vodka to calm her nerves. Looking at Thomas, who was oblivious to the real reason she had suggested dining out, Klara was once again struck by how innocent and trusting he could be at times. *How am I ever going to do this?* As Thomas prattled on about hospital gossip and an irritating patient, Klara was thankful that a few uh huhs and nods of her head were enough for him to think she was listening.

"It's already been thirty minutes and we still don't have our table," said Thomas, looking at his watch. "I'm going to go speak with the hostess."

"Thomas...?"

"Don't worry," he said with a wink. "I'll try not to bite her head off. I promise."

Once Thomas left to harass the hostess, Klara motioned to the bartender and ordered a second round of drinks. The first vodka had calmed her nerves; she hoped the second would numb her enough to get through the evening. Thomas was shaking his head as he ambled back to the table. "She said ten to fifteen more minutes. Can you believe it?"

"It's nice sitting here in the lounge. I don't mind, really," said Klara. "As long as we have a few minutes, I think I'll go freshen up." As she stood and slipped off the stool, she saw Thomas watching her appreciatively in the mirror behind the bar.

"You're still as beautiful as the day I met you," he said. "I'm one lucky man."

In the ladies room, Klara placed a wet towel behind her neck and tried to calm down. *Can I actually do this? Can I really say something that might destroy this man?* Looking up from the sink at her reflection, Klara could find no trace of the carefree girl she once was. *Perhaps, after tonight, I will finally be unburdened,* she thought. Still staring into the mirror, Klara did not hear the door swing open or notice the woman rushing toward her until she was almost upon her.

"Klara, thank goodness...!"

"Lotte, I almost had a heart attack! What in the world are you doing here?"

"Klara, I hate to tell you to stop talking, but stop talking. I only have a minute before Thomas sends out the troops to look for you. I'm on a covert mission for Sam. I've been standing outside for about ten minutes, feeling like a fool, peering through the window," said Lotte. "When I saw Thomas alone in the bar, I snuck past him and followed you into the ladies room. Sam called about forty minutes ago and asked, no begged me to deliver a message. I swear, Klara, I have never driven so fast in my entire life!"

"What's the message?"

"Have you said anything at all to Thomas about...you know?"

"No, I was hiding in here, trying to work up the courage."

"Good, good. Sam has new information. He wouldn't tell me what it was, but he's convinced that it will affect what and how you tell Thomas. He's flying to Atlanta in the morning."

"And you have no idea what he's talking about?" asked Klara."

"No, but he sounded desperate for you to hold off telling Thomas anything."

"Okay," said Klara without hesitation. "I'll wait until I see Sam, and speak with Thomas tomorrow. I'm actually relieved. Maybe whatever he has to say will give me the courage I need. And, Lotte—thanks for breaking the speed limit for me. You're a special friend."

"I love you, too," said Lotte. They hugged. Lotte waited near the bathroom until Thomas was distracted enough that she could slip out of the restaurant. Klara walked back to the table thankful that she could protect her husband from being hurt, at least for one more night.

THIRTY ONE

Sam hopped out of the taxi, and raced up Lotte's walkway. Klara was already pulling open the door, having spotted the approaching car as it came to a stop. "You're here," she cried, as she stepped outside into Sam's awaiting arms. Burying her face in Sam's shoulder, Klara held tightly to the man she had loved for most of her lifetime.

"Why don't you two move your reunion into the house?" Lotte called out. "My neighbors don't need anything else to gossip about."

"Gladly," said Sam with a wink, as he took hold of Klara's hand and escorted her inside.

"Sam, every time I see you I think it's a miracle. You were lost to me for so long."

"I'm here now, and I have something to show you. Why don't we sit down?"

"You are acting very mysterious," said Klara. She sat down on the sofa. "What on earth do you have that could be so important that you had to fly here at once?"

"Klara remember when we spoke the night before your accident?"

"Of course."

"When we met that night, I told you I believed that Thomas manipulated us in some way. I always thought it was strange that my unit was suddenly given new orders, and that the note I left for you mysteriously disappeared."

"Yes, I remember."

"Klara, after your accident, once I knew you were going to be okay, I did some digging," said Sam. "I tracked down the nurse, the one I gave the note to that morning. She wasn't too difficult to locate; she's actually still in the army. Anyway, I got a response." He retrieved the letter from his briefcase and handed it to Klara.

While Klara read, Sam and Lotte took seats on either side of her. "Thomas! My god, you're right! Thomas orchestrated *everything*!" She crumpled the letter in her hands. "If I had gotten this, I would have waited for you," she said turning to Sam. "We would have had a life together. We *should* have had a life together! You should have had a life with Tommy." With her head buried in her hands, Klara began to sob. Lotte encouraged her to let it all out, patting her. Sam took Klara in his arms and comforted her.

For the next several minutes, Klara cried for the life that could have been, of years wasted with a man she did not love, and for the pain of having her son denied the joy of knowing his real father. When her tears subsided, Lotte quietly left the room to make everyone a much-needed cup of tea, and to give Sam and Klara a chance to be alone.

"Klara," Sam implored. "Klara, look at me. Let me help you."

"I have been such a fool," whispered Klara as she slowly raised her tear-stained face to look at Sam.

"Klara, no...you were manipulated by a master. I probably was, too. I haven't been able to prove it yet, but I know he had something to do with my orders being changed."

"Sam, do you really believe that? Could Thomas be capable of something so horrible? Changing your orders put you in harm's way. Sam, you would never have been shot, never have lost your leg." With that realization Klara began to cry once again.

"Please, Klara stop. Listen to me. Do you know what this means? You're finally free. You've spent half of your life guilt-ridden about how you tricked poor innocent Thomas. He wanted you to believe he was selfless. He needed to be your savior. It was always Dr. Compton to the rescue...but it was all a lie, Klara, a lie."

Sensing that the tenor of their conversation had shifted, Lotte walked back into the room with a tray laden with a steaming hot pot of tea and enough small pastries to feed the entire neighborhood. "I thought some of my homemade sweets might make Klara feel a little better."

"I don't know about Klara, but I'm willing to test out your theory," said Sam as he popped one of Lotte's rugelach into his mouth. "Hmm, I'm not sure I feel better yet. I may have to eat a few more." Stuffing a few more into his mouth and barely able to speak, Sam motioned for Klara to try one. Sam's performance already had Lotte smiling, and soon Klara could no longer suppress her own grin as she saw the look of anticipation on both of their faces.

"Okay, okay. I'll try one," said Klara as she popped a tiny filled pastry into her mouth. "It's amazing," she said with a smile.

"See, I told you so," said Sam, taking Klara into his arms once again.

"What now?" asked Klara, when she finally felt ready to talk.

"Now it gets a little easier. We go to your home, and we confront Thomas together. You aren't alone, Klara. I'll be with you every minute."

"Thomas is working," said Klara. "He won't be home till after six o'clock, and there is something I need to do before he gets there. I'm not certain, but I believe he kept your letter all these years, and I may know where it is."

"Well, if that's the case he's either very stupid, or very sure of himself."

"Trust me, Sam. Thomas is not stupid."

Klara and Sam spent the next several minutes discussing how best to confront Thomas with their newfound information. Sam didn't want Klara to go back to the Compton house without him, but understood that his presence would undermine her search for the letter by alarming Eugenia. The plan was to meet back at Lotte's at five, and then to drive to the Compton home together.

Sam had learned that morning from John Lassiter that the arrest of Reinhardt Frank was imminent, and if he wanted to be in on the action he needed to get back to Washington as soon as possible. He told Klara that he was hoping that Klara would go with him, as he didn't feel right leaving her in Atlanta, and he wanted them to be together when Frank was arrested. The big unknown was Tommy. Klara thought that she should probably drive to Athens to break the news and explain the circumstances, to try and help him comprehend that everything she had done over the last twenty or so years had been for him.

When Klara pulled into the driveway, she was relieved when she saw that the garage that housed Eugenia's Lincoln was empty. She went directly to Thomas's study, the room where she and her husband had so often shared after-dinner drinks. She rarely spent time there without him, and it was a strange sensation to be snooping through his personal belongings and mementos. Thomas's books were arranged by subject, and Klara knew exactly where he shelved his wartime diaries. She clearly remembered the evening she had unexpectedly walked in on him holding a tattered piece of paper in his hands.

Thomas knew that Klara hated discussing the war and avoided reading anything about it, so he would have known that his collection of journals would make a logical hiding place. As Klara was pulling volumes off the shelf, she heard the unmistakable sound of the garage door announcing her mother-in-law's return. Working as quickly as possible, Klara continued her methodical search. Just as she was about to give up, she found one more journal tucked in behind the others. Suddenly, the letter Sam had tried to deliver to her so many years ago was in her hands.

Wanting nothing more than to leave the house without confronting Eugenia, Klara walked quietly outside, leaving the discarded volumes strewn across the floor. There was no point in hiding her discovery. Regardless of whether she tidied up or not, Thomas would know she had discovered the truth soon enough.

With the letter tucked safely away in her handbag, Klara raced back to Lotte's and the safety of Sam's arms. "I found it!" sang out a jubilant Klara as she raced up the walkway and flung open Lotte's door. "Sam, it's true—he held onto it all these years." Klara pulled the note from her bag and handed it to Sam, who once again read the letter he had penned on an early rainy morning in the waning days of World War II.

Reading the letter together had a profound effect on Sam and Klara. They understood the circuitous route their lives had taken when the quickly scribbled note had been intercepted and never delivered. "Sam, you know I would have never left."

"I know, Klara. I know."

THIRTY TWO

When Thomas arrived home, he noticed that Klara's car was not parked in its usual spot in the driveway. Expecting her shortly, he continued to his study, and sat down with a drink in hand to enjoy a moment of solitude. Within minutes the door opened, but instead of Klara, his mother walked into the room.

"I'll have whatever you're having," drawled Eugenia, taking a seat in a comfortable chair across from her son. "Where's your lovely wife? She's usually home by now."

"I'm sure she'll be here in a few minutes," said Thomas.

"I must have just missed seeing her," said Eugenia. "My bridge game ended early, and I was only in the house for a few minutes when I saw that little red car of Klara's tearing down the driveway. Really Thomas, I do think she drives too fast. She already caused one terrible accident."

"Mother, please, just stop. I've had a long day." Getting up to refresh their drinks, Thomas noticed some of his beloved books spread across the floor. As Thomas stared at the half empty shelf, it finally registered that the hidden journal was also in the pile. His gut-wrenching scream startled Eugenia enough that she spilled her eighth drink of the day all over her silk blouse.

"Are you nervous?" asked Sam as they neared the Compton home.

"Yes, very," Klara said. "All these years being married to Thomas, and I am now not sure if I ever really knew him. In a way, I always felt

222

responsible for his happiness. 'Saint Thomas' is how I used to think of him; I thought he martyred himself for me. I had no idea he manipulated me from the very beginning. So yes, I am nervous. But I am also furious and more than a little sad. For whatever reason, Thomas decided to play God, changing the course of so many lives."

"He saw something he wanted and he took it," said Sam. "He grew up in a world that told him that he was entitled—that he deserved the best, the most beautiful things in the world—and that included you."

"I know you won't agree, but I have to accept my own complicity in everything that happened after you left. Thomas may have intercepted your letter, but he didn't force me to marry him. I did that all on my own and I will have to live with that knowledge for the rest of my life," said Klara. "Now, for Tommy's sake, I wish I had been stronger."

"Klara..."

"No, Sam. I know you are going to try and tell me that I was young and traumatized by all of my experiences. That may mitigate some of my guilt, but it does not make me innocent. Once I was settled, once I was secure in my life as Mrs. Thomas Compton, I grew too selfish to put you or our son first. I should have told the truth regardless of the consequences. Tommy had a right to know, and so did you." Klara had been so somber throughout the ride that Sam was surprised when she suddenly looked up with a big grin on her face. "I just thought of one exceptionally good thing coming out of all this."

"What, that the two of us can now be together?" said Sam.

"Well, there is that tiny little thing..." said a still-smiling Klara. "But I just realized that after today, I don't ever have to see Eugenia Compton again!"

THIRTY THREE

Klara used her key to enter the only home she had known since arriving in America. The house was uncharacteristically quiet. Klara suspected that Eugenia already sent Beulah home and that she and Thomas were waiting for her arrival. Drawing strength from Sam's strong grip on her hand, Klara led the way to the study. As soon as she entered, Klara knew that Thomas and Eugenia were more than a little drunk.

"Well, good evening, daughter-in-law. I was unaware you were bringing a guest for dinner. Unfortunately Beulah has already left for the evening...so...I'm afraid we are just eating leftovers tonight and there's barely enough for the three of us." Tottering up from her chair, Eugenia made her way over to Sam and Klara, who were still standing by the door. "Thomas, you are being ill-mannered," she said, turning to her son. "Please get up so our dear Klara can make introductions."

"I know who he is," muttered Thomas sotto voce.

"What did you say, Thomas? You know my hearing isn't what it used to be."

"I said, I *know* who he is."

"Then I must be the only one who has not met your acquaintance. I am Eugenia Compton," she announced, taking Sam by the arm and ushering him into to the room.

"Eugenia, this is Sam Rosstein," said Klara. "Thomas and I met him during the war."

"How nice to meet you, Mr. Rosstein. I was unaware that Klara kept up with anyone from those days."

"Mrs. Compton, it's likewise a pleasure. Would you mind giving Klara, Thomas, and me a few minutes alone? I promise we won't be long," said Sam.

"Mother, just stay put. And please, all of you, stop with the phony pleasantries," yelled Thomas. He got up from his chair and stepped toward Klara. Unsure of Thomas's state of mind, and protective of Klara, Sam moved in front of her, blocking Thomas's path.

"Get out of my way. And get out of my house!" roared Thomas. "You have no business being here!"

"Thomas, you should calm down," said Sam. "We both know I have *every* reason to be here. I located Shirley Mosley. Remember her? She was one of the nurses at the Evac Hospital in Buchenwald. She was the nurse, in fact, who I asked to give my letter to Klara when my unit was redeployed in the middle of the night. She entrusted you with that letter, and you promised to give it to Klara, but you never did."

"I don't know what you're talking about."

"You know exactly what I'm talking about. Klara and I were in love, and she agreed to marry me, but you let her think I'd run off and ditched her," said Sam. "What I'm not sure of is whether or not you had anything to do with changing my orders."

"Please, Thomas. Answer him," pleaded Klara. "He lost his leg because of those orders. Please tell me you weren't involved."

All color had drained from Thomas's face, and Klara instantly knew the truth.

"Klara, I...I did it for you, for us. You were too good for him. Don't you see that? I had to protect you."

"Oh my god, Thomas.... You deliberately sent him into harm's way! He could have been killed!"

"It would have been better for everyone if he had," said Thomas.

Without thinking, Klara walked the few steps that separated her from her husband and slapped him hard across the face. Staring at her hand, Klara realized that her debt to Thomas had finally been paid.

The sound of the slap had a resounding effect on Thomas, who clearly recognized that the marriage he had so carefully orchestrated and nurtured was over. "Klara, everything I did was for you! I needed to protect you. I married you, even though I knew Tommy wasn't my son."

"You knew?"

"Of course I knew. I'm a doctor, Klara. I'm not an idiot. You don't think I recognized the signs? But I pretended. All these years, I pretended."

For the past several minutes, Eugenia had been standing silently by, observing and listening to the secrets that were spilling forth. "What are you saying?" said Eugenia. "Tommy's not my grandson?"

"Eugenia, you are his grandmother in every way except biologically, I swear," said Klara. "He loves you, Eugenia. He adores you. Please don't turn away from him."

"Klara, Thomas, Mr. Rosstein...I'll leave the three of you to your sordid mess. I need to rest," said Eugenia as she carefully walked from the room.

"I'm sorry, Thomas. Even your mother didn't deserve to hear about Tommy like that. I know you've had too much to drink, and Sam is the last person you want to see in your home, but I need you to listen to me. You owe me that much," said Klara. "What you did to me, to Sam, is unforgivable. You took advantage of a young, frightened camp survivor, making me think I had been abandoned by the man I loved, and then stepping in to save me from an uncertain future. You knew you were my best chance of getting out of Europe and that I would fall for your savior act, that I would grasp your helping hand and hold on for dear life. Thomas, you played on my vulnerability and offered me hope. I felt indebted to you. I have felt indebted to you for the last nineteen years. I was a dutiful and loving wife because I thought I owed you everything."

Thomas sat silently, staring down into his drink.

"I have come to terms with my own complicity. I lived a life of deceit in this home and willingly acted a part in our personal Greek tragedy, because I kept my truth from you," said Klara. "The Nazis had taken everything from me not because my parents were political activists but because they were Jewish. I am Jewish. I did not think you would help

226

me if you knew. Over the years I thought about telling you the truth, but then you would make some comment, some distasteful anti-Semitic slur, and I was afraid you would hate me, too. All these years, I have lied to you, but more importantly, I lied to myself. Did you guess that too? Did you know I was Jewish when you complained about the Jews at work or the pushy ones who were trying to get into that precious country club of yours?"

"No, Klara, I didn't know. If I had…well, you're right," said Thomas. "It might have made a difference in how all this turned out."

"Thomas, what are you trying to say?"

"You figure it out, Klara. Or ask Sergeant Rosstein. Now, the two of you get out of here. I need to check on my mother."

For several minutes, Thomas sat quietly on the sofa, waiting for the sound of Klara's car pulling out of the driveway. It was only once he was sure they had left that he allowed himself to cry. He thought about the person he had been before he manipulated the chessboard and secretly moved all the pieces. He could vaguely remember the man who once possessed a proper moral compass, the man who had chosen to become a doctor to help others. For the first time, hearing Klara speak, he began to acknowledge his own guilt. He had hurt her then to help himself, and he had continued to live with the secret of his machinations for nearly two decades, even though he suspected it was tearing Klara apart.

He decided then to let Klara believe the worst of him. He decided to let her go.

THIRTY FOUR

Klara felt both relief and sorrow. So many times she had imagined revealing the truth to Thomas but in the end always lacked the courage to do so. In a way, she had loved Thomas, and she wanted to protect him from the pain and hurt of finding out the truth about Tommy. She was shocked to discover that he had always known that Tommy was not his son, because even though he and her child had shared few interests in common, Thomas had always treated him as a loving father. He had always made time for him, and been a definite presence in Tommy's life, cheering him on at tennis matches and swim meets, reading him tales of adventure late into the night.

"Do you think he loves Tommy?" a bewildered Klara asked Sam.

"Yes, Klara, he did, and I'm sure he still does. I was watching him the entire time you were talking. There was a change in his demeanor that I almost didn't catch," said Sam. "I believe he finally understood what he had done, and wanted you to leave without remorse. In the end he actually *was* thinking of you."

Sam and Klara had been driving for about ten minutes when Sam pulled over to the side of the road.

"Why are we stopping?" asked Klara."

"Because my dear, I can honestly say I have no idea where we're going. We have to regroup. I need to get back to D.C. John said they are planning to arrest Frank tomorrow. I should be there, but I don't want you going to see Tommy on your own," said Sam. "Come back with me, and I promise, after the arrest, we'll fly back to Atlanta and drive to the university together."

"Sam, we've waited all these years to be together. One more day is not going to matter to us...but it might to Tommy. I've thought this through. I need to be the one to tell him, and I think it's best I speak to Tommy alone," said Klara. "I have to try and explain, and honest to God, I have no idea how he'll react. I'm scared to death he'll never want to speak to me again. Meeting you at the same time will only make it more confusing. As much as I would like to be nearby when Frank is arrested, talking to Tommy is more important. There is, however, one insect in the ointment."

"Fly in the ointment, Klara. It's 'fly in the ointment.' What's the problem?"

"Yes, yes, whatever," she said. "Other than my handbag and the clothes on my back, everything I own is back at the house. So, if I could make a slight detour and find a store, I need to pick up a few things. Oh, and I just remembered a second fly in the ointment," Klara added with a smile. "I am a little short on cash."

THIRTY FIVE

After settling Klara into a room at a downtown Atlanta hotel, Sam caught the last flight out to D.C. "Glad you made it back. We'll be ready to roll in a couple of hours," said John when Sam walked into his office the following morning.

"Yeah, me too. Thanks for waiting. You know this means a lot to me."

Thus far, the Office of Special Investigations had managed to keep the investigation under wraps. But now that the arrest was imminent, John discreetly leaked the date and time of the arrest to a reporter from the *Washington Post*. The prosecution of one of D.C.'s social elite as a suspected Nazi war criminal was major news, and the Justice department wanted Frank's attorneys to be as busy salvaging his tarnished reputation as they would be at building his defense.

When Ronnie Frick answered the telephone, the last thing he expected to hear was the panicked voice of his chief of security announcing that agents from the Federal Bureau of Investigation had entered the building. After hanging up, Frick adjusted his tie and cufflinks, touched his hand to his perfectly coiffed hair, and waited for the knock on the door.

"Come in, gentlemen, come in. I usually see visitors by appointment, but in your case I have no doubt I need to make an exception," said Frick, concealing any trace of curiosity or concern about their unannounced visit.

"Reinhardt Frank, also known as Ronnie Frick, you are under arrest for violation of the immigration laws of the United States of America and for falsifying documents relating to said immigration," said the imposing figure of John Lassiter as he stepped in front of the two agents who had accompanied him and Sam.

Gentlemen, you have me at a loss. I do not know what you are accusing me of, but I legally entered the United States in 1949 and became a citizen of this great country of ours in 1956."

"You'll have plenty of time to mount your defense in the coming months, but for now, stop talking and come along with us quietly. I'm sure you'll make bond by this evening."

Frick turned to his secretary. "Vivian, call my attorney," he demanded. One of the agents produced a pair of handcuffs. "I'm obviously cooperating. Is that really necessary?"

"I'm afraid so," said John. "Regulations and all."

"You'll pay for this," said Frank as he held out his wrists. "I have friends in very high places."

"We'll see who will be paying for what," said John, as he and Sam followed Frank out of his office. "And I doubt your friends will want to help once they learn who you really are, and all you've done."

The group of men entered the lobby. Not expecting reporters or photographers, Frank failed to hide his face, and was bombarded by the flash of several cameras and a microphone thrust close to his face. Within hours he would see his own face sneering up from the front page of the *Post*'s evening edition, showing him in a rare unguarded moment as he glared menacingly into the camera. The photograph was picked up by UPI and syndicated in newspapers across the United States by the next day. Overnight he became a celebrity, albeit an infamous one. Reinhardt Frank's years of solitude and safety were over. He could never again hide behind the identity of Ronnie Frick. The press not only published the photograph, but also printed details about Frick's suspected identity and alleged war crimes.

The Office of Special Investigations team was ecstatic but realized that winning the opening round mattered little if the fight was lost. Days later, Frank answered the charges in an interview with a *Post* reporter. Categorically denying that he had falsified his identification papers in order to immigrate, Frank presented his documents so that they could be reproduced in their entirety. He also repeated the story he had told for years about his wartime past. He claimed that he, like so many others, had been a victim. He asserted that he had never joined the Nazi party but had instead resisted—and claimed that he had ultimately paid for that resistance by being interned in a camp, which he survived by sheer determination and a little bit of luck. "I decided early on that starvation was worse than being shot, so I took my chances and stole food, and that is how I survived," he was quoted as saying.

Sam and John were not troubled by Frank's denials. The passage of the Jencks Acts in 1957 had given federal prosecutors some leverage. They did not have to supply the defense with a list of potential witness or their statements until those witnesses testified on direct examination during the trial. As long as they were able to keep the identities of Klara and Gertrude hidden, they knew they had a reasonably good chance of winning.

A week after the arrest, Klara was due to arrive at Dulles airport in D.C. After coming back from Athens, she stayed at Lotte's for a few days. There she had struggled to accept the idea that Tommy never wanted to see her again. She had no idea how she had found the strength to drive back to Atlanta, so distraught had she been by the look on Tommy's face as it changed from bewilderment to disgust and then to rage. Fortunately, Sam had been right about Thomas. He did and always would love Tommy, and when Klara called and told Thomas how upset and angry Tommy was, her soon to be ex-husband had driven to the university immediately to talk to him. He promised to tell his son the truth about his own complicity in the twenty-year charade in which Tommy unknowingly participated. Thomas still hadn't told Klara he was sorry, but she hoped that someday he would.

Thomas had allowed Klara to go Compton house when Eugenia was out to pack up some clothes, photographs, and personal belongings.

Klara took only the barest of essentials, leaving behind all of the expensive gifts and jewelry Thomas had purchased for her over the years. She almost walked out of the room before remembering to unhook the strand of pearls that had graced her neck almost everyday since their purchase in 1945. With time, she hoped she and Thomas would stop being so angry toward each other, and someday find a way to forgive.

THIRTY SIX

On a hot muggy morning four months after the arrest, the case came to trial in the nation's capital. Although Klara would not be called to testify for several days, she had been a nervous wreck for months. While John acknowledged that the chances of Klara and Frank running into each other were slim to none, Justice Department officials still demanded Klara remain sequestered in an apartment they rented for her until the day of her testimony.

During the long wait, Klara tried to make amends with Tommy, but whenever she called him, he hung up the minute he recognized her voice. *If only I could see him!* But that was out of the question until the trial was over. Sam had been wonderful, bringing her all sorts of books and magazines to keep her occupied. Twice he had bent the rules and whisked her away to a drive-in movie theater across the border in Maryland. The irony of the situation did not escape her: she was a prisoner once again, while Frank was still enjoying his freedom.

Jury selections in the *United States v. Ronnie Frick/Reinhardt Frank* took the better part of three days. News of Frank's suspected past had been covered extensively in print and on television, and it was hard to find someone who had not already formed an opinion. Opening arguments were scheduled to begin in the late afternoon; Klara was warned that she would probably be called to testify the following day.

Sam had no role at the trial other than as an observer. His relationship with Klara could be interpreted as prejudicial, and John had been careful not to involve him in any of the proceedings. Sam hated sitting on the sidelines but understood the possible complications if the defense team tried to convince the jurors that Klara had been coached.

For the past three nights, Klara had bombarded Sam with questions the moment he walked through the door. Her fear of seeing Frank again had shaken Klara to the point where she almost imagined he had supernatural powers. With Klara's testimony scheduled for the next day, Sam decided to risk angering John, and spent the night at her place, but even Sam's presence could not calm her jitters.

Around three in the morning, Klara finally gave up trying to sleep. She needed some fresh air. Since taking a walk was out of the question, she settled for a sitting on her balcony. "I hope I didn't wake you," said Klara when, minutes later, Sam appeared.

"Nope, not even close," Sam said. "Didn't know if you wanted company. I won't be insulted, Scouts' honor."

"Oh, you and your Scouts' honor. Were you ever really a Boy Scout?"

"Yep, for one day. I hated the den mother. She had a big mole on her chin with one long hair sticking out, and to tell you the truth she scared me."

"So your entire scouting career was one day?"

"Scouts' honor," Sam said, holding up two fingers in the Boy Scout salute.

Smiling, Klara got up and curled her five-foot-six frame onto his lap. "You know I love you," she said. "I didn't think it was possible to love someone this much." Breathing in Klara's scent, Sam drew her in closer, and the two of them tried to forget, if for only a few minutes, the pain and suffering the trial would undoubtedly bring.

Finally falling asleep just before dawn, Klara could barely move when the alarm went off two hours later. In the bathroom mirror she took a moment to study her reflection. She had been only a few months shy of eighteen when she first met Reinhardt Frank. She had not changed all that much in the ensuing years. Would he still think of her as a young frightened child? The last time she had seen him he had been wearing his SS officer's uniform. Now he was finally being forced to answer for his crimes, and Klara was terrified she wouldn't be up to the task of challenging him. *What if they don't believe me?*

"Klara, are you almost ready?" asked Sam as he joined her in the bedroom and offered her a much-needed cup of coffee.

"That's a loaded question," answered Klara. "I'm not sure anyone could ever be ready for something like this. I'm terrified just to see him again. I really cannot believe the hold that monster still has over me."

"Klara, look at me. He is a man, nothing more. He has absolutely no power over you, and he cannot ever hurt you again. Do you believe me?"

"I'm trying, Sam," said Klara, reaching for her handbag and sweater.

"I know, darling. I know."

Throughout the jury selection process and opening arguments, Reinhardt Frank had conveyed the confident demeanor of an innocent man to all those present in the courtroom. No one, other than perhaps his long-dead mother or his estranged wife, would have noticed the slight change in expression that passed over his face when John Lassiter called Klara Werner Compton to the witness stand.

Klara's purposeful walk belied her nervousness. She was grateful to have the sweater draped over her shoulders to cover up the perspiration dripping down her back. After she was sworn in, Klara forced herself to look directly at the man who had flippantly sent her mother, brother, and countless others to their deaths. Plastic surgery had altered his appearance, but she would have known him anywhere. *Sam is right*, she thought. *Without the uniform, he is just a middle-aged man with thinning hair and a thickening waistline.*

Looking away, Klara tried to find Sam in the crowded courtroom, knowing that a nod of his head or the sight of his smile would give her the strength needed to get through the next several hours. Finally, she located him toward the back. His grin did give her courage, but she was equally encouraged—and shocked—to see Tommy and Thomas flanking Sam. When Sam realized that Klara had seen them, he placed an arm around Tommy's shoulder, indicating that a resolution between all three of the men in her life had somehow been reached. Lotte, sitting behind the trio, gave Klara a little wave and an encouraging smile.

John rose from his chair, and Klara steeled herself for his first question. She knew from her preparation that the first few hours of testimony would be spent answering questions about her family and her childhood in Berlin. As Klara spoke, the reminiscences from the poised and beautiful woman describing life in prewar Berlin soon captivated the jury. Klara became so lost in the retelling that she didn't notice the door to the courtroom swing open, or see that her mother-in-law had also taken a seat in the courtroom.

"Klara, when did life begin to change for you and your family?" John asked, when Klara reached the point in her story where it seemed appropriate to interrupt.

"Oh, there were changes right away, as early as 1933, when Hitler came to power. Jews were forced out of civil service jobs and university and judicial court positions. I was very young then, and since those particular laws did not affect me, I was probably not so aware of what was happening to some of my parents' friends," she said. "By 1937, we were further segregated from the rest of our fellow Germans. I could no longer attend public school or go to the theater or the cinema. I loved the movies and I missed them terribly," Klara added with a slight smile, prompting several members of the jury to offer her one back.

"But I have to admit, even with all those changes, I felt secure because I was just a child embraced by the love and security of my parents." Klara continued, sharing with the jury the events of the next several years. She described Kristallnacht, the Night of Broken Glass, which had precipitated the arrest of her father. She described how he had been beaten to death. She explained how her mother had eventually fled with Klara and Ernst to France, where the family managed to remain hidden until 1942, when they were captured by the Gestapo in Paris.

Klara's oratory had thus far not prompted any objections by Reinhardt's attorney. Other than periodically looking at his nails or jotting down a few notes, Frank stared at the witness dispassionately throughout her testimony. For her part, Klara followed the advice of John and Sam and purposely directed her statements toward the jury.

As the court recessed for lunch, Klara turned once more toward Frank and was unnerved when he looked back with the slightest of smiles.

Noticing the exchange, John led Klara quickly to a private area adjacent to the courtroom. Sam was already sitting inside when Klara walked in.

"Tommy is sitting with you? Sam, what in the world is going on?" Klara asked, bewildered by the sudden appearance of her son and husband. "This is not the day for surprises. He has not spoken to me in months, and now I see him here...today of all days, having to listen to the gruesome details of the life I have tried so hard to keep from him!"

"Klara, we can argue about this when the trial is over, but for now just listen," said Sam. "For several months now, I've been visiting Tommy in Athens. All those days when I told you I had business out of town? Well, I did. I had *family* business. I needed to make things right for you and for Tommy, and I needed to find a place in my son's life. And, by the way, in case you haven't noticed, the kid is really stubborn. The first time I tried to see him, he slammed the door in my face. I went back the next day, and he inched it open. I suppose he was a little curious about what I looked like. That time he said he wasn't interested in anything I had to say and told me not to come back. I waited a week and showed up again. When he cracked open the door, I told him he must have inherited his engaging personality from me."

In spite of herself, Klara laughed.

"I suppose he finally decided that the only way I'd leave him alone was to let me in and have it out. Over the next couple of months, I flew down once a week and we got to know each other. We spent most of the time talking about you and what you went through during the war. Klara, I won't lie. He's still angry, and having a hard time dealing with all the deception from both of you, but at least he knows the truth, and he's willing to listen. And he's willing to talk to you. He *wanted* to be here, and he convinced Thomas to come, too. Klara, he's an adult; he can take it."

Klara's emotions were raging war within her. She was angry with Sam for visiting Tommy without first discussing it with her, but she was also grateful he had been able to manage what she hadn't...getting

Tommy to see her again. "Sam, I understand you were only trying to help, but the last thing I need are more secrets." She was about to say more when John stepped into the room with bags of sandwiches and chips.

"Klara, you only have a few more minutes. Eat something," said John. "You're doing great, by the way. Just keep it up. I know this afternoon's testimony is going to be a little rougher than this morning's, but stay focused on me or the jury. You'll get through it. I promise."

"Okay, I'll do my best," said Klara as she gratefully took a bite of the sandwich. "Sam, let me just get through today. And stop looking at me with that puppy dog expression. I still love you, and I always will. And thank you for bringing Tommy." They hugged, and then it was time to return to the courtroom.

"She's coming back in," yelled a spectator, prompting Judge Andrew Heller to forcefully bang his gavel. Once again, Klara took her seat in the witness box. All eyes were upon her, but as before she focused only on the jury.

"Klara," John began. "This morning you described your life in Berlin before and during Hitler's rise to power, your escape to France, and finally your family's arrest in 1942. Now, if you please, can you describe your first encounter with the defendant."

Unlike the morning, when Klara's testimony had elicited no response from the opposing counsel, each statement Klara declared as fact was now met with an objection from Frank's attorney. Klara understood that she would need to brace herself for his eventual cross-examination. Frank was a survivor, and he was not about to surrender without a fight.

Between the starts and stops, Klara was able to piece together her story and answer the remainder of John's questions. She identified defendant Ronnie Frick as Standartenführer Reinhardt Frank, and as she spoke, long-repressed memories came rushing back. She described how Frank had manipulated her into believing he would save her mother and Ernst from deportation and how he had promised that they would survive if she accompanied him willingly to his home in Paris. She confessed to her own immaturity and gullibility, and acknowledged that it was only later that she realized that he could have taken anything he wanted regardless of her so-called choice.

"I was so young and naïve," she said, with tears streaming down her face. "It was all a game to him. He never had any intention of saving my mother and brother. That first time, when he raped me in his office, I could have resisted, although he told me that doing so would mean the end for them and for me. Instead, I chose life, and acquiesced to his brutal treatment. I told myself that I was keeping them safe...I was helping Mama and Ernst. I told myself, 'Just close your eyes and think of something beautiful.' And that is what I did. I would try and picture our garden, our home, the faces of my loved ones. Eventually even that was impossible, and I became inured to the daily assaults, the horrible abuse."

"Klara, did Frank ever admit that he ordered your mother and brother to be deported?" "No, but I knew. The letters stopped coming and he never mentioned them, so I just knew."

Frank's defense team objected.

"Did you ever overhear other conversations about roundups or deportations of Jews in Paris?" asked John.

"Hearsay," Frank's attorney objected again.

"Denied," Judge Heller replied. "I'll allow the witness to answer. Please continue, Mrs. Compton."

"Yes, all of us. We, the prisoners, everyone who worked in his house. We all overheard. The Nazis never asked us to leave when we served their coffees and cakes. They knew their secrets were safe. We would never be able to use our information, as we were all to be deported and killed."

"Thank you, Mrs. Compton."

Arising from his seat, Joseph Buell, Frank's high-priced and high-powered attorney, demanded attention by his size alone. Six-foot-three and close to three hundred pounds, Buell towered over Klara, and his overpowering presence gave Klara pause as she readied herself to answer his questions. "Mrs. Compton, again, please inform the jury how old you were when you first met Reinhardt Frank?"

"Not quite eighteen."

"And, now you are what, thirty-nine?"

"Yes," Klara answered.

"So you have not seen this man in twenty-three years?"

"Objection, Your Honor. Mrs. Compton has already established that she was a prisoner in Frank's home in Paris for two years, so that would make it twenty years since she last saw him."

"Sustained."

"Twenty years, then," said Buell. "Can you concede that twenty or twenty-three makes little difference, but that it is nevertheless a long time?"

"Not so long that I cannot recognize the man who violated me almost daily for two years," said Klara, aware the defense counsel was planning to call her identification of Frank into question.

Buell cleared his throat. "Since his arrest, my client, Ronnie Frick, has categorically stated that this is a simple case of mistaken identity. He was himself a prisoner, arrested for trying to stand up to the Nazis. He left Germany after the war because he could no longer stand to live in a country that had perpetrated such heinous acts on so many innocent people."

"Objection," shouted John. "Is there a question somewhere hidden in all those accolades?"

"Sustained. Do you have a question for the witness?" asked the Judge.

"Yes, yes. My apologies to the court," said Buell. "Mrs. Compton, please answer very carefully, for a man's reputation and freedom are at stake. Are you *absolutely positive* that the man seated at the defense table is the same individual you remember in Paris?"

"Mr. Buell, for two years I was repeatedly raped, beaten, and imprisoned by that man sitting next to you. Yes, yes, yes. I am *absolutely positive*."

Klara's testimony had taken up the rest of the afternoon. The proceedings were adjourned at a little after five o'clock. Exhausted, Klara was relieved to be allowed to step down from the witness box... until she remembered that Tommy would be waiting for her. John complimented her on a job well done, then ushered her through the same room where she had waited previously. She was now free to join her family. Walking into the corridor outside the courtroom, Klara eyed them, the odd congregation. What a strange concept, to think of Tommy, Sam, and Thomas as her family, but when she saw them together, she realized that for better or worse, that was what they were, her family. When Lotte joined them, the tableau was complete.

As Klara approached, Sam whispered something to Tommy. Sam and Thomas stayed back while Tommy walked toward his mother. "I'm proud of you, Mom," he said.

"You are?"

"Yeah. Still angry, but really proud."

"I see your dad is here. How did you manage that?" asked Klara?

"Which one? I seem to suddenly have two," answered Tommy, with the first smile Klara had seen in months.

"Thomas. I mean Thomas," said Klara.

"I talked him into it," said Tommy. "The two of them have hardly said a word to each other, but they both came here for me—and, of course, for you."

"My son, the diplomat," said Klara.

"Oh, and I need to warn you. Gran..."

"What about Gran?"

"She's...um...she's here, too. In the bathroom."

"Tommy, please, you must be joking. What possible reason did she have for coming?"

"Because I asked her. Mom, I wasn't blind growing up. I know how she treated you. She needed to be here."

"You really are a diplomat," said Klara.

Eugenia emerged from the ladies room. She only nodded hello in her daughter-in-law's direction, but Klara understood that by coming to Washington, Eugenia was acknowledging that their twenty-year war was finally over. *Of course,* Klara thought with a laugh. *The divorce would be final in another month, and that alone was probably providing Eugenia with some comfort.* When mother and son walked over to join the others, Klara recognized that a détente among all the significant people in her life had been reached. Years of secrets and lies could not be forgotten overnight, but at least the wounds they had caused one another could finally begin to heal.

For the first night in months, Klara slept soundly. She planned on being in the courthouse the next morning, even though as a potential rebuttal witness, she was still barred from the proceedings. The prosecution was wrapping up its case in the morning. Klara hoped the testimony of Gertrude Frank would be enough to convince the jury of Frick's guilt.

Court reconvened promptly at nine. Before going into the courtroom, Sam promised Klara that he would give her a blow-by-blow account of Frick's reaction when his estranged wife appeared.

"Your Honor," said John. "The prosecution would like to call Gertrude List to the witness stand." John could barely suppress his own excitement about the reaction her appearance would cause when Frank's wife's identity was revealed. Sam had chosen a seat in the courtroom that would allow him to gauge for himself any subtle changes in Frank's demeanor, but thus far he saw nothing. *He's more robot than man*, Sam thought. *He has no feelings.*

John began. "What is your relationship to Reinhardt Frank?"

"I am his wife. We were married in 1933, and since I have never signed any papers of divorce, we still are married."

A murmur of surprise rippled through the courtroom. Prompted by John's questions, Gertrude recounted how the two had met and eventually married. "Frau Frank, is the man sitting at the defense table your husband, Reinhardt Frank?"

"Yes, without any doubt. I see a few subtle changes here and there, but yes, I would recognize him anywhere. Although I must say, Reinhardt, that I liked the look of your old nose better than the one the plastic surgeons have given you." Gertrude smiled at her husband. The courtroom erupted with laughter.

"Objection," Buell screamed, as he jumped out of his chair.

"Sustained. Frau Frank, please just answer the questions. No embellishments," he added. Sam could see now that Frank was on the verge of exploding.

"I am sorry, Your Honor," Gertrude added, smiling again at the defense table.

"Frau Frank, when your husband was stationed in Paris, how often did you visit?"

"As often as he would allow. I loved him, so I tried to see him as much as possible. I went every few months and usually for a week."

"Do you remember meeting any of the prisoners who were working in the home?"

"Yes, I remember them all. One in particular, a young girl, in her late teens I would say. She was a beautiful thing, but like a little mouse. Always scared, always scurrying about the house, dusting, polishing, trying not to be noticed. But I *did* notice her, every time I went. I believe she was there for about two years, right up until the time Reinhardt fled Paris. I felt sorry for her. She was so young, so terrified. I should have helped her and I did not. I never even spoke to her except to ask for things, like coffee or the morning papers. I am not proud of that. So...I am here now to make amends."

"Do your remember her name?"

"Yes, although I only knew her first name. It was Klara."

"One last question. Before today, when was the last time you saw your husband?"

"Ah...after the war. He forced his way into my parents' home."

"What happened on that occasion?"

"He took everything of value—jewels, silver, the small Modigliani right off the wall. Reinhardt, do you still own the Modigliani we both loved? Or did you sell it to pay for your false papers?"

"Shut up, you old Schreckschraube! I paid for that painting!" Frank hissed, no longer able to keep his temper in check.

"Objection, Your Honor!"

"Sustained."

"Your Honor, for the record, I'd like to point out that the defendant has just called his wife a 'battleax.' Thank you, Frau List. That will be all," said John, trying to suppress a smile. "The prosecution rests."

The remainder of the afternoon was taken up by the defense, which produced expert after expert, each insisting that Frick's documents were authentic. Reinhardt Frank, also known as Ronnie Frick, did not take the stand. The jury deliberated for only a few hours before Judge Heller read the findings: Reinhardt Frank had illegally entered the United States, illegally used forged documents to become naturalized citizen Ronnie Frick, and concealed his wartime record, which allegedly included numerous war crimes. The judge then ordered the immediate revocation of his citizenship and deportation to Germany, which would be notified of the allegations against him.

Outside the courtroom, Sam found Klara and Tommy waiting for him with identical worried expressions on their faces. After all these months, he still marveled at how much they looked alike.

"Guilty! They found him guilty," Sam yelled as he approached. Tommy pulled both of his parents into a fierce bear hug.

"You did it, Mom," he whispered. "You really did it."

When the three of them finally disentangled, Klara realized that Gertrude List was quietly standing nearby.

"Klara, her testimony really nailed Frank," said Sam. "She corroborated everything you said."

Seeing Gertrude for the first time in more than two decades, Klara felt conflicted. The woman had done nothing for the frightened child, but she was now seeking absolution from the adult Klara. Looking first at Tommy and then Sam, Klara realized for the first time in years that she was at peace. Forgiveness was easier now. Klara walked forward, crossing the short distance that separated her from Gertrude, and offered her hand.

EPILOGUE

Several days after the trial, Thomas asked Klara to meet him for breakfast. "I wasn't sure you would show up," said Thomas, as Klara took her seat in the booth.

"Thomas, I am glad you called. The last time we spoke, we were both so angry. Perhaps now we can...what is the expression...clear the air," said Klara. "You came to the trial, and I know that could not have been easy for you."

When the waitress appeared, Thomas ordered for both of them, knowing exactly what Klara liked. "Sorry," he said. "Force of habit."

"We were married for many years. I understand," said Klara.

"Since the night you left, I've had a lot of time on my hands. I've been trying to make sense of what I did and why," said Thomas. "You know, I think I fell in love with you the first moment I laid eyes on you. I was obsessed with having you and nothing was going to stand in my way. I convinced myself that I was saving you from a life of drudgery."

"A life with a Jew."

"Yes. There was that, too," Thomas said, as he reached across the table to hold Klara's hand. "Please don't look at me like that. I'm ashamed enough. Klara, I was raised a certain way, with certain prejudices. They were not easy to break. You've seen where and how I grew up, so you know."

Pulling back her hand, Klara asked, "Would you have still wanted me if you had known that I was a Jew, too? Would you have brought me home to your mother and your big house in Atlanta?"

"I'd like to think so, but honestly, Klara, I really don't know.... And that is the honest-to-god truth. And while I'm telling the truth, I need to also confess something else. I did have Sam's orders changed. I knew you loved him, and I was desperate. But I swear.... I mean, the war was almost over, and I never thought he would see any more action, let alone be injured. It's not an excuse, only an explanation. I will have to live with what happened to him for the rest of my life."

Klara sat for several minutes, pushing away the plate of food that had just been placed before her. "Over the years I have also done many things of which I am not proud. We are quite a pair, no? I hope you can forgive me for all the lies."

"I already have."

"Did you really know that Tommy was Sam's child?" Klara asked after several more minutes had gone by in silence.

"I had my suspicions, but it never mattered. I loved him the moment I laid eyes on him, and I still do," said Thomas. "I'm also still in love with you, Klara."

"I know, Thomas. I know."

Three years after the trial, and the denial of a multitude of appeals, Reinhardt Frank was officially deported to Germany. The Israeli government was now hoping to have him extradited based on evidence found in the deportation documents Gertrude List had turned over to the Justice Department.

Klara knew that she would someday be called to testify again, but for now she was enjoying the daily pleasures of being married to the man she loved. The summer following Tommy's graduation, Klara, Sam, and their son decided to take a month-long trip to Europe to celebrate Tommy's accomplishments—and to put to rest any remaining ghosts and demons from Klara's past.

Klara was surprised how much Paris had changed. She was determined to enjoy the sights and sounds of the city. Tommy and Sam had forged a comfortable relationship, and Klara took joy in watching the two continue to grow closer. On the last day they were to spend in Paris, Klara decided that she could not leave the city without visiting the house of her nightmares. The home Reinhardt Frank had occupied was no longer a private residence. It had been purchased by a group of doctors who now used it for their medical practice. When Klara told them about the building's history and why she wanted to visit, they readily agreed.

The first time she had walked into that house was the day she had been separated from her mother and brother. The place had been her prison for the next two years. Now that she was walking up the stairs with the support of the two most important people in her life, she was determined to leave the past where it belonged.

The house had been renovated to suit the needs of the doctors, and at first Klara had difficulty getting oriented to her surroundings. "Here," she finally said. "This is where I slept. And over there is the office where Frank would meet with other officers of the Third Reich." Finally Klara located the room that had once served as Frank's library. The mahogany bookshelves and the volumes they held were long gone, as was the dark leather sofa that Klara remembered in such vivid detail. Sam and Tommy knew that this was the room where Klara's childhood had been brutally ended.

Looking around the room, Klara realized that the room was now used as a play area for children waiting to be examined. The four walls that embodied her terrifying real-life nightmares had been redeemed, turned into a space where healing could begin. Klara couldn't imagine a better end—or a better beginning. Embraced by the two most important people in her life, Klara walked down the steps for the last time, and knew she would never look back.

ACKNOWLEDGMENTS

I would like to thank all of my readers, you know who you are.

More thanks to my editors, particularly my husband Ozzie Berman, daughters Erin Berman and Annie Rosenberg, sister Gail Ross, niece Michelle Gilhooly and friends Jane Leavey, Jennifer Campbell, and Judi Ayal.

I would also like to thank my friends and family who supported me throughout this process. I could not have completed the book without your encouragement.

Sandy Berman is an archivist and museum curator. This is Sandy's debut novel. She lives in Atlanta, Georgia with her husband and enjoys spending time with her children and grandchildren.

CPSIA information can be obtained
at www.ICGtesting.com
Printed in the USA
LVHW040623100122
708131LV00006B/1010

9 781497 339927